CONVICTION

CONVICTION

Samuel H. Pillsbury

Walker and Company
New York

First published in the United States of America in 1992 by
Walker Publishing Company, Inc.

Published simultaneously in Canada by Thomas Allen & Son
Canada, Limited, Markham, Ontario.

Library of Congress Cataloging-in-Publication Data
Pillsbury, Samuel H.
Conviction : a novel / Samuel H. Pillsbury.
p. cm.
ISBN 0-8027-1225-8
I. Title.
PS3566.I5135C66 1992
813'.54—dc20   92-10952
CIP

Printed in the United States of America

2 4 6 8 10 9 7 5 3 1

for all my mentors in the law

CONVICTION

ONE

Walter Buris, assistant United States attorney, watered the last living plant in his office from the dregs of his coffee mug. He liked the idea of greenery in the office—a touch of nature and innocence in a place where neither usually appeared. But though he cared for his plants, they never seemed to last. It might have been the air or light, or maybe they died of aggravation. The windowsill was lined with plastic pots of soil, each with a long white tab sticking up like a gravestone, identifying the plant it had once held.

"He kills people, you know." The words came from Roscoe, Walter's chief witness in the case against Ted Jeffries.

"Not that again," Dan Matti responded, his voice weary. Matti was the FBI agent assigned to the case.

"Shut the fuck up, J. Edgar. You don't know shit," Roscoe said.

Matti took off his steel-framed glasses and rubbed the kidney-shaped marks they had made on the bridge of his nose. Then he stuck them back on and faced Roscoe. An ex-marine and a star football player in high school, Matti had a way of setting himself that threatened force.

"You finished?" he asked.

"Yeah. I'm finished."

"You got a bad attitude. And if it doesn't improve, you're gonna find yourself somewhere they do kill people. I'll see to that."

"Kiss my ass."

Matti's hard face grew harder as he stared down Roscoe.

"Okay, enough," said Walter. "Dan? Maybe you can give us a few minutes."

Matti nodded and slowly gathered his papers. He looked up at Walter twice before slamming his briefcase shut. Matti considered Roscoe his responsibility and resented Walter's interference. But since Walter had developed the case, there was little Matti could do.

"Call me," he said.

Roscoe laughed quietly as Matti's footsteps echoed down the hall.

He adjusted his polo shirt so that it fell without wrinkles from his shoulders. It was a pastel pink that set off the light brown of his skin. He had smooth features and deep, watchful eyes.

"You shouldn't do that," Walter said.

"That asshole's been all over me for months. He's—"

"—a senior FBI agent with a case about kids being turned into junkies and prostitutes, that depends on a career coke dealer who likes to jerk his chain," Walter said. "Leave him alone."

Roscoe shrugged.

Walter looked out his window over East Los Angeles. The city appeared as a study in beige: the concrete-lined Los Angeles River and the railroad yards in the foreground with a sea of industrial buildings beyond, blurred by the June haze and the gritty window screens. It was Saturday, and with the air-conditioning off the room felt thick and stale.

Defense attorneys loved to complain about the "awesome resources of the federal government," but in a case like this, it was a bad joke. Walter could just imagine how Ted Jeffries—the subject of their investigation—was spending his day. No doubt he was somewhere in his beach house, the doors flung open to the ocean breeze, and if his reputation were true, some beautiful girl was going down on him. Meanwhile his attorney, Gary Driesen, would be making final preparations for trial in the comfort of his high-rise Century City office, surrounded by associates eager to do his bidding.

"I can't live on what you're givin' me," Roscoe said.

Walter turned back. "I'll see what I can do, but I'm not promising anything. I spent all week fighting with the FBI over who was going to pay for the two charts we need at trial."

Roscoe nodded and examined his nails. "You think we're gonna take Jeffries down?" he asked.

"You worried I can't handle it?" Walter asked.

"Uh-uh. I've seen you in action." The response came too quickly to be entirely convincing.

"Some people think I can't handle it," said Walter. "But they're wrong. They get fooled by my good looks."

Roscoe laughed.

"It's true," Walter said, deadpan. In fact his wife, Laura, had always maintained that he was not taken seriously in the office because of his boyish looks and sense of humor. He did not fit the image of the hard-bitten prosecutor.

"Tell you a story," Walter said. "You know I used to manage a rock band, before I went to law school? Well, we did one big tour, all across the country, and basically we played anywhere we could get a date. We got a gig at a redneck roadhouse somewhere outside of Tulsa. It was a scene straight out of some Lynyrd Skynyrd song, you know? Anyway—"

"Walter—"

"Yeah?"

"Maybe later—okay?"

"Sure." Walter sat down, deflated.

"You know this is my last chance," Roscoe said.

"Yeah, I know that."

"I do my thing in court, I get a new name, new place for my family. I get out of the business. My kids get a chance to make something for themselves. I don't want them to come and see me in prison anymore. But that means we gotta take this guy down, you know?"

"It's guaranteed," said Walter.

Roscoe laughed, but whether out of humor or some other reason Walter could not tell. Roscoe left a few minutes later, saying he had some things to do before the trial started. Walter stayed in the office, going over old investigative reports, trying to anticipate the defense cross-examination of Roscoe and others. It was late afternoon when he left for home.

He lived in a small bungalow perched off a side street near the western ridge of Elysian Heights, northwest of downtown. The rear of the house looked over the sprawling Southern Pacific rail yard and, beyond it, the beginnings of the San Fernando Valley. At the time they bought the house, it was the most they could afford. When they started to make money, Laura wanted to move to a more upscale location, but Walter resisted. He liked living in what realtors called a "mixed" neighborhood. Built around a hill, it was poor and Mexican at the bottom, whiter and middle class at the top, where single-family houses surrounded Elysian Park.

On weekdays the park was a restful place of grassy slopes and tall eucalyptus trees, joggers and walkers. On Wednesday nights and weekends it drew gleaming low-riders from across the city, the pickup trucks and big American sedans cruising slowly through the neighborhood, stereos up full, bass pulsing through the trees. The Hillside Stranglers had dumped several of their victims in the park's underbrush.

After checking the mail and his answering machine Walter dropped onto the living room couch and watched the sky turn pink, then deep purple. He was tired and hungry, but more than anything he needed to relax. He thought about a beer, but he was in training for the trial and needed to keep his edge. He reached behind the first row of books in the bookcase for the old-fashioned cookie tin. He pried open the lid and sniffed the sweet dirt smell of marijuana. Like everyone else he knew, he started smoking in college, but unlike most he had never stopped. It was hypocritical now that he was a prosecutor and spent his days pursuing drug dealers, but there it was. Nobody's perfect.

He took in the sharp smoke, watching the red ember flare at the joint's end and held it down until the first trickle of relaxation spread out from his head. Then he let the smoke escape his burning lungs. He felt it first in his forehead, like a hand smoothing his brow, and then a tingle above his nose. But it was mostly cerebral, a set of pleasant associations that played back like an old and favorite song he had not heard for a long time. He took another toke and put it out. He decided to call Laura.

"Hello, Mrs. Buris?" he asked when the phone was answered.

"I'm sorry, there's no one here by that name," Laura answered.

"Do you own your own home?" he asked.

"We're not interested."

"Hi, Laura. It's Walter."

"Walter, what have you been smoking?" Laura demanded.

He could imagine her tossing her hair from her face and looking intently across the room. She had large brown eyes in a narrow face that made her look vulnerable, but her mouth would be set in a line, a sign of her inner strength.

"I'm trying out a new career in telephone sales," Walter said. "We have a special on home improvements. We can remove the sparkles in your ceiling for just twenty-nine ninety-nine. Think of it. A ceiling that doesn't glitter, yours for just twenty-nine ninety-nine. Call now, our operators are standing by."

Laura laughed. There was a click on the line signaling another call. "Hold on," she said. Laura was a literary agent in the movie business and was always juggling calls according to their importance. Walter hated it.

"Sorry," Laura said, coming on again. "I'm expecting another call. Sara wants to say hi."

"Hi," came the voice, soft and high. She breathed fast into the phone.

"Hi, Sara. What did you do at school today?"

"I did a project. We got some feathers from Jason, and with the paints and all the milk cartons we collected and paper bags we made costumes. I was a fairy princess," she said in a rush.

"That sounds nice. Are you going to wear it to the ball?"

"We're not having a ball. We're having a parade."

"Sounds like what I do—dressing up and showing off."

"Oh, Dad," Sara said in mild reproof.

"Can I talk to Mom?" he asked.

"Hi," Laura said. "How's the case going?"

"Fantastic. Monday we have motions and then we pick a jury Tuesday. I hope you can come down for that."

"I'll try," she said. "Did you get my letter?"

"Yeah."

"So what do you think?"

"Laura, I'm right in the middle of the biggest case in my life. I can't think about anything else."

"That's what you said six months ago."

"It was true then too."

"Walter, we've been separated for almost a year. And no matter how many funny phone calls you make we're not getting back together."

"I know."

She sighed. "We still on for next Sunday?"

"Sure. Absolutely."

"Good. Sara's been looking forward to it." There was another click on the line. "Gotta go. Good luck." She hung up.

Walter put down the phone softly. How did anyone have a private life that worked?

"Mr. Buris." The judge's voice bit, cutting off Walter in midphrase.

The judge leaned forward over the high bench and fixed Walter with blue eyes that glittered with warning over his reading glasses. It was the moment when United States District Judge August F. O'Brien took command of the courtroom.

Because the chief judge was sailing to Hawaii on vacation and the case had drawn international media interest, it was being tried in the chief judge's courtroom. The largest of the courtrooms, it was a broad rectangle of high white walls, brilliantly lit by floodlights in the ceiling, above dark wooden spectators' pews and rails. Its quiet dignity reminded Walter of the Episcopal church where he had sung in the choir. Stiff portraits of former chief judges ranged along the sides of the room; behind the judge's bench appeared the seal of the United States, like a halo over the seated jurist.

The judge had interrupted Walter's argument opposing the last of the defense's pretrial motions in the case.

"When I was with the United States attorney's office," O'Brien continued, "we had a policy on the use of perjured testimony." The judge paused. He used silence well, but he plunged on before the last wave of anticipation had crested. "We didn't do it."

"That hasn't changed, your honor," Walter responded. The tone was good. Clear, confident; he thought of it as the voice of reason.

"Then what's going on here?" O'Brien snatched off his reading glasses, face flushed. "From what we've heard today from your star witness-informant, this drug dealer lied before the grand jury." The judged flicked his glasses toward Roscoe. "Under oath he said he never supplied drugs to the children, only the defendant. He was quite clear about it. Now he says he sold to the kids. He lied, Mr. Prosecutor, and you relied on that lie to get your indictment," O'Brien said. The judge leaned back, his high-backed chair creaking.

Ted Jeffries, the defendant, flicked a gold pen between his index and middle fingers. Walter noticed that he had let touches of gray emerge at his sideburns, which made him look a few years older than his forty-six years, but more distinguished. In his dark blue suit he looked more like a senator than a television producer.

Meanwhile Roscoe swayed back and forth in the witness chair.

Walter checked his anger. He could not get mad at the judge, and getting mad at Roscoe would be worse. He reminded himself that coke dealers do not make the most reliable witnesses. Still, there was no reason. Roscoe was an admitted dope dealer. But he had drawn the line at selling drugs to kids.

"Look, I did the stuff with Flash and Jeffries," Roscoe had explained to the grand jury. "I knew they were giving the shit to the kids. They called it candy for the candy store. But that was on them. Not me. I seen what it does to kids."

The grand jurors had believed him, just as Walter had. Walter trusted Roscoe. But then prosecutors always want to trust their informants.

For most of the afternoon Roscoe had kept Gary Driesen off guard. It seemed as if Driesen was putting on a show for his client. Pretrial motions could be like that, a ritual of cross-examination and legal argument, ending in denial. For more than an hour Roscoe kept Driesen mired in unimportant details.

"So the second time you met this guy Sandy was in January?" Driesen had asked.

"I think."

"You don't know?"

"It was raining."

"Huh?"

"It was raining. So it was probably in the winter. But it was a while ago. I can't really say when I met Sandy."

The dull thuds of Judge O'Brien's shoes against the bench quickened, a sign of impatience. "Why don't we move to another area, counselor," O'Brien had finally suggested.

[6]

Driesen had edged away from the lectern but kept a hand on it. Practice in the federal courts in Los Angeles was formal, and judges required attorneys to stay at the lectern during questioning. It was one of the ways federal judges kept lawyers in their place.

Walter saw Roscoe look over at Jeffries. Their eyes locked for a moment.

"You occasionally sold drugs to Mark and some of the other kids, didn't you?" Driesen had asked.

"I sold to Flash."

"But you also sold to the kids. Directly."

Roscoe didn't answer right away. The pause sent a trickle of sweat down the inside of Walter's arm. His suits lasted only a day in court before they needed cleaning, but he usually let them go for three. The smellier he was, the closer Walter liked to stand to his opponents during the sidebar conferences where they huddled at the judge's bench. Driesen would not like that; he always smelled of expensive cologne.

"You also sold to the kids, didn't you?" Driesen demanded.

"Once or twice, maybe. I dunno," Roscoe answered.

It took Driesen forty-five minutes to drag the rest out of Roscoe. Roscoe claimed that he wasn't asked before, that he had forgotten, that it didn't seem important, but finally he admitted that he had lied—he had sold marijuana, though not cocaine, to a few of the older kids.

"Mr. Buris, when did you learn that your witness lied to the grand jury?" the judge asked.

"Just now, your honor."

O'Brien sent him a long look, then shook his head. The judge was a former United States attorney and he held prosecutors to an impossibly high standard of skill and integrity. He frequently roasted the government's representatives with his dragon's breath of sarcasm and outrage. It hurt because O'Brien knew what he was talking about. "I don't mind saying that the government's conduct in this case has been sloppy. At best." The judge paused. This time he waited the extra instant, until the balloon of tension blew out full. "We'll be in recess for fifteen minutes. I will rule on all pending motions when we resume."

The courtroom was suddenly full of motion as O'Brien rose from the bench and disappeared behind the door to his chambers, his black robes billowing behind him.

Walter sighed. It would get a lot worse, he knew. He walked out of the bustling courtroom to the small men's room down the hall. He was standing at the urinal when he sensed someone behind him.

"I like your style." It was Jeffries, unzipping his fly. Even in that simple act he seemed self-assured. "Really. You don't let anything faze

[7]

you. I want you to know I don't take this thing personally." Jeffries's eyes met Walter's. They were a pale blue and registered nothing.

Walter zipped up and turned toward the sink.

"I think I know your wife," Jeffries said.

Walter stopped.

"Not personally, of course. But she's sold some stuff to our company. Small world, isn't it?"

Walter shrugged.

"I guess you're not supposed to talk to me. You could get in trouble, right?" Jeffries said.

"Something like that," Walter added.

Jeffries shook his head. "If we could talk we might be able to work something out."

"You can't talk your way out of this one," Walter replied.

"You're naive," Jeffries declared.

Walter stared back at him, in a way he hoped looked tough, then pushed out of the bathroom. He thought he heard a small laugh as the door swung shut behind him.

"I have considered the motions and I rule as follows," Judge O'Brien intoned. He gave his rulings, mostly in favor of the prosecution, but here and there excluding small portions of the government's case. "I reserve ruling on the admissibility of the second video, that found in defendant's car. I have serious reservations as to the constitutionality of the search but wish to look at the cases submitted by the government at oral argument today.

"As to the motion to dismiss or in the alternative to suppress the testimony of Roscoe Brown, I find that the government did not willfully present perjured testimony to the grand jury. Mr. Brown may testify in the case-in-chief. Jury selection will begin tomorrow at nine-thirty."

Jeffries slapped his pen on the table, hard.

"Court stands in recess," the judge said.

Gary Driesen put a hand on his client's shoulder. "I told you it was a long shot, Ted," he said.

"Yeah," Jeffries responded. The tone was accusing.

"Ted. We had a very good day. Roscoe may testify, but after this, who's going to believe him? And he's their whole case."

Jeffries nodded. "See you tomorrow." The reporters were already crowding around, looking for a quote. Driesen indicated he might have something to say outside.

TWO

All night wet ocean air moved inland, settling over the ground in a thick, even mist. A small pickup truck made scattered stops along the hill, a boy bundled in a windbreaker and Dodgers cap in the back, tossing out newspapers into driveways and yards. The truck and the boy made a rhythm—engine revving, squeak of brakes, thud of paper, engine revving. In the distance the freeway rumbled.

Walter was deep in sleep when the phone rang. Some part of him heard and answered, but the rest of his mind remained far away, as if under water, struggling to surface. He recognized Dan Matti's voice but could not understand him. Something about Roscoe being gone. He wondered how Matti knew that Roscoe had taken off.

"He's dead," Matti said.

When Walter understood, an awful tingle started in his groin, shot up his spine, and spread across his shoulders. He remembered Roscoe's smile from the weekend and Jeffries's dark face after O'Brien's rulings and felt guilt's grip tighten around his chest. Roscoe had tried to warn them, but they had not listened.

Outside it was a June morning, the colors made gray by the fog. Traffic on the Harbor Freeway moved swiftly, the early commuters intent on beating the coming rush. Going through downtown at seventy, Walter imagined himself in a magical kingdom setting off on a desperate errand. On either side of the freeway the tall buildings stood massive and mysterious in the purplish gloom. Once he had finished the case he might work in one of those towers, in a cool hushed office, an attractive, efficient secretary beyond his door screening his calls, handling his visitors. Maybe then he could escape the madness.

The city came into hard focus when he left the freeway—a jumble of fast-food signs and graffiti-covered walls bordering drab streets. The mist had lifted enough to leave the city in clear tones of black and white. Tired dark-skinned people, more women than men, waited for the buses beneath the small white, red, and orange RTD signs.

He thought he would recognize the scene immediately. He had

seen it often enough on television—a clump of onlookers and reporters milling around a location marked for importance by police cars and the yellow tape of a crime scene. But the house was marked only by a small strip of tape across the front door. There were no crowds, no reporters. Across the street a woman dressed for work unlocked her car.

Driving past the house and all the others like it, windows barred against the world, Walter's chest tightened again. That Roscoe would risk his life was a given; he was dope dealer caught red-handed. It had nothing to do with his being black. Maybe Matti would have had more patience if he were white, but it wouldn't have made any difference, Walter thought.

He found the small, brightly lit donut shop that Matti had described and saw the FBI agent through the window. Dressed in slacks and a windbreaker, he seemed smaller than in a suit. His thick hair was combed back straight above a wide forehead and dark eyebrows. His gray eyes looked dull and tired.

"How long have you been here?" Walter asked as he sat down beside him.

"We got called around midnight," Matti said.

Walter nodded. Matti could have called him then, but Walter did not mind; he had no taste for corpses.

They drank bitter black coffee and ate jelly donuts. Walter drew circles in a mound of sugar that had spilled on the table.

"Looks like a drug rip-off," Matti said. "There were a couple bindles of rock cocaine under the couch and some plastic wrapper with coke residue. It looks like it would have been about a kilo. There was no sign of forced entry, so it had to be someone he knew."

"Who knew where he was."

"Yeah."

"The coke could be a setup, something to get us off track," Walter said. "You didn't know anything about him dealing again, did you?"

"No."

"And Roscoe said he never dealt street amounts. He only worked wholesale. If there were bindles it had to be a setup."

"Unless he needed the money," Matti said.

Walter nodded, remembering Roscoe's complaints.

Matti spread out before him Polaroids of the murder scene. Walter looked at them quickly and then turned away, his insides quivering.

The pictures were gory, but that was not the worst of it. It went deeper than that. It was like a science fiction movie where a person was made inhuman. Roscoe had been an important witness the day before, a friend in some ways. He was a husband and a father. He was a dope dealer and a pain in the ass. Now he was a thing to be photographed, scraped, bagged, dissected, and disposed of. It was an ugly, degrading end.

Walter took a deep breath. He would not lose control.

"For now LAPD's handling the investigation. If anything turns up that it's connected to us, we come in," Matti said.

"Okay." Walter was surprised. The FBI did not have a good reputation for sharing cases.

Walter called the office from a pay phone near the rest rooms. He asked his supervisor, Rollie Jackson, to send someone down to get a continuance from O'Brien.

"You coming in?" Rollie asked.

"Maybe. Probably—I don't know," Walter responded. He tried to decipher the block-lettered graffiti carved into the wall by the phone.

"Don't blame yourself," Rollie said. "He was a doper."

"Yeah."

Walter met Matti outside.

"What about Sharon?" Walter asked, referring to Roscoe's wife.

"I called her. I think she'd already given up on him," Matti said.

"Think I should call?" Walter asked.

Matti shook his head. "She said she'd call me if she needed anything."

Walter nodded. "This ever happen to you before?"

"What do you mean?" Matti asked sharply.

"Had someone you were working with get killed."

"In Korea." He made it sound like a challenge.

"You want to go for a drink?" Walter asked.

Dan looked at him strangely, then shrugged. "I know a place up around USC."

Walter followed Matti's dark sedan north through rush hour traffic while listening to the insistent jabber of the morning disc jockeys. He remembered in high school when the jockeys always sounded stoned and played music in sets according to theme: train sets with old R&B songs about going home and leaving home, leading up to the Dead's "Casey Jones"; sets about love revenge (Jimi Hendrix, "Hey Joe") and sets about being sad (The Beatles, "Eleanor Rigby" and "Blackbird"). Now it was all preprogrammed, and the songs and commercials sounded the same.

The place was a lounge-restaurant that catered to USC students and staff. Blowups of 'SC football stars lined the walls. The empty lounge was dominated by a big-screen TV tuned to one of the morning news shows. A reporter spoke breathlessly about a decision by the Supreme Court. They had cut back on some constitutional right, but that was all Walter could make out. He ordered two beers from a bartender with brush-cut blond hair who looked as if he had just come off the beach.

Walter lifted his glass. "To Roscoe," he said.

Matti lifted his glass in response and they both drank.

Walter laughed. "Roscoe would think this was pretty funny. Two feds toasting him."

Matti just grunted.

"What do you think we should do?" Walter asked.

Matti shrugged. "It's your case."

Walter studied him for a minute. "I know you didn't like Roscoe, so I know you're not that broken up about him. And you say it's my case, I should worry about it. So what's eating you?"

"The Bureau doesn't like it when people in our protection get killed," Matti said. "It sets a bad precedent. But it'll make my supervisor happy. He's been after my hide for years. In a couple months I'll be doing background checks in Topeka."

"I'll stand up for you," Walter said.

Matti chuckled. "Thanks." A smile formed at the edge of his mouth.

"I'm not giving up," Walter said.

Matti looked at him, quizzical. "Nobody said anything about giving up."

"Good," said Walter. A long silence extended between them. Walter finally drained his beer. "See you tomorrow."

He went home to remember. He had an idea that by running it all through his head he could work it out.

He had been halfway out his office on a Friday night in January, one arm in his jacket, briefcase open on the table by the door, when the phone rang. He was taking a last push through the papers on his desk for an FBI report he had to read over the weekend, and he was already fifteen minutes late to meet a college friend for a drink.

It was probably someone calling about something Walter should have done weeks before and he would have to make up a story about being in trial that would allow him to put it off for another few weeks. Except that it was Friday night, and no one in government works late on Fridays—and it might be his friend, wanting to change their plans—or maybe the girl he had met at the beach the weekend before—Terri, Sheri, something like that—who had promised to call. She had a neatly rounded bottom, perfect in her tight bikini, the kind that drove him crazy.

He picked up on the fifth ring. It was a tired narcotics detective working out of Compton who asked if Walter knew a subject by the name of Reginald Douglass Brown, also known as Roscoe, who they were holding for possession of two kilograms of cocaine. That was nearly four and a half pounds, worth maybe forty thousand wholesale.

"He says he has to talk to you." The detective yelled at someone in the distance to shut up.

"What for?" Walter asked.

"Huh?"

"What does he want to talk to me for?"

"How the fuck do I know?"

"Maybe you could ask him."

"Shit."

There was a loud clack as the detective dropped the phone. Echoes of human traffic came through the line. Walter was about to hang up when a new voice came on the line.

"Detective Perez. He says it's big. Has to do with kids, some big shot in Hollywood. That's all he'd say."

"What do you think?"

"What do I think? I think we've got his balls in a nutcracker and he'd fuck his mother if he thought it'd help."

Walter smiled at the mixed metaphor. Cops liked them almost as much as judges did. Perez sounded like a burned-out bureaucrat, refusing to pass judgment. Walter tried to wait him out, hoping he would speak his mind. Finally the detective continued.

"Look. The guy's scared. Maybe he's making up stories. But who knows—maybe it's righteous. Only one way to tell for sure."

Walter did not want to go. The station was in the heart of South Central, at the center of the city's chaos zone. The detective was probably taunting him. Walter had seen the way cops treated lawyers who came to bail out their clients. Still, if you want to win the sweepstakes you have to play, his father always said.

The station was quieter than he expected. There were no screamers, no ravers, no bloodied suspects. It was not Hill Street. Although new, the building looked worn from the stream of people that passed through daily. In the main lobby and in the halls Walter felt hard eyes watching him. Both police and citizens were suspicious. In his dark gray suit he looked like trouble.

The duty sergeant took Roscoe out of the holding cell and handcuffed him to a chair in an interview room, a small rectangular space harsh with fluorescent light. A gun-metal gray table took up most of the room, with metal chairs scattered around it. The walls were made of acoustic tile that had been gouged out in a line by detectives tipping back in the chairs.

[13]

"Man, I did not expect you to come," Roscoe said with a smile.

"Me either."

"You're gonna like this."

"I hope so."

"But hey—before I start, I need some guarantees, up front. Like you'll get these turkeys off my back." He spoke fast, with a cadence, a rhythmic up and down that carried as much weight as his words. "Man, you should have seen that bust. No warrant, no nothin'. I answer the door, get a gun upside the head, they tear up my place, scare the old lady, my kids. Then they find two kilos on the kitchen table. If you believe that. Shit. If I had two kilos you think I'd leave it out on the kitchen table?"

"Enough," Walter said sharply.

"Man—"

"You'll get a lawyer, tell him about it."

"It's a bullshit case, you gotta—"

Walter stood up to go.

Roscoe took a deep breath. "Okay."

Walter leaned against the door, wearing a look of professional boredom, the one he always used on defense attorneys who wanted a favor. Roscoe began again.

"Heard of a TV guy, big deal, loaded like you would not believe, Jeffries? Made that TV show 'One Big Happy Family.' I can give him to you."

"For what?"

"Dealing coke to the kids that stayed at that house for runaways. He made videos with them, hard-core stuff. And he . . . it's like he played games with them."

Walter sat down.

"I need protection," Roscoe said sharply.

"Roscoe, you know how it works. You tell me what you have, then we'll see.

"The guy's bad."

"Roscoe, you deal with Colombians, right?"

"They got the best shit."

"And you're telling me this guy's bad?"

"Worse."

"Then why call me? If they got you on a bad search you can beat it. If not, you know how to do time. Sounds like you've got a score to settle," Walter said.

Roscoe shook his head. "It's not like that."

"So?"

"The guy is sick."

[14]

Walter sighed. It sounded like a chance encounter between the powerful and the powerless, a wild card Roscoe had saved for his inevitable arrest. Still, Walter was there, and Roscoe seemed rational. There was none of the surging wildness that signaled craziness. Walter had heard of Jeffries and recalled something, some kind of allegations, but then there were nasty stories about virtually anyone famous. The part about the videos was promising. That could be child exploitation, a federal charge.

"Tell me about it," Walter said, sitting down.

"I need a cup of coffee and some cigarettes," Roscoe said. "Kools. And get me offa this chair." Roscoe rattled his handcuffs against the chair arm.

Walter found the coffee and eventually bummed some menthol cigarettes off a pimp waiting to bail out one of his charges. Finally he needed a tape deck to record the interview, but all the station's machines were broken or lost. Roscoe offered the cassette deck in his car, which was in the impound lot across the street. Walter retrieved the machine and bought tapes at the corner 7-Eleven. The handcuffs required negotiation, but eventually the sergeant compromised on one hand cuffed to the chair arm.

Walter lit Roscoe's cigarette. He inhaled deeply, let his head drop back, and blew the smoke at the ceiling.

"After I got out—this was a couple years ago—I used to hang out at this place in Hollywood. I knew the guy who ran it, and it was a good spot."

"For business, you mean," Walter said.

"Right. I wanted to upgrade, you know. I woulda gone out to the Westside but they see brown's your color and not your tan, the bouncer's all over you."

"Mm," said Walter.

"Anyway, first this guy that used to have a stable, you know—ladies—this guy Flash came in to see me. Flash said he worked for a guy who wanted to establish a business relationship. Says his guy wants grass and coke, quality stuff, but not killer. He flashes a wad—that's why they call him Flash. Pays me five hundred dollars for an ounce of sinsemilla and some toot.

"His guy liked the stuff. Every couple weeks, we do business. Then Flash comes in with Jeffries. Very smooth. He smelled of money. You know, the hair, the clothes. Usually, somebody like that comes in, especially a white guy, to a place like this, he's a mark and everyone's on him trying to rip him off. Not with him. He had this, like, aura: Don't fuck with me. First I thought the guy was in the business the way he talked. He wanted to know whether I'd done time, whether I'd ever been a snitch. Testing. His eyes looked straight into you. I knew this was going to be something. I didn't know what, but it was going to be something."

And so Roscoe began his story. He told of a rich man intrigued with the underworld, into drugs, making connections with a dealer, gradually buying more. Walter had heard similar stories. But at each familiar sound, there was a twist, something that didn't fit.

Although Jeffries was an expert judge of quality he never used what he bought. "He would take a little taste of the coke, rub it on his gums. I couldn't tell if he even liked it," Roscoe said. "I never saw him drink anything except a glass of wine. He said he got the stuff for his friends, for parties. At first I figured that was just what rich white people did, you know.

"Then he started talking about his kids, the kids at the House. He took me over to see the place. I'll never forget the way we came in that door and they were all over him. And this was for real. You can tell with kids, see it in their faces when they just want something. This wasn't like that. They called him Dad. It was all fucked up."

Roscoe described a man who was always in control, even when he acted crazy.

"I remember one time, he was taking me somewhere, real late, we were on the 405, going north," Roscoe said. "He's got this wild dark green Jaguar XKE from before they put any of that smog shit on it, and we pull up beside this CHP car. Ted waves at the guy, gives him the finger, then steps on it. Puts it up to a hundred and forty, then all of a sudden he slows down, pulls over, and pops the hood. He tells me to get out and wait in the bushes. The CHP comes screaming by, lights and siren going. He sees the Jag, screeches around, tires smoking, and backs up real fast. The cop jumps out with his gun, sticks it in Ted's face.

" 'Hands up and spread 'em, motherfucker!' " Roscoe yelled, using his free hand to imitate the policeman's gun.

"Most people would have been shitting in their pants. But Ted's real cool, puts his hands up and says, 'We must have some sort of misunderstanding here, officer,' like he was some banker or something. He goes on about how Jags overheat and it's cuz it never gets hot in England. The Chippie's screaming at him about reckless driving, but Ted says it must have been another Jaguar and asks the cop if he got the license plate. The cop is ready to shit, but Ted tells him he's a big producer and the cop runs his license and it comes back clean. And the cop realizes there was somebody else in the car he saw. He never actually says he's sorry, but he does kind of. After he takes off I get back in, Ted humps it again, and we pass the CHP doing a hundred—and both flip him the bird. There was no way he was gonna catch us." Roscoe laughed.

"I could never figure out what the guy was about," Roscoe said. "Just when I thought he was a total shit he'd go see some kid in the hospital dying of cancer that he just heard about and spend about three hours making him feel good."

While Roscoe filled tape after tape, word circulated in the station that it was big. Fresh coffee, cigarettes, and new tapes appeared along with officers who wanted to listen in. In the quiet of Saturday morning they heard the stuff of headlines and gossip. Later they could say they were there.

By the time Walter left, the day was grainy with the approach of dawn. He packed up his tapes and notes, told Roscoe he would be in touch, and made sure that he was booked into the county jail on keepaway status. Walter drove home high on fatigue and caffeine and Roscoe's secrets. If he could get corroboration, and he was sure he could, it would be big. People would remember him for it. Yeah, he's the guy who took down Ted Jeffries, they would say. It was not quite his fantasy of single-handedly stopping a shootout in court, but it was close. He would show this decadent, selfish city that someone could stand up for right and win. Walter knew it was childish, but he wanted to be a hero.

Now he looked back in wonder. How could he have thought that it would be that easy? All along, Roscoe had tried to warn him, but he had never really listened.

And now it was too late.

THREE

Judge O'Brien called a status conference on the case for late Wednesday afternoon.

"I assume, gentlemen, that we will be ready to begin next week," the judge stated from the bench.

"The government stands ready to proceed," Walter loudly announced. Now more than ever he had to project confidence.

"That's fine, your honor," Gary Driesen said.

"No chance of a pretrial disposition I take it," O'Brien said. He had been pushing for a plea from the start of the case, but neither side was enthusiastic.

"Our present position is that the government will accept nothing less than a plea to all counts of the indictment," Walter said.

"The case is going to trial and we expect complete exoneration," Driesen declared.

"Very well, gentlemen. I guess that's what we get paid for. Case adjourned until next Tuesday at nine."

Driesen tapped Walter on the shoulder as the courtroom emptied. "I need to call you," he said. "You'll be in your office in about an hour?"

"Yeah."

Walter wondered what Driesen wanted. Driesen's tone was friendly and professional, which meant that he wanted something, probably a continuance. Driesen had insisted that Jeffries wanted the earliest possible resolution of the case, but maybe things looked different now that the trial was about to start.

It was nearly seven-thirty when Driesen called.

"Sorry this is so late," Driesen said. "I was talking with Ted and he likes to talk."

"What's up?" Walter asked.

"Despite what we said in court today I wonder if we could talk disposition. I was thinking maybe dinner. How about tomorrow?"

"You've got something to say you haven't said before?" Walter asked.

"I believe so. And so should you. Things have changed."

"They have and they haven't," Walter replied.

"Look, you want to try?"

"Sure."

It seemed as if all the big prosecutions in the city were doomed. Despite a videotaped drug transaction and a massive trial effort the United States attorney's office had lost its case against car maker John DeLorean. After months of courtroom proceedings the handsome executive strolled out of court a free man. Walter had watched him on the courthouse steps, signing autographs and accepting flowers from well-wishers. Across the street in the state courts the DA's office had found its own Vietnam in the McMartin preschool child molestation case. The rule for prosecutors seemed to be the more sensational the charges, the worse the result.

The restaurant was a trial lawyer's hangout, a place of dim light, red leather booths, and strong margaritas. Driesen was already installed at a table in the back. He was drinking a Dos Equis from the bottle and munching tortilla chips heaped with green salsa.

"Good to see you, Walter. Especially without the entourage. It's hard to talk with your FBI friends around."

Walter smiled. "Matti wanted to come."

"Tell me about it. Ted was ready to can me for not letting him tag along. You can forget about client control."

Walter nodded. Driesen was in a selling mode if he was talking about client control. It usually meant a defense attorney's ability to make a reluctant defendant plead guilty. Although it could be a critical skill, defense attorneys did not like to talk about it, at least not with the opposition. It went against the image of the zealous defender.

"The guy's incredible," Driesen continued. "You know that *Rolling Stone* interview? He managed to tell me about it the day before it came out. He pays out six figures for my advice, then ignores it."

"Yeah."

Walter knew the tidbit was meant as an icebreaker. Driesen was suggesting that they were the sensible ones, mediating between crazy clients.

Like all good lawyers Driesen could work in a variety of styles according to need. In court he had been the lawyer's lawyer, precise, tough, respectful to the judge and critical but not personally nasty toward the government. That would change in front of a jury. He had not seen Driesen's current approach before, but knew it was carefully calculated.

"Walter—there's one thing I want you to be very clear about," Driesen said. "I know most prosecutors think defense attorneys are scum. And believe me, some are. But mostly we just have a slightly different take on things. We have rules too, things we won't do. I wouldn't be here if I thought Ted Jeffries had anything to do with Roscoe Brown's death."

"Okay," Walter said, noncommittal.

Driesen crooked a finger at him. "You have any reason to believe otherwise and I want to know about it. I don't represent people who off witnesses."

It was amazing how fast he could turn on the intensity.

"Yeah. You never know when they might want to off their lawyer," Walter replied.

"I'm serious," Driesen insisted. "Look, I've got some other clients who are, shall we say, in the same line of work as Mr. Brown. They tell me that he had a reputation for coming up a little short. That can be a dangerous practice."

"Interesting. Who should we talk to about this?" Walter asked, pulling out his pen.

"You know it doesn't work like that." Driesen took another chip. "You're probably worried about the beeper."

"The beeper?"

"Yeah. It was on the news. On TV or in the paper, I can't remember where. Brown had one on his car, so it could be tracked. The police found it."

Walter nodded. He had not heard anything about a beeper.

"Check it out. I'm sure you'll find some law enforcement type put it there. If not on this case, then an earlier one."

"We'll check it out," Walter said.

"Jeffries will not plead to anything having to do with the kids," Driesen said. "I don't care what you think, that part of your case is bullshit."

"That's what it's about," Walter replied.

"Past tense. What it was about. What you have now is a possession case—the stuff you got out of his car. He'll plead to a misdemeanor possession of cocaine."

"It's a felony amount."

"Which you would never file on. It's below office guidelines. We would never have filed it when I was in the office and that was a long time ago."

"So?"

They went back and forth, arguing, going off on tangents about the case and lawyering. Finally Walter tired and made Driesen put his final offer on the table—a plea to a felony count of possession, no deal on sentencing. Jeffries would face a potential five years. Walter knew that O'Brien would consider it a drug case; he might look at the distribution allegations, he certainly would not consider the child exploitation charges. Jeffries would probably get a split sentence—maximum six months.

Walter shrugged. "I won't accept less than a plea to child exploitation."

Driesen exploded. "Jesus, Walter! What the hell have we been doing here for the last hour." He sat back. "Is this the way the front office sees it? Or does it come from Washington?"

"Just me."

Driesen shook his head. "You can't play cowboy on a case like this, Walter."

"It's my case. And I'm going to see that your client does serious time."

"I've seen this happen before, Walter. It happened to me when I was in the office. You get involved in a case, it gets personal, then when things fall apart you get desperate. It's a mistake. We're lawyers. We get paid to stay detached."

"I appreciate the advice," Walter said.

"You're in over your head."

Walter walked into the meeting Monday morning a few minutes late. Everyone in Bridewell's office seemed to have a copy of the Metro section of the morning's *Los Angeles Times* folded to the story about the upcoming trial. The story reported on speculation that the prosecution was looking for a deal now that its star witness was dead.

"Walter. Glad you could join us," Rollie Jackson said, taking the pipe from his mouth. Jackson was the chief assistant, the attorney who managed the criminal division. He was a champion squash player, a Rhodes scholar, and a Yale law graduate. He thought Walter was a lightweight; Walter considered him a stuffed shirt.

"Hi," Walter responded and sat down in the corner next to the window and an outdated set of *U.S. Law Weeks*. The focus of silent attention shifted between himself and Paul Curtes, another prosecutor, who sat to the right of Jonathan Bridewell, the United States attorney.

Walter looked around. Also in the office were Dan Matti and his supervisor, Andrew Dadden: two dark blue suits with Samsonite briefcases by the window. Matti gave Walter his Efrem Zimbalist, Jr., smile.

"I know it's late in the game, Walter, but I've assigned Paul here to second chair the case with you," Bridewell said. "With what's happened I think I agree with Rollie that you need some backup."

Walter nodded. For months he had been fighting Jackson's efforts to put someone else on the case. "Fine," he said. Curtes was young and full of himself, but he worked hard and had a reputation as a great organizer, which Walter was not.

"Any developments?" Bridewell asked.

"No. Roscoe's still dead. But I'm pretty sure who did it." Walter paused for their full attention.

"You suspect Jeffries," Bridewell suggested.

"That's right. Friday I had dinner with Driesen. He wanted to talk disposition, something about a plea to a drug count. I told him to go fuck himself."

"Walter, don't you think—" objected Jackson.

Bridewell held up his hand, cutting off his assistant.

"Anyway, Driesen was trying to get my confidence, so he played like he had inside information about what happened," Walter continued. "Says he's heard from some of his other clients in the drug business that Roscoe had a reputation for cheating his customers and that's why he was whacked. Except it's bullshit. Roscoe was a professional. He took pride in being good at his business. All that stuff found at his house was a setup."

Matti shook his head slightly.

"You think different?" Walter asked him.

"We can talk about it later," Matti said quietly.

"Maybe we ought to hear about it now," Jackson said.

Matti glanced first at his supervisor and then at Bridewell.

"Go ahead, Dan," said Bridewell.

Walter was surprised that the two were on a first name basis. But then Matti could move in all circles. It was why he was so good undercover.

"Well, it's just that Roscoe did have that reputation," Matti said. "For shorting people. That's how he got caught in the state case. He shorted somebody, or at least they thought he did, and they set him up. I figure that's why he kept talking about being a professional. It's a bad rap to have when you're in that business."

"You never told me," Walter said.

"It never came up," Matti replied.

"You never told me about the beeper either."

Matti blinked, but responded fast. "It's in the police report." He turned to the others. "They found it in the bumper of Brown's car. We don't know if it's connected or not."

"In any event, the investigation continues, right?" Bridewell said.

"Absolutely," replied Walter.

"Well, we just wanted to get things squared away," Bridewell said. "You know that the office is one hundred percent behind you, Walter. Whatever resources we can muster are yours. Just keep us informed."

At fifty-five, Rachel Martin was the oldest probation officer in the county with a full case load, and she still worked longer hours than anyone else in her division. She was at her desk by seven-forty-five and rarely checked out before six. Since her children were grown she devoted more time to causes and most nights she went out to a meeting. She smoked, got little exercise, and every morning before her third cup of coffee, when her smoker's cough seemed most persistent, she wondered how long she had left. A variety of supervisors had urged her to take a desk job but she refused. They might have forced her out, but after thirty years in the job, she knew too much. She scared them.

Lately she had been thinking about retirement though. Her county pension was vested, her small house in the Valley was paid off, and her younger son had just graduated UCLA. She thought about selling the house and moving north, someplace where the air was clean and the people friendly.

In February she had asked her supervisor not to give her any new cases, hinting that she would resign by the summer. Then one Sunday in March her supervisor called her at home and told her to report to the federal building in Westwood. The feds had raided the Hollywood Youth House and did not know what to do with the kids. Once she got involved with the case she could not let go. It seemed to bring everything back into focus.

Monday morning she went in to see Walter Buris. They had spoken before, but Buris had never paid her much attention. Now that Roscoe Brown was dead, she thought he might be more receptive to her ideas.

"I think you should start a real search for the house in the hills," she said when she finally got in to see him.

Walter sighed. "The house in the hills." It was the El Dorado of the case, a mysterious ranch-style house located somewhere in the Hollywood hills where all the movies had been shot. Several of the Youth House residents had described being taken there, but always at night. They could only describe the location generally.

"What's the point?" Walter asked.

"I know the place must have been cleaned out since Jeffries's arrest, but too much happened there for them to cover up everything," Rachel said. "Finding it's just a matter of legwork. We know enough about it to find it through public records and some knocking on doors."

"We start trial next week," Walter said.

[33]

"You know it was Jeffries that killed Roscoe," she said. "He'll do anything to get people out of his way."

Walter nodded, considering her words. She was a hard person to take seriously. She wore loose dresses with florid scarves and kept glasses on a chain around her neck. Her red hair was set in a permanent at least twenty years out of fashion. She spoke with the hint of a Brooklyn accent in a voice that still crackled with passion. She always seemed furious underneath. And she smoked. "No one else seems to think that," Walter said as she lit another cigarette.

"They don't know Jeffries," Rachel said. "It's his standard MO. Usually he doesn't have to do anything, he just threatens. But when he has to, he'll do anything. I've been working in Hollywood for years and I know a lot of people who've dealt with him. They're scared to death of him."

"Maybe that's just a front. A Hollywood thing," Walter suggested.

"People in Hollywood know the difference," she replied. "You know about Tommy DeWit?"

"I've heard stories."

"Then you know about how he disappeared from the House after having a falling out with Ted and no one's seen him since. Everybody loved him, but the kids won't even say his name now. Something happened to him. Just like Roscoe."

Walter studied Rachel. He needed someone he could trust, who thought the way he did. "Have you heard anything on the news, or anywhere else, anything about a beeper being found on Roscoe Brown's car after he was killed?" he asked.

"No. And I've read or watched just about everything on the case," she said.

"Can you find the house?" he asked.

"By myself?"

"Yup," Walter said.

"Yes," she said finally.

"Then raise your right hand and repeat after me," Walter said, his right hand raised in the position for administering an oath.

Rachel looked quizzical. "Okay," she said finally. She cocked her arm so that her right palm faced Walter's.

"I, Rachel Martin, state probation officer, do hereby promise to faithfully and cautiously assist in the criminal investigation of *United States* v. *Jeffries* under the direction of federal authorities, so help me God."

". . . so help me God," Rachel concluded.

[24]

"Welcome aboard, Rachel. I hope it's not a sinking ship." Walter extended his hand.

"I don't know what I just did but I'll help any way I can," she said. "You need a haircut, you know."

Walter laughed.

"No, you do," Rachel said. "It's not the sixties anymore."

"You sound like my mother," Walter said.

"Uh, Walter?" Paul Curtes appeared in the doorway.

"Hey, Paul. This is Rachel Martin. She works with the kids and is going to be helping us."

"That's great," Curtes said with an awkward smile.

"Well, I guess I better get to work," Rachel said.

Curtes sat in one of the chairs opposite Walter's desk, adjusting it so that he faced Walter directly. It was one of his little quirks. His office was immaculate, even in the middle of trial.

"I want you to know that I volunteered for this assignment," he said. "I've worked with Dan Matti before and I have the greatest respect for him. As far as I'm concerned he's one of the great investigators of our times. But I want you to know that I totally understand that it's your case and you call the shots. Just tell me what you want me to do." He pulled a Cross pen from his suit jacket and prepared to write on a yellow legal pad. Curtes was younger than Walter and had started in the office two years after Walter, but he had a reputation as one of the hot young prosecutors.

"Perhaps you have some ideas," Walter said.

"Well," said Curtes, removing a typewritten sheet from a manila folder, "I have noted some organizational problems. I spent most of the weekend going over the files." He gave Walter a copy of his memo and went through it, detailing problems with the exhibits and witness list.

"And I think we need a media strategy," Curtes continued. "They're killing us on this stuff in the paper and the courthouse steps TV bits. I was thinking if you don't want to leak something then maybe we should file something inflammatory in the trial memo. You know, make it public record. We have to match fire with fire."

"I'll think about it," Walter replied.

"And—now you tell me if I'm out of line here, but I don't know about letting somebody like Rachel Martin get involved. I read her memos about the case. She's a total loose cannon. If she oversteps her bounds, Driesen could hand us our head in a basket. Have you ever had a case with him?"

"No," said Walter.

"My first summer of law school I worked for him. Got to know him pretty well, so we've got a good rapport, if you need a liaison or anything. Anyway, he's good. Very good."

"So I hear," Walter said. He could see that Curtes did not think the same of him.

FOUR

"I'd like to hear your opening statement," Ted Jeffries told Driesen.

Driesen nodded. Trial was to begin in a few days, and like most defendants, Ted was on edge.

"I'll probably defer that until we begin the defense portion of the case," Driesen said in his calmest voice. "The prosecution puts its evidence on first, then—"

"I know how it works," Jeffries said sharply.

They sat in Driesen's Beverly Hills office in a building that overlooked most of the Westside. It was expensive and inconvenient to the courts downtown but had an impressive view of monied Los Angeles, which put his fearful clients at ease. They figured he could not afford it if all his clients were put away. The office had been professionally decorated in what his wife called legal Colonial—lots of dark wood furniture, framed diplomas, and prints of English barristers in horsehair wigs. At least once a month Driesen was tempted to throw it all out, but then he would have to find something better.

Jeffries glared at him from across the desk.

"Why don't you tell me what you had in mind?" Driesen asked. Many clients disliked his strategy but few had ideas of their own, at least that would stand up to scrutiny.

"I want an aggressive opening," Jeffries said. "With lots of facts. Stuff the reporters have to use in their stories."

"Such as?"

"Like I'm going to testify. Like we'll prove their witnesses are lying scum trying to save themselves."

Driesen nodded carefully. He was not a lawyer who would throw a case away on the strategic whim of a panicky defendant. He would take his best shot at every opportunity—by negotiation, by litigating pretrial, trial, and appeal, taking no more chances than necessary, waiting for the prosecution to crack. It took determination and a lot of patience.

"We can talk later about your testimony—whether you'll testify," Driesen said.

"I am taking the fucking stand," Jeffries said quietly.

"There's not much use you paying me the kind of money you are if—"

"I'm not paying you shit. To me it's shit. It's big money to you, but not to me. I'm paying you because you're good. Not because you're God. I'm not one of your Colombian slimeballs. We're talking public relations and I know public relations."

"It's a trial, Ted. A jury trial."

"Public relations."

"You're very astute about a lot of things, Ted—"

"Don't talk shit."

Driesen tapped his pen against a manila folder.

"Okay. You were right about the *Rolling Stone* interview."

"Fuckin' right. Turned this case around. Before that I was a world-class pervert. Now I'm a self-made man, a successful businessman, a backer of liberal causes who is fighting for his life and reputation. Now we have a shot at it. A good shot."

"Okay. But at least I should have been there."

"No way. If I'd had you there it would have been a bullshit story and everyone in the world would have known it. The writer would have been all over me. Me doing it alone, that writer knew he was getting the real shit. The truth sings, and he heard it, loud and clear."

"You gave them ammunition for cross-examination."

"I'm innocent, Gary. That's different than not guilty. Innocent. I didn't do any of this shit. Yeah, I said some things they can use to make me look bad. I made mistakes. But I owned up to them. I'm not what they say I am."

Driesen nodded. It had been an extraordinary move—doing a day-long interview with a nationally known writer, no ground rules, no lawyer—and Jeffries had pulled it off. The psychology was just right. From the article Jeffries appeared personally devastated by the charges but righteous in his own defense. He came across as the victim of circumstances. The story was picked up by the wires and played prominently on television, providing Jeffries's side of the case more effectively than any of the courthouse steps comments Driesen had made. It had also changed the lawyer-client relationship. Now Jeffries thought he could dominate the legal process the way he dominated everything else. With any other client Driesen would demand the right to set basic strategy and risk losing the client to another lawyer. But Driesen wanted the case. The case could make his career. In a few weeks he could go from a prominent LA lawyer to a national figure.

He would never have to hustle clients again. They would all come to him, and he could pick and choose.

"Okay, Ted. This is what I'll do," Driesen said. "I'll give an opening statement, right after Buris. I'll tell the jury that we'll be calling witnesses and give a general outline of the defense. But I won't make any reference to you taking the stand. That's way too dangerous for any number of reasons."

"Sometimes you gotta put your balls on the line."

"That's right. But you don't do it when you don't have to," Driesen responded.

Jeffries laughed lightly. "I'd like to hear it when you have it ready."

"I'm not in the habit of auditioning for my clients."

Jeffries stood. "I'd like to hear it when you have it ready," he repeated.

Driesen finally nodded.

"Oh—and you know this new prosecutor they have on the case, Curtes?" Jeffries said. "He's their weak link."

"How do you know?"

"I have my sources."

Driesen looked at him hard.

"It's just if you have to lean on one of them, I'd choose the young one, Curtes," Jeffries said.

Driesen nodded again, but doubted his client's advice. Curtes was less experienced than Buris, but Driesen had known Curtes since he was a law student and thought of him as smart and tough, probably smarter and tougher than Buris, who was known as something of a flake. What did Jeffries know that he did not? Driesen wondered.

Walter spent Saturday pushing through the pile of juror questionnaires for the third time. It was frustrating work. The questionnaires provided basic background information, but not enough. He had to know more than their ages, occupations, and knowledge of the case. More would come out in court, but even then body language and verbal nuance meant more than the actual answers given. Jurors invariably used the same meaningless platitudes. Yes I can be fair even though I read about it in the paper. No it doesn't matter to me that the police arrested my brother three times but he was never convicted.

The questions Walter wanted to ask he could not put to most of his friends. They were the kind that had to wait for the right moment, the right buzz of human warmth and trust to permit a personal intrusion. How old were you when you first had sex? What was it like? Have you ever enjoyed pornography? Have you ever used cocaine or known anyone who did? It couldn't be done, at least not in open court.

"Walter?" It was Curtes, standing in the doorway. "Got a minute?"

"Sure."

Even on a Saturday he wore a crisply laundered blue shirt and unwrinkled khaki pants. His thick, blown-dry hair looked perfect.

"I noticed the witness list," Curtes said.

"Yes?"

"Flash is listed as the first witness."

"That's right," Walter said.

"Whatever happened to starting off with the strongest witness?" Curtes asked.

"He's dead," Walter replied.

Curtes nodded and sat down. "Walter, as I understand it, Flash is a pimp, a doper, and a three-time loser. And comes off like one. But Dan headed up the search team, he can get in some statements, the pictures, lay the foundation. You know we had a case together—that political corruption thing in Orange County? It all depended on credibility. He did some of the undercover work and—"

"I know," Walter said, cutting him off.

"Anyway, it wasn't an easy case," Curtes continued, "but after Dan testified the jury was eating out of my hand."

"Mm," Walter grunted.

"People believe him," Curtes said.

"Okay," Walter said. "Tell Dan he'll go first."

"Great. You won't be sorry."

After Curtes left Walter realized the mistake he had nearly made. They needed to start with credibility, not sleaze. Walter saw that going with Flash had been a way of denying Roscoe's death.

He missed Roscoe. With Roscoe, Walter could swear, lose his temper, tell wicked stories and dirty jokes. Curtes was too uptight, and Matti was a different generation. And Walter could talk to Roscoe. Walter told him about the breakup of his marriage. In a strange way Roscoe seemed wise about women. He seemed to know Laura without ever having met her and knew where Walter had gone wrong. He told Walter that when he was in prison even the guards used to come to him for advice. Not that it helped in his own private life.

Walter went home in the late afternoon and took a run through the park. He ran hard and felt almost relaxed as he broke the imaginary tape he always set for himself by the fire hydrant half a block from his house. He was walking back, hands at his hips, T-shirt stuck to his skin, when he heard the faint sound of the phone ringing in his house. He grabbed it on the sixth ring; it was Erica Praiz, a woman he had met at a meeting of the litigation section of the county bar a few weeks before.

"I just decided I'm not going to work all weekend even though I really should," she said with a slight laugh.

"I know what you mean." Walter felt guilty leaving the office, but after months of preparation there was little more to do. He had promised himself no distractions during the trial, but it had not started yet and he felt the old hunger. If she was calling him that meant she was lonely and wanted to see him. It was up to him.

"So, you doing anything tonight?" he asked. "Maybe want to go out and get something to eat?"

She hesitated a moment, then agreed. Two hours later he picked her up outside her building in the Valley.

"Interesting," Erica said, spreading her long skirt around the vinyl seat of his six-year-old Toyota Corolla, taking in its sparse, black interior.

"It's a statement," Walter said. "It says I can't afford a BMW."

Erica laughed.

For years Walter had ridden a motorcycle, but when Sara came he bought the car from a friend. It had belonged to a woman stockbroker who had died of a heart attack at twenty-seven. He had found her hash pipe in the trunk, and old lipsticks under the seats. The car was not much fun to drive but it always worked.

Erica was a few years younger than he, with short blond hair and bright blue eyes. Her body and face seemed soft, rounded in a childlike way that gave her a deceptive vulnerability. When she smiled she seemed much younger and almost mischievous. When serious her eyes were focused and intense. She was a lawyer who worked in a small but prestigious Century City firm best known for its entertainment practice, although she did mostly business litigation.

It was early evening, the sun low and searing against his arm and face as he drove. The Ventura Freeway was clogged with vehicles that glinted harshly in their eyes. Something about the scene reminded him of the old Eagles, so he slotted a tape of theirs into the car's deck.

When the too-sweet sound got to him, Walter punched in a Lynyrd Skynyrd tape and turned up the volume. His favorite cut on the album, "Gimme Three Steps," came on, and he sang along, loud. It was his favorite kind of barroom rock and roll.

"You have a good voice," Erica said.

"Thanks. In another life I'd be a rock singer," he replied.

"Little different from being a federal prosecutor."

He turned down the music.

"I don't know. You get up in public and make a fool of yourself. Lots of drugs involved. Maybe it's just you're on different sides." He switched into the fast lane but had to brake fast as traffic suddenly slowed, a serpent of red lights flicking on in front of them. "What about you?" Walter asked. "What would you be? You know, if you could."

"An astronaut. Not like on the space shuttle, though, going up twice in twenty years to launch spy satellites. I mean like Sigourney Weaver in *Alien*. Or Captain Kirk."

"Yeah. Beam me up," Walter said.

By this time traffic had ground to a complete halt. They laughed.

At dinner they drank a bottle of wine and traded stories about office politics and wondered at all they left unsaid. They wondered about the night ahead, and after, but could not mention either for part of the wondering was wondering what they wanted. It was better to leave it unsaid and to work on the sensation of a night out of time, like a moment stolen alone in the quiet and cool of a bathroom at a loud party. It was enough not to be alone.

Walter listened and probed carefully, following her through the maze of her life, tracking the scattered clues as she left them, some obvious and others apparent in omissions and little gestures or a change in tone. He liked people, especially women, especially getting to know them. When he was on, when he made a connection, they became transparent. He could know their thoughts before they spoke them, sense their feelings before they did. Laura had been like that. She had been astonished at the way they talked like old friends within an hour of meeting. Later, much later, she turned opaque and Walter feared their conversations. Talking with her became like stumbling through Sara's room at night, the floor littered with sharp-edged toys.

Erica flickered in and out of view. When she was calm he could see her clearly, but then something would happen, and she would fly off, like paper caught by a gust of wind and she would be talking at double speed, leaving Walter to sip his wine and wait until she alighted again.

She wanted to talk about the Iran-Contra affair. "Isn't it so per-fect—Reagan selling arms to the Ayatollah and then not even knowing it? But I guess you see it differently. I mean working for the government and everything."

"Not really. We're pretty independent from Washington."

"So what are your chances? From everything I read it sounds like a long shot."

"We're going to win." The buzz of alcohol and the thrill of her eyes looking into his made him absolutely sure. Winning was a matter of tapping into the public power source, of finding and channeling the urges that make people laugh and scream, and if tonight he could connect with this woman he barely knew, he could do it with twelve jurors.

Outside it was dark, the air cooling, and from the freeway the city was casually but elegantly lit, the lights dotting the landscape far into and around the distant mountains.

"I love this place at night," Walter said as he drove. He kept the radio off, enjoying the night's soft peace.

"It makes me think about being rich," Erica said. "I think about having a big house in the hills, behind gates, with big high trees, and never coming out except at night, like a vampire."

Walter smiled. A few minutes later he pulled the car up to the curb by her building. There was a moment's pause.

"You coming up?" she asked.

"Sure."

She had a townhouse in a complex. The downstairs was decorated with Central American fabric works, fantastic landscapes of brilliant colors done in thick quilting. Walter opened the French doors to the rear and felt the night air sweep in.

"Do you want to dance?" she asked.

"Sure."

Erica knelt at her stereo and looked for a station, without success. Walter put a hand on her shoulder.

"Let me," he said. He set the radio on a station that played quiet soul.

"Thanks—you know, I listen in the car," she said, "but somehow I never do at home and—"

He put a finger to her lips and began to move to the beat. She followed. They never touched but watched each other and moved in response. Finally they kissed and she led him upstairs.

In the bedroom they had to work because they were neither frantic nor familiar. The signals had to be clear and simple, the moves slow, deliberate. It felt as if they were under water. Yet with all the slowness, he soon felt the edge of hunger, felt himself grow strong and saw the flush come into her cheeks and neck. Then, as they became familiar, she worked with her own motion, still anxious, clutching at him, desperate that he stay with her to the end. He did that, he was good at that, and when her nails dug into his side and she gave out a long grating sigh he felt warm inside. She lay back, soft and languorous, like an infant after feeding, and with her hips led him swiftly to the same place.

He lay beside her, his face against the cool sheet, feeling his breath and the beat of his heart. For the first time in days he was relaxed and wanted to lie there motionless until sleep took him away.

"This is the only time I wish I hadn't given up smoking," she said. "You know, I always love those scenes in French movies in bed afterward. It's like a nightcap or something."

Walter propped himself on an elbow to look at her.

"Walter—can I trust you?" she asked.

"Trust me? Yeah, I guess so."

"I like to smoke a joint before bed. Is that going to, like, freak you out or something?"

"No."

"You really are a sweetie. I don't see how your wife let you go." She reached into her bedside table, removed a small tea box and a tightly rolled cigarette. She lit it with a match and drew in deeply. "You know, when I first met you I thought you were kind of wimpy," Erica said, her voice thin in her throat. She exhaled, blowing out smoke. "But I guess it was just because you were quiet."

She offered the joint to him, and with a shrug he took it from her, their fingertips meeting around its slim width.

"I'm generally misunderstood," he said, smiling.

FIVE

Leslie Montaigne sat at her desk in the study facing the garden. Through the French windows she watched a small bird poke for worms in the freshly watered soil. It was her favorite place in the house, reminding her of a nineteenth-century classical painting where barely draped gods and goddesses danced in lush gardens beneath pink skies. She used the room for reading and for making calls. Working for Ted Jeffries meant a lot of calls.

"Maury? Leslie here. Did I wake you?" she said in her cheeriest voice.

A grunt was the only response.

Leslie did her most important work of the day in the early morning, making calls from her home. She caught people before they left for work, and as second-in-command to the premier syndicator in the business they had to take her calls. She liked to catch them still groggy, without their calendars and with their minds in a fog.

"So sorry," she replied. "I wanted to follow up on that matter about which we spoke on Wednesday." She cut off his response. "If you haven't been able to find out anything, I understand. We're all busy people."

She paused to let him make further excuses.

"Yes. I understand. I just want you to know how important this is to me."

He began an explanation.

"Maury, I respect your ethics. I don't want anything confidential, just what knowledgeable people know."

She paused for his answer.

"Sorry you couldn't help. And on that reality show, we are casting now, but I don't think any of your people are quite right. You know how it goes. Ciao."

She slammed the phone down. Maury was a partner at the agency where Buris's wife worked but said he knew nothing about Buris.

Maury did not want to get involved. When it was all over he would realize his mistake.

Leslie had always been a gossip. Ever since she was a child she wanted to know everything about the people around her. She wanted to read their letters and diaries and hear their private conversations. In school she was a small and rather mousy girl who found power in what she knew about others. It did not win her friends but it guaranteed attention and that was enough.

When she started to work in the entertainment business, an enterprise dependent on personal relationships, she saw that her knack for gossip could be valuable. As a woman accountant, though, no one paid her any attention—until she met Ted Jeffries. She had spotted him early on as a force in the industry and sent him choice bits of information picked up from her accounting contacts. Jeffries was highly appreciative. When he finally made his move and formed his own company, he asked her to join him. In addition to handling the details of his business he gave her a list of his contacts.

"Take care of this," he said. "It's worth more than you can imagine." It included someone at virtually every important studio, agency, and production company in town.

She went down the list, name by name, and took each to a meal or to drinks to establish credibility. By the time she was done she felt like a spy master. She expanded the network until it covered all organization levels, from top-level executives to the mail room at big agencies to waiters at the hot restaurants.

Within the entertainment business, Leslie knew no limits. But she fought a sense of dread when she approached the world of police, courts, and jail. Several times she had been caught up in the criminal system and each time barely escaped its bony grasp. The last time had been the worst. Two pudgy, polyestered policemen appeared in her office at the studio and started asking questions. Only Jeffries's intervention had prevented a conviction for embezzlement, and probably a prison term. Nearly ten years later she still had nightmares about it.

She would have been lost except for a source that Jeffries had developed years before. The source was difficult, often uncooperative, but well placed. Among the first items the source supplied was the FBI's background report on Walter Buris, done when he was hired by the United States attorney's office. She read the report the way a scholar reads another academic's paper, with more attention to the sources than the text. She doubted that a rookie or burned-out veteran—the sort assigned to background checks—would find anything of interest about him. She would go back to the sources herself, if she could do it discreetly.

Walter R. Buris was born January 5, 1952, in Tarrytown, New York. His parents looked middle class—father Henry was a marketing executive with IBM, mother Ellen kept house and raised the three children—John, Walter, and Kate. They moved around a lot. In those days people used to joke that IBM stood for "I Better Move." Buris did moderately well in high school and went to a private college in the Northeast with a strong academic reputation. He did moderately well there as well, majoring in political science. He worked as a salesman in an electrical supplies company in Connecticut for nine months. Probably something his father arranged, which Buris took for as long as he could stand it.

Then for two years he managed a rock band, unnamed in the report. After touring for nine months they ended up in Los Angeles, where the band split up after a recording deal fell through. He worked in a grocery store, and in 1977 started law school at USC, where again he did moderately well. Three years later he went to work for a downtown firm that Leslie's contacts told her liked to hire good-looking WASPs for its old-line clients. She laughed when she heard that; she found it reassuring that even in Southern California the old prejudices survived. She liked the old ways for their predictability. After two years in civil litigation Buris applied to the United States attorney's office, criminal division. He had been there for five years, trying a variety of cases, many of them involving narcotics trafficking. That seemed to be much of what federal prosecutors did.

She wondered what his soft spot was. From what she had seen of Buris she knew there was something. Growing up in Pennsylvania, she had known enough young men like him. They went to good private schools, played sports, drank, and studied only when they had to. They were charming, smart, and ambitious, but underneath they were vulnerable.

She read carefully the newspaper clippings on Buris provided by her service. When he was quoted, his remarks were studded with words like *justice* and *right*. He was both arrogant and naive. He had never stood the pressure of a major public controversy. If she could just turn the harsh white spotlight on him, he would squirm, pale-faced and helpless, until he cracked and made a mistake. Then they would tear him apart and Jeffries would be saved.

With the extra trip home to shower and dress, Walter had to rush Sunday morning to meet Laura and Sara at Griffith Park. He found them at the front of the line to ride the model trains.

"Daddy, you're thirteen minutes late," Sara said, looking at her watch.

"Sorry."

"You're always late."

"I said I'm sorry, Sara."

A scale model yellow Southern Pacific diesel locomotive pulled up, towing a line of cars with small seats. A man in his fifties wearing a greasy engineer's cap and railroad patches on his jacket swung off the locomotive. It always reminded Walter of the man in the raincoat who rode the tricycle on "Laugh-In." In a quick segment he would pedal furiously and then keel over.

"Do you want me to ride with you?" Walter asked Sara.

"No!" she replied.

"Okay."

"She wanted to wait for you so we could both watch her," Laura explained.

Sara climbed in the first car. Soon the cars were loaded with children and parents and the driver blew the whistle. The train moved out of the miniature station and across the yard designed as a world in miniature, with scale bridges, tunnels, barns, and the remnants of a western mining town. Walter followed Laura over to the sunlit benches. He noticed the hills had turned their summer colors—the grasses tawny, the brush a dark, oily green. The morning sun was already a fierce white, burning the color out of the day. It would soon be hot.

Laura shaded her eyes from the sun, watching Sara's train as it stopped for a signal. When they separated Walter had thought he would enjoy living on his own again. He imagined staying up late at night, going to hear music in all the clubs, reading all the books and doing all the projects that he had put aside since Sara was born. But instead he just missed his family. He even missed the whining and the arguments. He missed being needed.

"So?" he asked finally.

"I'm fine," Laura replied. "I signed two new writers this week. Sara's fine, although she's scared about you and this trial."

"Did you tell her anything?"

"No. I don't know if it's something she saw on TV or heard from Rosa or the kids at school or just vibes she picked up from me. We don't have anything to worry about, do we?"

"No."

"How does the case look?"

"We miss Roscoe. You remember him."

"I remember you talking about him." She paused. "Do you know what happened?"

"I've got a pretty good idea."

"I don't want to hear about it," Laura said quickly. "It's bad enough

[38]

reading the paper every morning. After hearing about your cases I know we're never safe."

"I'm sorry," he said. He knew what she meant. It was why all the federal agents and police he knew lived in all-white suburbs hours from the city. After seeing the madness firsthand they feared it more than anyone.

"You were wearing your guilty look before," Laura said. "When you came over, you wouldn't look me in the eye. You kept arranging your clothes."

"Laura—come on, I—"

"I don't care," she said lightly. "You're not cheating on me anymore. You're free to do whatever you want."

"Yeah," he said, looking away. Then he turned to her. "I'm not so bad, you know."

"I know you're not," she said and put a hand on his shoulder. Somehow that made him feel worse.

When Sara returned they had an early lunch beneath a tree in the park. Sara told him all about school and wanted to know about his work, but there was nothing he wanted to say. He never thought he would have trouble making conversation with his own daughter, but she was like Laura, she wanted to know what was really happening and he could not answer that. He lacked the energy to tell his usual jokes and stories or to ask her probing questions about the world around them. Usually when they went to the park they had long talks about the plants and trees, insects and birds. Now Walter just dug his fingers into the thickly rooted grass and wondered when he could leave. He would see her again soon, they would do something without Laura and that would help, he told himself.

"Well, I gotta go," he said finally. "I have to drive out to San Bernardino with somebody to see a witness."

"It was good to see you, Walter," Laura said, giving his hand a squeeze.

He gave Sara a hug and was off.

The drive to San Bernardino was bleak. The freeway was gray and cracked from overuse and the high walls at its edge pushed the eye back to the crowded roadway. The sun and pollution turned the sky a glaring white.

Walter would have turned on the radio but Rachel Martin wanted to talk. He would have turned on the air-conditioning but his car had none. He handled the steering wheel with his right hand and leaned his head on his left, his elbow resting on the narrow window rail. The wind roared in one ear while Rachel's rough voice attacked the other.

"So anyway, I've almost got the list made up. If I can just get the building department to let me use their computer, we're all set," Rachel said.

"Yeah."

"Of course maybe Eleana can help."

"You think she will?" Walter asked.

"You can never tell with kids. They don't know themselves from one minute to the next. I think she knows a lot more than she's told us."

"Yeah."

"I'd like to do the talking if you don't mind," Rachel said. "We've spent time together. You haven't."

"And I'm a man," Walter added.

"That too."

"No problem."

Urban sprawl followed them eastward from Los Angeles. The farther they traveled the fresher it seemed, as if the asphalt and high signs, discount department stores, malls, building and rug emporiums, were native to the land of hot brown haze. In the blurry distance beige mountains loomed.

They were to meet at a McDonald's in a mall. After a half hour's wait in the bright and overcooled space, a bad taste in his mouth from the shake he had downed, Walter began to feel uneasy. A more experienced attorney would not be doing this on the eve of trial. He would be polishing his opening, reviewing jury instructions, or just relaxing. He was wasting himself here, waiting with an obsessive probation officer for a teenager who would never show. Rachel lit her fifth cigarette. He closed his eyes and tried to relax.

"Eleana, you're late," Rachel said sharply.

Walter looked up to see Eleana, hand on one hip, standing before them. He was surprised again by her beauty. Her skin looked pale against the black of her hair, which was cut to frame a long oval face. Her eyebrows were dark streaks above brown eyes that darted like minnows in shallow water, though whether from fear or interest he could not say. Her nose was thin and straight, cut short at the end in a hint of a pug, her lips full and expressive. It was a face that had the beauty of simplicity.

She wore an Elvis Costello T-shirt and tight jeans. She took one of Rachel's cigarettes and sat down.

"The traffic," she said and shrugged.

"You know Mister Buris," Rachel said.

"Yeah."

They nodded at each other.

"You've been okay?" Rachel asked.

"When can I get outta this asshole of a town?" Eleana demanded.

"I'd like to talk about the House," Rachel said, ignoring her question.

Eleana did not react. Walter saw that she did not expect anything from them. She had met them because she had nothing better to do. Or no choice.

"I dreamt last night I lived on a big ranch where the grass was green for miles around and everyone had horses and was going to Europe or just coming back," Eleana said. "It was great except the horses all had these huge boners and if you got off they'd stick you with them and rip you in two."

Walter raised his eyebrows in what he hoped was a sensitive but noncommittal reaction. He knew she was trying to shock him, but he could hardly laugh it off, given what she had been through.

She ground out her cigarette and reached for Rachel's pack. "Mind?" she asked, a new cigarette already in her mouth.

"Go ahead," Rachel said. "Now about the House."

After taking two deep drags Eleana began to talk about the House. As far as Walter could tell, it was the same old story. She said that every time she had gone it was at night and she knew they were in the hills but she could not tell where. He listened carefully, trying to put what he knew of Eleana together with the girl sitting across from him. One minute she seemed a typical California teenager, staring at the gangly boys who passed by, complaining about school and not having a car. Then she said something that reminded him why he was there.

"I wish I was a dyke sometimes. You know I used to sleep with a girl at the House, Tawney. She named herself after that girl on the news, you know, with the makeup and the virgin-whore look? Ted used to talk about that. The virgin-whore look. Anyway, with Tawney it was cool because you didn't have to get anything stuck up inside you, you really got off, better than doing it yourself, but she got all hot and bothered about me and Ted. She got all the wrong idea."

Then Eleana talked about the episode of "Dallas" that was on Friday night and how she wanted a ranch like Southfork so she "could be a total bitch and still have a place where you could walk for miles and just smell the grass, you know?"

She and Rachel dueled for nearly an hour, Rachel asking about the House and whether she was going to school and staying off drugs, Eleana either ignoring the questions or suggesting that she spent her days cutting class and doing coke. Walter could not tell whether she was lying or telling the truth. Finally Rachel went to the ladies room and he was alone with Eleana.

"You're kind of cute," Eleana said.

[41]

"Thanks," said Walter.

"I'm not gonna testify," she said, lighting another of Rachel's cigarettes.

"I know."

"So don't try and make me. I'll screw your case if you do. I'm very believable."

"I can see that."

"I guess you wasted your day."

"That doesn't matter. See, I just wanted an excuse to spend some time with Rachel. I'm very attracted to her." He said it with a straight face so that she looked worried. When he smiled they laughed together.

"Talk about horses," Walter added dryly.

Eleana giggled. Walter took out a business card and wrote his home phone number on the back.

"Call me if you feel like it, any time."

"Okay."

"I know you're scared. But sometimes you have to fight back," Walter said.

Her eyes flared then, as if saying, What did he know?

"Where do you live?" she asked, looking at the card.

"In Los Angeles."

She was a navy brat, the product of a sailor and a nurse who lived at various ports around the country until their divorce. Her mother ended up in San Diego with Eleana and her brother. To outward appearances her mother was an exemplary parent. She worked a steady job, kept the house clean, and saw that her children were clothed and fed. She liked her men friends though, most of them sailors, and she liked to party. Eleana never knew who would be in the house when she came back from school or when she woke up in the morning.

When she was ten a sailor friend of her mother's climbed into her bed smelling of whiskey to read her a bedtime story. He was one of the ones she liked because he paid attention to her. She struggled and cried when Bill put his finger inside her and made her rub his red stiffness. No one came to help. When she told her mother she did not believe her, and when Eleana showed her the stains on the sheets, she asked what was the man doing in her bed in the first place. She called her a slut.

Other sailors visited Eleana's bedroom after her mother passed out from drink or pills. She screamed and fought until she learned the simple ways to accommodate their needs. But Bill wanted more. He insisted on a wet kiss and somehow that was worse. When she was eleven Bill came by the house with a bottle of her mother's favorite whiskey; by midnight she was lost to the world, sprawled on the living room couch, an old Elvis tape playing on the stereo, and Bill knocked on Eleana's door. He told her it was time that she became a woman, although she had not yet had a period. He raped her and said that if she were good she would get it again. He proved to be a man of his word. When Bill returned the following night Eleana tried to stab him with a kitchen knife she had hidden beneath her pillow, but he knocked it away and laughed.

"I like a girl with spunk," he said. Bill became a regular visitor at the house.

At thirteen she ran away. She took the drugs her mother had stolen from the base PX, packed her clothes and her favorite stuffed Snoopy in a knapsack, and with the money she had saved in her piggy bank and taken from her mother, she bought enough gasoline at the filling station down the block to fill two empty gallon milk containers. She told them her mother's car had run out of gas. When Bill and her mother were asleep, Eleana soaked the floors of the house. She woke up her little brother and left him on the steps of the next-door neighbors, then lit the house afire.

Bill and her mother survived, although both were badly burned. One side of her mother's face looked like that of a plastic doll that had been left on a hot oven. It was enough to put off Bill and most other men. Walter had met her shortly after Jeffries's indictment and been chilled by the hatred she felt for her daughter. He wondered if it predated the fire.

Eleana hid out for the night in a park where she could watch the fire and the next day took a bus to Los Angeles. She rented a motel room in Hollywood, just as she had done on family trips when her mother had been drinking. She spent her nights at the hangouts that stayed open all night—the fast-food stands and restaurants, the video arcades, and all the parking lots where street people gathered. Word got around that she had a supply of interesting pills, and for a while she made enough to keep going. Tucked in her clothes she kept a knife with a long thin blade that flicked out at the snap of a wrist. Six days after she arrived in Hollywood a sixteen-year-old gang member tried to grab her bag and she stabbed him in the gut. His gang friends threatened trouble, but the manager of the Pollo Loco where it happened called the police and they took off. Tawney, who had been on the street for six months, led Eleana away while the sirens neared. The next day they met Ted Jeffries and registered at the Hollywood Youth House.

On the way back to the city Walter fought the sinking feeling he always got when he came too close to the dark side. He did not know how those in the state system—the deputy district attorneys and public

[43]

defenders, the probation officers and the cops—stood it. The rapes, robberies, burglaries, and murders they handled were rancid with hopeless lives, people caught in never-ending cycles of pain and carelessness, so hurt they hurt anyone they could. There was an underworld without rules, only a stupid, spasmodic lashing out. It was hell on earth.

"I'm going to put that son of a bitch away," Walter said calmly, squinting into the sun even though he wore his dark glasses.

"Good," said Rachel. "Eleana gave me a new clue on the House."

"Oh?"

"Yeah. The next-door neighbor had a dish. One of those satellite TV things. I mean, put that together with the signs that you're supposed to be able to see from the house, the tile we know from the video, the pool, the electrical service, and some other things, we've got a lot to go on."

"Great." Walter knew Rachel wanted to talk, but Walter lacked the energy. They drove the rest of the way in silence.

That night the weather changed. Instead of a cool mist drifting in from the Pacific he felt the uncomfortable, restless stirring of a Santa Ana. The hot, dry wind started in the eastern desert, gathered force in the mountains, and then swept through the city on its way to the sea. The palm trees swayed and their dead fronds rustled loudly. Summertime, he thought.

SIX

"Mrs. Garcia. You said you don't like a lot of the things you see at the movies and in those newspaper boxes on the street," Driesen said from the lectern. "Even if you had to see some of those things in this case, and maybe worse, do you think you could give the defendant a fair trial?"

The small, heavyset Mexican woman pondered the question.

"Yes," she answered. "I am a married woman."

The courtroom exploded with laughter. Mrs. Garcia smiled broadly.

Driesen forced a smile; he had asked one question too many. Mrs. Garcia fit their bad juror profile perfectly—working-class Catholic mother with a high school education. He was not putting her on the jury. But by her answer she had proved herself the sort of salt-of-the earth observer the other jurors would expect to serve. If he kicked her off the panel they would suspect him of racism. Still, he could not take the chance.

"Your honor, the defense would respectfully request that the court thank and excuse juror number forty-three, Mrs. Garcia," he intoned.

Overall, jury selection had gone better than Driesen had expected. O'Brien had surprised him by allowing him to question the jurors personally, something almost unheard of in federal court, although it was required by California law in the state courts just across the street. Driesen used the opportunity to probe and begin his presentation, gently and not so gently establishing the presumption of innocence as the personal, moral obligation of every juror.

The pool of prospective jurors was promising. There did not seem as many from Ventura, Riverside, San Bernardino, and Orange counties, or as many retired government employees and suburban housewives and businessmen as he remembered from past federal panels. Not one of those who made it to the jury box was a retired postal carrier with an RV, and there were no born-again fundamentalists who had three relatives in law enforcement and claimed they could be absolutely fair.

And though jury selection was critical, he could not remember a case where the decisions on whom to challenge and whom to take were easier. The background information that his team had developed and collated meant that he knew more about each person called into the jury box than he usually did in state court after two hours of individual questioning. They had condensed all the information into a ten-page document of tiny print so that it would not seem as if the defense had any secret weapons. He had wanted to load it all into a laptop computer, but Jeffries had vetoed the idea, arguing it would look bad. "Nobody wants to be picked by a computer," he said.

Jeffries had been a surprise. Polite and reserved in the courtroom, he deferred completely to Driesen. On jury selection he was perceptive and cooperative. He let Driesen make the close calls; on the others they agreed. They would not take the thirty-nine-year-old Westside real estate agent who had never married and "was not bothered" by pornography. His background revealed he had been arrested once for prostitution, probably in one of the local stings where policewomen went after the johns. He also would not look at Jeffries. They decided the case would hit too close to home and he might turn on them.

They decided to take the young nurse from Torrance who thought child abuse was a terrible problem. She looked everyone in the eye, including Jeffries. They knew she had a brother who had a problem with cocaine and she had gone to a liberal college where she was an arts major. Jeffries was sure she was a lesbian. Driesen could not tell, but he liked the skeptical way she considered the proceedings. She was a wild card, and wild cards favored the defense. It took twelve to convict, but a single holdout could hang the jury. Driesen took a pessimistic view of the case, as he always did, and would be happy to gain a mistrial.

Walter wondered how he looked to the jurors. He had an image of himself as the dashing trial lawyer—tall and lean, head held at a slight angle, hair a little wild, his smile slight but provocative. He saw himself as handsome, but a little awkward, just enough to make him seem trustworthy, like Jimmy Stewart. When he made a mistake, he was the first to smile. Of course it was all fantasy. When he watched videos of himself, he thought he looked goofy.

For jury selection he wore the same dark blue suit he had bought five years ago for his first trial. He had been impossibly nervous then, his fingers drumming on the lectern, sending an echoing sound through the microphone. He had asked Laura to come watch, and he looked over at her for her opinion on each juror. He had asked her to come down again for the Jeffries jury selection, mostly for luck. He had never lost a case where she saw him pick the jury. But she had not shown.

Looking at the jury Walter saw only two clearly sympathetic faces. Mrs. Thompson, the retired teacher-librarian from San Gabriel followed him closely and smiled pleasantly. Walter hoped he reminded her of one of her three sons. The accountant from Torrance, an older man with a broad middle, also looked to him for support. The rest of the panel left no strong impression. There were eight whites, two Hispanics, and two blacks; seven women and five men. Half the panel was single or had been divorced at least once. Walter found that discouraging, as he always did. These were all ordinary people who had regular jobs and pensions and kids and they could not keep a family together. Walter hated it because he hated it when his parents had divorced, and he would soon be doing the same.

"Would the clerk please swear the members of the jury," O'Brien requested.

The twelve jurors and three alternates rose and faced the court clerk, who stood before the judge's bench. Walter took a deep breath. After the jury was sworn, jeopardy attached, meaning that the trial had officially begun. If Walter or the judge screwed up now the case would stop, and under double jeopardy it might not be retried.

"Raise your right hands and repeat after me," the clerk intoned. "We, the jurors in the case of *United States* versus *Theodore Henry Jeffries*, do solemnly swear to try the case according to the law of the United States of America, so help us God."

O'Brien then reminded the jurors not to talk about the case among themselves or with anyone else and sent them off for lunch. When they were gone, he addressed the lawyers.

"Counsel. We have one further matter before opening statements: defendant's motion to suppress what has been called the second tape— the video found in the defendant's car following his arrest. I have studied the cases carefully and find that the search cannot be justified as a search incident to arrest. The car was too far from the point of arrest and the search took place too long afterward. Therefore it must be excluded from the case-in-chief under the Fourth Amendment. Use of the video for impeachment will be considered if the occasion arises. Opening statements will begin at one-thirty."

Curtes and Matti looked at Walter, dumbfounded. Walter could only shake his head. "Son of a bitch," he muttered.

In his office, Curtes raged. Walter had never seen him so mad.

"The Supreme Court could find a hundred ways to keep that video in. This was not cowboy cops, it's the FBI. And that video is critical to our presentation. Just because O'Brien used to be U.S. attorney he thinks he knows how to try our case better than we do. That's what he does, knocks out just enough of your case to make it interesting. That way he can never get reversed. And of course he waits until the jury's sworn and we can't appeal. He's a disgrace to the federal bench."

"It's a problem," Walter said.

"We should move to reconsider, then if he denies it we can blast him in the press. Liberal judge kicks out critical evidence. Film at eleven."

"O'Brien's not a liberal," Walter said.

"Anybody who throws out evidence like that is a goddamned Communist as far as I'm concerned," Curtes replied.

"Have you ever listened to yourself?" Walter asked.

"When you get hit you have to hit back twice as hard. That judge's got us by the you-know-what and we aren't even screaming."

"I appreciate the advice," Walter replied.

"You're not going to do it?" he said in disbelief.

"No, I'm not. He's our judge and he's not going to change his mind and getting him mad won't help," Walter said. "Now I need some time to think."

Driesen took his group over to Phillipe's, the French dip sandwich place northeast of the courthouse. It was a throwback to the thirties and forties when Los Angeles was a small desert city with midwestern tastes. It was a big, crowded place, with long tables and stools and a broad counter displaying freshly baked pies and pickled eggs swimming in large jars of purple liquid. They took their lunch upstairs to a small room with brick walls. Driesen was not hungry, he never ate before a trial began, but he noticed that Jeffries took big bites from his sandwich on which he had slathered the restaurant's special hot brown mustard.

The group, which included two associates and three paralegals, was in an upbeat mood because of O'Brien's ruling. Even Driesen admitted the case was breaking their way. Unlike most judges, O'Brien took the law seriously. He followed precedent even when it meant an unpopular ruling.

"If it wasn't for some sleazy pimp we all wouldn't be here, you know?" Jeffries said to the group. "June, 1969. I'm working at a studio over on Santa Monica in Hollywood. I was a gofer. I was there late for some reason and I go out for a burger. There's hookers all over the place usually, but that night there was just this girl at the corner of Santa Monica and La Brea. Long red hair down her back, parted in the middle the way they all wore it in those days. Looks like she's eighteen, *maybe*. Name was Karen."

Some at the table turned to Jeffries. Others concentrated on their meal.

"We talked a little and I asked if she was hungry. We went to a burger place, and sitting in the corner was this greasy little guy in a fringed leather jacket giving us the eye—her pimp.

"Anyway, we ate and then she wanted to see what a studio looked like so I took her back. We were watching them set up for a shoot when something pokes me in the back. It's her pimp and he's got an ugly-looking 44 Magnum jammed in my kidney. He starts going on about taking his 'lady.' Karen looked like she was gonna faint. I was a little worried until I saw the shine in his eyes and that gave me an idea. I said I had some coke in my office. He said okay."

By now Jeffries had the group's full attention.

"We go into this back room where they keep supplies. It's real dark and I say I have to get out the stash. I explain that it looks kind of different because it's pure rock stuff from Colombia. I wasn't into drugs at the time, never have been, but they were all over the place in the business. Anyway, I lay out this white stuff on the desk and give him a straw."

Jeffries spilled salt on the table to demonstrate.

" 'You gotta take it fast and hard,' I say, and so he gets down real close and snorts the whole line like that." Jeffries leaned close to the table, finger to one nostril and acted it out.

"There was about a second delay. Then he started screaming." Jeffries paused, making sure he had everyone's attention for the punch line. "He'd just snorted a line of crystal Drano."

The paralegals broke into astonished laughter. The associates looked bemused and shocked.

"All hell breaks loose. Karen and I run out of there with this guy screaming and firing off his gun.

"She didn't have anyplace to go, didn't have any money. Her pimp took everything she made. I don't know, I guess I'm a soft touch, but the cops would have put her in jail, her pimp would have beat the shit out of her, her family didn't want her back. I knew about that, about being in a place where nobody else gives a shit about you. So she stayed at my place for a while.

"I could never get very far from the streets. Once you've been there, it's always with you. I spent too long out there hustling just to forget about it. It's like I don't really even have a choice."

Walter waited until the courtroom was absolutely silent to begin. He had spent an hour pacing in the stacks of the ninth circuit library at the top of the building, going through a revised opening in his head. It sounded okay, but thin.

Judge O'Brien had given the jury preliminary instructions on the case: how opening statements and closing arguments were not evidence, how they were to disregard the objections made by counsel unless they were sustained by the judge. O'Brien gave the instructions with warmth and charm and an aura of kindly paternalism. O'Brien assured them that they were not missing any of the "fun stuff" when he excused them to listen to the arguments of counsel. The courtroom filled with pleasant laughter. Finally he read the indictment and turned center stage over to the government.

Walter waited for the last shifting of weight, the last coughs to cease.

It was the moment he lived for, when all eyes and ears were upon him, when the spotlight picked him out of the darkness and his voice filled the space. It was like a power that he drew from them all, a rush better than any drug because it was real. Only a few times in even a big trial did such moments come. Once during the opening, at least once during the closing. Maybe once during a big cross-examination, or some other time when the whole creaky process of the trial seemed to move, when his weight on the levers had an effect.

The first five minutes of the government's opening statement could be the most important of the whole trial because that was when first impressions were made. He would lay out one or two powerful ideas, images he could build upon and invoke throughout the trial until by final argument their simple mention would bring back the government's case in rich detail. After that he would lay out the basic facts of the case, going for as long as forty-five minutes, knowing the jurors would take in only a fraction of what he said. That would not matter as long as they heard, and believed, his first five minutes.

"This case is about betrayal," Walter began. "The defendant, Theodore Henry Jeffries, a successful television producer, decided some years ago to help the runaway youths of Hollywood, and so he established the Hollywood Youth House. It provided shelter and counseling for many runaways and many good services. It, and the runaways, were also the defendant's playthings. He played with their bodies and minds. He fed them drugs and had them star in movies. You will see one of those movies. It will speak for itself.

"The indictment, as you have heard, is in six counts, which charge a total of five offenses: possession of a controlled substance, cocaine; conspiracy to distribute controlled substances to persons under age twenty-one; distribution of controlled substances to persons under age twenty-one; conspiracy to sexually exploit children; and sexual exploitation of children.

"The facts of the case are simple. On March fifteenth of this year, at the time of his arrest, the defendant possessed nearly a gram of cocaine. You will hear testimony that although the defendant rarely used drugs he was generous with them with his friends. That included the children, or at least some of the children, at the Hollywood House.

"On several occasions over the last two and a half years the defendant supplied either marijuana or cocaine to children at the House. He wanted them to have a good time, he said. He wanted to make sure they did not buy it on the street, he said.

"The defendant also used several of the children to make movies. Short, graphic movies. Movies of children, persons under the age of eighteen, engaged in sexual activity. The movie you will see depicts a boy of fourteen in graphic and prurient detail, masturbating to climax."

Walter let that sink in for a moment. The jurors were still with him, their eyes leaving his face only to measure the reactions of Jeffries and Driesen. They hoped, as jurors always did, to find some clue in the faces of the defendant and his counsel about what they really thought. But Walter saw the jurors did not seem upset, and he needed their anger to counter what was sure to be Driesen's appeal to sympathy.

"We will present a series of witnesses who will tie the defendant to this movie. By a variety of circumstances, including when the movie was made, that the boy in the movie was a resident of Hollywood House and close to the defendant, and an expert's examination of how the movie was made, we will establish beyond doubt that the defendant personally made this movie.

"Before I go over the case in more detail I must give you a final caution. This may be Los Angeles and the case may be about Hollywood, but this," he said, gesturing around the courtroom, "is not television. It is not the movies. There will be no dramatic resolution after the last commercial. You will have to work hard to see what the defendant did here. Because he was, and is, a clever man.

"You will be hearing about the underworld of Hollywood, the world of chickenhawks and runaways, of Dumpster diving and sleeping in abandoned buildings, about children who should be in school who instead sell their bodies to survive. Ted Jeffries said he would save them from this. But instead he took brutal advantage."

Gary Driesen knew what he was going to say but until he heard the government's opening had not decided how to say it. He liked to keep himself open to the moment, to respond to the swings of the courtroom. It required enormous preparation to be ready for any eventuality and a quick, agile mind to make last-minute decisions. Many criminal lawyers prepared thoroughly; many could strategize on the spot; few could do both.

Buris had given him the perfect opening. He would answer Buris's anger with anger, outrage with outrage. He would even use Buris's theme. He was surprised that Buris did not see how easily it could be turned against him.

"The prosecution is right. This case is about betrayal. The betrayal of a good, caring man, Ted Jeffries." Driesen paused, but only briefly. When he began again his voice was loud. "To the prosecution he is only the defendant, but he has a name: Ted Jeffries. He is a self-made man in every sense of that phrase. He decided to help runaway kids in Hollywood because he knew what they were up against. He's been there. You don't know and I don't know and Mr. Buris doesn't know; there's probably no one else in this courtroom who knows what it's like to be a teenager, living on the dark streets of Los Angeles, without friends or money. But Ted Jeffries does.

"Ted Jeffries, you will hear, pulled himself out of the streets to become one of this city's most successful television producers. A man with wealth and power. He did not have to help, but he did.

"Now let's not kid ourselves. He made some mistakes. Some things went wrong, terribly wrong. There were drugs and there was at least one video made of a young man who spent some time at the Hollywood House. We do not deny this now, nor will we ever. These things happened. The question, ladies and gentlemen, is who did them. Who betrayed the children? Who betrayed Ted Jeffries?

"The betrayers—or at least one of them—will testify for the prosecution. His street name is Flash. A small-time drug dealer and pimp, he became associated with the House as a youth counselor. He admits supplying drugs to the children. He has been convicted of living off the proceeds of a prostitute. When the FBI questioned him he was a man in deep trouble. Like others in this case he did the only thing that would get him out of it. He squealed. He tried to bring down the biggest man he could find—Ted Jeffries.

"You will find, ladies and gentlemen, that at every step in this case there is less to it than meets the eye. This is a case that the prosecution has put together with Scotch tape and paper clips.

"Think about who you would expect to testify in a case about the exploitation of children. See if they testify. See if any of the victims of these charges take the witness stand."

Driesen cocked his head and looked over at the witness chair, quizzical. He paused a moment before turning back to the jury.

"Ladies and gentlemen, this case is not about whether bad things happened to some young people while at the Hollywood Youth House. It is about whether Ted Jeffries did them. The evidence in this case will show that he did not."

Driesen was not comfortable with the last line, he did not like to commit himself to an affirmative proof when the burden was on the government, but Jeffries had insisted. The jury seemed to like it, though, and he could always argue reasonable doubt in closing. Maybe Jeffries was right.

Walter was leaving the office at eight that night when he noticed Eddie, one of the office clerks, still working at the photocopying machine.

"Don't tell me we're paying overtime these days," Walter commented.

"Nope," Eddie said gruffly, squinting against the roving bright light of the machine. "But Curtes said not to leave until all this was done. I'll just come in late tomorrow."

Walter looked at the copies coming out of the long machine.

"I can't believe he wants you to copy my notes for opening argument," Walter said. "And these Justice Department reports?" The confidential memoranda detailed Roscoe's criminal background and involvement with the case.

"He said everything."

Walter shook his head. It seemed strange, but Curtes probably decided that if he gave Eddie any discretion, he would leave out something important. It was just like Curtes to want a full duplicate file for himself.

SEVEN

Rachel Martin stood in her kitchen, sipping coffee, admiring the sun's bright gold on the lacquered green of her backyard. When collecting the paper from the driveway she had felt the sun's heat beat back the last of the night's cool. How marvelous it would be to get a book and some magazines, her beach chair, and a cooler and set off for the beach, she thought. Soon she would do that. She would prove them wrong about being a workaholic. She would take care of Ted Jeffries and then she would go to the beach.

She sat at the kitchen table to plan her day. She did her best thinking at the worn Formica surface in the small room that reminded her of her son Rob, who now worked as a carpenter in Oregon. Sitting at the table, she could see him in all his sizes, the toddler walking with stiff legs and swaying arms upstretched, the serious grade-schooler, working at his homework, and the looming teenager peering endlessly into the refrigerator, as if by staring he could improve its offerings. She had lived in the same house since her husband left her nineteen years earlier.

Spread out before her was a checklist of addresses, a Thompson's map book of Los Angeles County opened to the Hollywood hills, and a yellow legal pad. She had narrowed her list to 213 addresses, but they were scattered throughout the hills on the winding roads that looked so peculiar on the map of otherwise straight lines. Just finding the houses would be hard, for streets in the hills circled crazily and had similar names. Oceanview Terrace looped around Oceanview Point and intersected twice with Oceanview Street. None of them could boast an ocean view, except on those rare winter days following a storm when the air was scrubbed clean.

Once she found a place, she would check her nine points of reference, the four definites and five possibles. She would have to make detailed notes on each address so she could rethink the process if she came up empty. All this assumed that someone at each address would answer her questions.

She wondered if even Ted Jeffries was worth it. She had seen plenty who were worse, certainly many who had done worse. People who killed or tortured for the fun of it. Parents, boyfriends, girlfriends, baby-sitters, who flung their rage at helpless children, leaving them so battered they grew up like human bonsai trees, stunted replicas of human beings. She had seen so many who did these things casually and felt no sorrow but that of self-pity, who would blame anyone except themselves, including their child victims. Through her job she had met hundreds, maybe thousands of people who made her ashamed to be a member of the same species.

Ted Jeffries was different. In his own strange way he cared about the kids. When it suited him he tried to help them. But mostly he liked the feel of fresh lives in his strong hands. That was part of it, but the worst was his arrogance, the way he acted as if he deserved all the power, all the money he had made. He was worth hundreds of millions, all because of a few game shows. For a life of grinding social work she had only her small house in the Valley, a vested pension, and a ten-year-old Mazda. It was her version of the American dream that even a poor worn-out state probation officer could bring down the mighty if she worked hard and long enough.

By early afternoon her blouse stuck to her back, her mouth was dry, and the combination of sun and smog had started a pounding between her eyes that she knew would last the rest of the day. The smog seemed worse in the low hills than in the flats because here the wind stacked it up against the steep slope like hot air near the ceiling of a closed room. From the hillsides, where the houses perched on narrow strips of land, the hard edges of the city were blurred by the brown veil it laid across the horizon.

She had planned to visit fifty addresses that day, but it was three o'clock and she was working on her fourteenth. She had gotten lost several times. At most of the addresses no one was home or would answer her questions. She had faced snarling dogs and thought she saw a pistol held behind the back of one man who answered the door in his boxer shorts at eleven-thirty in the morning, red-eyed, an enormous hairy paunch wobbling above the white of his underwear.

She had vowed not to stay at any address for more than seven minutes, but at the fourteenth house, when the frail woman with the cane invited her in for tea, Rachel accepted.

Helen Meyers lived alone in a small house overlooking a neighbor's pool and Laurel Canyon Boulevard. She insisted on giving Rachel a tour of her husband's memorabilia from the days when he worked in the civil rights movement in the South.

With tea in hand they sat in the sunlit living room and talked about the old liberal causes. Rachel's and Helen's ex-husbands had been active in some of the same groups; they were surprised they had never met before.

"Of course with who we have in charge now, I wonder why we bothered," Helen said.

"I know," said Rachel. "But conservatives must have felt the same way twenty years ago."

"Even then they had the money. And no shame."

"Well, you're probably right, but—"

"This thing you're working on—it's the same."

"Actually the defendant's a big supporter of liberal causes."

"Doesn't matter. You're not old enough to see it. When FDR, I'll never forget, I was a teenage girl, listening on the radio . . ." Her voice trailed off.

Rachel shifted to the edge of the sofa. "Mrs. Meyers, I appreciate your help—"

"Helen. Call me Helen, dear." She shook her head. "You're too young to see it."

"Yes, well I must be going."

"Leave me your card," Helen insisted as she walked Rachel slowly to the door. "I will make some calls," she said.

"You know, I appreciate that, but it's a little delicate, this is an official investigation—"

"You need help," Helen said.

"Of course, I work for the county." She sighed. "Here's my card—in case you hear of anything."

"Write it down," Helen said, pushing a pad of paper at Rachel. "All the things you know about the house. I have to know everything if I'm going to help."

Rachel sighed and wrote down the four definites and the five possibilities.

"You're too young," Helen said a third time as she held the door open for Rachel. "Everything changes but people. Only an old person can see how bad some people are. Young people don't want to see that."

Rachel nodded. She hoped she would not hear from Helen too often. Anyone who thought Rachel was young did not qualify as a skilled observer.

On the witness stand Dan Matti was all Curtes had promised he would be. In his crisp government blue suit he sat erect, looking forward into the courtroom, with an occasional glance at the jury. His voice was clear and powerful, his answers short and to the point.

Walter had planned to take the first witness and leave the later, lesser witnesses to Curtes, but Curtes had a special rapport with Matti, and Walter was glad to give up the hours of witness preparation that taking him as a witness would have required. He did not know why but the longer Walter and Matti worked together the more they grated on each other's nerves. Matti never said what he really thought, just left it to Walter to guess and Walter usually guessed wrong.

"Special Agent Matti," Curtes began. "Did there come a time when you conducted a search of the Hollywood Youth House pursuant to a federal search warrant?"

"Yes. That was on the morning of March fifteenth of this year."

"Please tell the jury what you first saw when you entered the House."

Curtes took Matti through the search, step by step. It was a classic direct examination, with Curtes asking just enough questions to structure the account but leaving the story to the witness. Walter could see why Curtes thought he should be in charge.

Matti's testimony brought back Walter's own memories of the search. It had gone down on a Sunday morning. The FBI had protested scheduling the operation for a weekend because of the overtime required, but Matti had pushed, and main Justice in Washington finally agreed. They hoped they would get lucky and catch Jeffries and the House residents unaware. They knew from state inspectors that they would find nothing in a raid during regular business hours.

On the Saturday afternoon before the raid Laura and Walter had been waiting to see their marriage counselor when Laura announced she wanted a divorce.

"I'm not going to forgive you, Walter. You just don't have an affair when you're having your first child."

"It wasn't an affair," Walter said.

"Right. You just slept with her a few times. I can't trust you, Walter. It's as simple as that." She walked out, leaving Walter to make the explanations to the therapist. The therapist did not seem particularly surprised.

Walter was shocked. As long as they were both trying, they could make it. He wondered if she had met someone else, but knew that was unlikely. She made decisions cleanly and would have told him if there was anyone.

That Sunday broke rainy and cold, the first day of a storm that had swept in suddenly from the Pacific. Sunday morning was always quiet in Hollywood but the weather made it seem especially silent and weary as Walter drove in. Parked along the block surrounding the House were unmarked FBI cars, conspicuous by their blandness and the bulky white men hunched inside. Walter could not stay, he might have to testify in court if he saw anything go wrong, so he drove to the FBI building in Westwood where he and Roscoe waited in the operations room. They listened to the FBI communications on the progress of the three teams—one at the House, one at Jeffries's residence, and one at the offices of Family Entertainment.

He hated the waiting. If the searches came up empty, if they could not find Jeffries and the others for whom they had arrest warrants, months of investigation would be wasted. If successful, if the searches turned up evidence and if the arrestees, or someone else, decided to talk, the case would be made. Although it seemed a distant possibility, the operation could also turn violent. Walter watched the rain stream soundlessly against the window and reminded himself that it was beyond his control. He had done his best and the rest was luck.

"Sara was in this ballet show last week," Walter told Roscoe. "You should have seen her. She's about up to here," he said, indicating his waist. "And she was in this white tutu with wings on her arms and she'd flap around the stage. And after the show she was just beaming, holding the flowers, curtsying. It was like she was all grown up."

"I would have liked to see that," Roscoe said.

"It makes up for a lot of getting up in the middle of the night."

"Yeah."

Roscoe told him about his children, Chris and Duane, who played baseball. Duane, the older of the two, had come home recently throwing gang signs.

"I have to get out of here," Roscoe said. "I don't want my kids doing that shit."

Eventually the agents called in to report their spoils: a video of a boy called Mark taken from his room in the House; marijuana found in three places in the House. The agents brought the residents of the House in for interviewing.

The noise level rose higher as the teams returned; success rang out with the crude male jokes the agents traded back and forth. Agents in the field reported that Jeffries was in custody and in possession of another video and cocaine. Matti obtained a full statement from one of the House residents tying Jeffries to the videos. An arrested staff member, Flash, wanted to cooperate. It was all falling into place.

Walter moved out to the division room, a broad cold expanse filled with desks and telephones, now crowded with agents. They came in with boxes of evidence and set up in groups to record it, one removing items from the box and describing them, another making up a tag, and a third securing the evidence in a clear plastic bag.

A nearby conference room held six of the youths taken from the House. Someone had tried to prepare for their arrival by laying out magazines—*Sports Illustrated, Boys' Life,* and *Seventeen*—along with playing cards and board games, packs of gum and thermoses of hot chocolate. But these were not kids, they were just young. Hard-eyed and sullen they sat slumped in their chairs, smoking cigarettes, chewing gum, and drinking coffee taken from the agents' machine. A cassette player blasted the latest from "X." They played at boredom, hardly glancing at those around them, but watching closely nevertheless. Each was called individually to speak with Dan Matti and Rachel Martin, who came in from the county probation department to handle relocation and "reorientation." Walter wanted to join in, but knew he had to trust Matti. One person might interview, two could question; any more was an interrogation, and these were supposed to be the victims.

From the beginning Eleana and Mark set themselves apart. Mark cruised the floor, eyeing the agents and their guns.

Walter was on the phone when he heard Mark's hoarse shout: "Freeze motherfuckers!"

Mark had a gun trained on a group of agents going through documents from Jeffries's house. He was in a shooter's crouch, gun in his right hand, steadied by his left. The agents looked pale. Around the office hands reached slowly for guns.

Then Matti stepped out of the interview room and walked toward Mark, not fast, but deliberately. Obviously unarmed, he ignored Mark's gun, focusing instead on the boy's eyes. Mark took aim at the agent's head, but when he came within two steps, Mark let out a high-pitched laugh and tossed the gun in the air. Matti neatly caught it with one hand, his eyes never leaving Mark's face.

"April Fool's," the boy shouted. He swaggered back to the conference room, where he received a hero's welcome.

Eleana, however, was unimpressed, especially when Matti handcuffed Mark to a chair. She came over and sat across from Walter.

"You're in charge here. These narcs all talk to you," she said.

"I'm a federal prosecutor. Walter Buris."

"Well whoopee doo. Got a cigarette?"

"No. I don't smoke."

"I don't trust good-looking guys."

"Don't blame you."

"You married?"

He showed her his ring.

Eleana nodded, as if it figured. "What happens to us?" she asked.

"That depends on what you want. Do you want to see your parents?"

"I don't have a dad," she said. "And I don't want to see Mom unless she's dead." She said it in the same flat tone of voice.

Walter nodded. He did not know what to say next.

"Well, see ya around," Eleana said and she was gone.

Matti's testimony went smoothly until Curtes offered Mark's video for admission into evidence. Driesen objected on relevancy grounds, arguing at sidebar that the video should not come in "until the government makes a showing that the defendant has something to do with it." Curtes argued heatedly in response but O'Brien denied admission until the government presented further witnesses.

Walter was angry. It was typical of O'Brien. He knew perfectly well that they had, or would have, enough to link Jeffries to the video. And he was smart enough to know that Driesen's objection had nothing to do with the rules of evidence and everything to do with strategy. If the government could show the video now, it would give punch to Matti's testimony. A big investigation by the FBI culminates in a big raid producing—this video. See for yourself. Delayed until later in the case, Matti's testimony and the good impression he made would be forgotten. Worse, they would have presented the first witness and not scored major points. Two in a row for the bad guys, Walter thought.

After lunch Driesen cross-examined the FBI agent. The defense attorney worked carefully, spending most of his time establishing negatives and normality—all the possible incriminating evidence the FBI did not find, all the signs of normality they did. Driesen treated Matti with cool respect, as if his testimony were unimportant. Only when Driesen asked about interviews with the House residents did he appear genuinely interested. Then he cocked his head while waiting for answers and asked his questions slowly, creating long pauses between phrases.

"Agent Matti. You spoke with Eleana Torelli on the day of the search, did you not?"

"Yes. I spoke with her several times."

"The first time you spoke with her, where were you?"

"That was in a room on the third floor of the house."

"I see. And were you alone with her?"

"Yes. Temporarily."

"And what sort of room was this where you had your encounter?"

"It was her bedroom."

"Yes. And where was she in the room?"

"She was in bed."

"What was she wearing?"

"A T-shirt."

"Was she wearing anything else?"

"No, just a T-shirt."

"That's it?"

"Well, underwear, you know, panties."

"What color?"

"What?"

"What color were Ms. Torelli's panties?"

"I don't know, I wasn't paying attention," Matti replied.

"But you noticed she was wearing underwear."

"Yes."

"Could they have been pink or purple?"

"They weren't distinctive. Probably white."

"Probably white," Driesen repeated. He looked through his notes at the lectern, then went over to counsel table to confer with one of his associates, as if to find something. Walter figured it was just a way to give the jury more time to wonder how Agent Matti knew the color of Eleana's underwear. It had nothing to do with the case and Driesen would not mention it in his argument. He was just blowing smoke.

"Now, Agent Matti, I would like to turn your attention to your interview with Mark Hanson of the same day. The interview which took place on the rear porch of the House."

"Yes."

"You recall that."

"Yes."

"Would you describe Mark's attitude prior to this interview?"

"He was generally uncooperative."

"Meaning he was hostile and wouldn't answer your questions?"

"Yes."

"Did he defend Mr. Jeffries to you?"

"Objection, hearsay," Curtes yelled, leaping to his feet. When he shouted his voice was reedy and piercing.

"I'll withdraw the question," Driesen said.

Walter gritted his teeth. Driesen knew the question was improper, he just wanted to plant the idea in the jury's mind. If Walter did that, O'Brien would have him drawn and quartered but O'Brien barely noticed when defense attorneys played games. It wasn't fair.

"After your porch encounter did Mark become more cooperative?"

"Yes, he did."

"He gave you a full statement, did he not?"

"Yes."

"During this encounter you struck Mark across the face, didn't you?"

"No."

This was new. Walter would have expected Driesen to make a motion if it were anything significant. Probably it was just Mark telling stories. Walter noticed Curtes did not seem surprised.

Driesen continued. "So that if others at the scene say they saw red streaks on Mark's face consistent with a slap from an open hand they would be lying, wouldn't they?" he asked.

"Yes they would."

"No further questions, your honor."

After court Walter asked Curtes to stay for a minute.

"It's bullshit," Curtes declared before Walter could say anything. "Driesen's blowing smoke like a diesel truck."

"You knew about this," Walter said.

"Dan told me it might come up."

"He just volunteered it? Because Driesen's never mentioned it. I've never heard anything about it."

Curtes shrugged. "I don't remember."

"Did he do it?" Walter asked.

"I don't know. The kid's a sociopath. Maybe Dan needed to get his attention. Don't worry, they're not going to make a big deal about it," Curtes said.

"How do you know?"

"It's not Jeffries's style. And Driesen would have made a motion if he really cared."

"I see," said Walter. "You might have told me."

"Yeah, sorry about that. Guess I just forgot in the press of business."

"Anything else you may have forgotten?" Walter asked.

"No, of course not. I said I'm sorry, Walter. It's not a big deal."

EIGHT

When Gary Driesen called and said that Ted had not shown up for court, Leslie panicked. Like many great men, Ted was not satisfied unless he broke all the rules. He assumed they did not apply to him, and usually he was right. But she dreaded the day he was wrong. She told Driesen she would take care of it and sped over to Ted's house in Beverly Hills.

"What are you doing?" she demanded as she burst into the downstairs den.

Jeffries was eating a light breakfast while watching game shows on two different televisions and reading the newspaper.

"Just playing a little hooky," he said lightly.

"God damn it Ted! This is not high school. That judge wants to put you in jail and so does half the country—"

"Leslie—" His tone was gentle but peremptory. "Calm down. I won't speak to you until you calm down."

"Don't patronize me, Ted."

"Leslie—enough of the angry mother act," he said in his warning voice. "I have an appointment to see Dr. Hunter in an hour and he'll verify that I had a severe migraine this morning. I thought that Ban Luk had told Gary, but I guess there was some miscommunication. That's one of the nice things about having a foreign-speaking housekeeper, it gives you plausible deniability."

"You promised you wouldn't play these games," Leslie said.

"You're just upset," he said, taking her hand.

"Are you going to listen to me?" she demanded, pulling back.

"I always listen to you," Ted said.

"Do you remember what you told me after you got them to drop the embezzlement charges? We were coming out of your lawyer's office and you said, 'Leslie, don't take more than you need.' "

"Sounds like good advice," Jeffries said.

"It was. Now you're the one who's greedy. You're acting as if you want to go to jail. Maybe I should just call up the FBI and say I want to

[63]

help," Leslie said. "I could tell them some things they'd find pretty interesting."

At that Jeffries stopped eating. "I'm sorry if I scared you, Leslie."

"You've never been sorry about anything."

"Leslie. This has nothing to do with you. You know the way I am. I need my space. Now nothing's going to happen, I guarantee it."

Leslie did not react.

"Have you been feeling okay?" he asked.

"I'm all right."

"You're eating?"

"I eat what I can," Leslie replied.

"You're still on the medication?"

Leslie nodded and brushed at her eyes with her free hand. "You know I'll do anything for you, Ted. But if you play games I can't take it. I just can't take it."

"I'm sorry, Leslie. I really am."

That afternoon Jeffries borrowed his housekeeper's car and drove to San Bernardino. Driesen would scream if he knew, but that was lawyers for you. They didn't play to win, just tried not to lose, and that was not good enough.

He found the high school easily and parked where he could see the students leave. Eleana was among the last out of the big swinging doors and he drove up beside her without attracting attention.

"Hey Slim," he called out.

Eleana turned quickly. Her eyes widened in surprise as she saw Jeffries in the car.

"I'll meet you at the park in ten minutes. Under the big tree," he said. Before she could respond he drove away.

It was hot and the air corrosive. His eyes watered and his throat scratched. Only the ignorant or weak would live here where the air was so foul, he thought.

He felt again the grinding in his gut. He could not take it much longer, this dodging and feinting when he wanted to stand up and fight. Last night it had become too much and he had fled the house to visit the clubs. He drank deeply of the city's night, returning just before dawn. Although he slept for only a few hours he felt revived. The case was wearing him down, making him small and bitter. If he was not careful, he would turn into the man the feds said he was.

He smiled as he saw Eleana crossing the park. He had given her the nickname "Slim" because she reminded him of Lauren Bacall with her long beauty and inner assurance. She tried to seem so tough. They all did, but she almost pulled it off. Not many people knew how much she hurt inside.

[64]

"What the fuck are you doing here?" she demanded when she came within earshot.

"I wanted to see how you were doing. Whether you were going to school."

"Right," she said, sarcastic.

Jeffries had brought some new music tapes he knew she would love but did not want to bring them out yet. He did not want her to think he was buying affection.

"Eleana—have I ever done anything to hurt you?"

"I don't know," she said with shrug.

"No—have I ever done anything to hurt you?"

She shrugged. "No."

"You'd tell me," he said.

"Yeah, sure," she replied.

"Because I don't want anybody putting ideas in your head," he said.

"What do you want?" Eleana asked. She sounded impatient, but Jeffries knew she was just feeling awkward. Like most kids her age, she did not know what to feel or how to act.

"I need your help, Ellie. If I go to prison there'll be a trust fund for all the kids but I'll need you to keep track of everybody."

"You said the trial was bullshit."

"It is but not everybody sees that. A lot of people hate me, Slim."

"They're just jealous, that's what you always said."

"Yeah. Well, as long as you kids are okay I don't care. Even if I have to spend the rest of my life in prison. I mean even if one of you kids testified against me it wouldn't matter. It wouldn't change the good times we had."

"Nobody's going to rat on you," Eleana said.

"Hey—I'll understand if they do. You have to look out for number one."

"I don't want to talk about it," Eleana said.

"Okay," Jeffries said. "You know I've been a little worried about you Slim."

"I'm okay."

"I wish you were happy."

Eleana shrugged.

"I remember the way you used to smile at me that always got me, all the way down."

Eleana tried to smile, but it was a weak effort that contorted her features.

"Oh Ellie," he said and hugged her. His arms enclosed her thin frame. "Promise you'll call Dad sometimes."

"I will, I promise."

Walter might not have returned Laura's call except for the break in trial caused by Jeffries's "migraine." He did not notice until he was dialing that his secretary had marked all the messages urgent.

"Walter. I'm glad you still know how a phone works," Laura said, taking his call immediately.

"I've been a little busy," Walter said. "Is Sara okay?"

"She's fine. People have been asking about you."

"What do you mean, people—reporters?"

"I don't think so. Maury said he was asked some questions. He didn't want to talk about it."

"I have nothing to hide."

"That's what I thought. I mean, you fool around, but that's not a crime."

"Really?"

"I just wanted you to know," she said, not taking the bait.

"Okay. Now I know."

"Fine."

"Look, I'm sorry. I appreciate you calling, Laura— I do."

"Okay."

"And Sara's fine?"

"Yes. She's great. She's upset that ballet's out for the summer but that's about it."

"Maybe there's something else she can do, you know, one of those programs in the park."

"She's fine. She likes to have something to complain about."

"You could bring her down to court if you want."

"Does it seem like appropriate entertainment to you for a five-year-old girl to watch her father try a child pornography case?"

Walter could see nothing wrong with it but wanted to avoid an argument. "Maybe not," he said. "How's your work going?"

"I'm doing fine, Walter. In fact I've got two lines waiting. Take it easy."

"Bye," he said and the line went dead. He had been feeling pretty good. Judge O'Brien was furious about Jeffries's failure to appear, and sooner or later that would hurt them. Meanwhile in witness preparation, Andrew Synes, otherwise known as Flash, was proving a more articulate and reliable witness than Walter had expected. He had no idea what Laura's call meant so he decided not to worry about it.

"Andrew, come on back," he called out.

Flash appeared immediately at the door, making Walter wonder how much of the conversation he had heard. In his early forties, he had the lined, sallow face of one who pushed his body hard. When Walter had first met him, he looked like a pimp, his shirt unbuttoned halfway down his chest to reveal a fistful of gold necklaces. Now he wore an expensive dark blue suit with crimson tie.

"How long have you had this place?" Flash asked, looking at Walter's bare walls. "It doesn't make the right kind of statement."

Walter's office did have a beaten, temporary look. Although crowded with charts and boxes from his many cases, government issue desk, chairs, and file cabinets, only a diploma and a trio of postcards decorated the dirty white walls. On the bookcase Walter had propped his personal photographs—a promotion photo of himself with the old band and his favorite picture of himself playing rugby in college. He had the ball in one arm and he was lunging forward out of the grasp of a desperate tackler.

Like most prosecutors Walter had neither the time nor the inclination to decorate. He was not going to be a prosecutor forever, and he liked the rawness. He liked it when high-priced defense counsel looked around in disdain. Then Walter could remind them of the difference between money and power.

"Just a couple more things," Walter said. "I think we're straight on the drug stuff. You just have to remember those dates, that's very important."

"Don't worry, I got it all up here," Flash said, tapping his head.

Walter grimaced. That kind of memory usually disappeared in court. They needed to develop a script that Flash could follow without thinking and a rapport that would allow improvisation if things did not go as planned. For in court, things never went as planned.

"You never heard anything about the house in the hills or the movies," Walter noted.

"I told you, I heard things but I can't remember what. Just bullshit, you know."

Flash had consistently stonewalled on the sexual side of the case. Walter was sure he was hiding something but he did not expect to find out what.

"Did you ever see Jeffries do anything with any of the kids?"

"Nah. He wasn't that kind of guy. 'Course he and Eleana used to fool around."

"What do you mean?"

"I don't know." Flash liked to tease. He seemed to think he would be treated better if he played hard to get.

"What do you mean?" Walter demanded.

"They used to look at magazines together."

"What kind of magazines?"

"You know."

"No, I don't. *Time, Newsweek? The New England Journal of Medicine?*" Walter did not like Flash. He did not mind making the deal with Roscoe, but cutting Flash loose from his parole violation charges in return for his testimony had been painful. Like Jeffries, Flash used people.

"*Penthouse, Playboy,* like that," Flash said.

"Anything harder core?"

"I don't know."

"What did the magazines show?"

"The usual."

"What's that?"

"Cocks and pussies."

"Were the men's penises erect or flaccid?" Walter had become accustomed to the strange words of official sex. They made sex sound like a medical condition.

"I don't know."

"What did Eleana and Jeffries talk about?"

"They laughed at it. Whether the guys were big, or the girls had big tits. The lighting. Whether the photographer was any good."

"Was there any physical contact between them?"

"She was sitting on his lap."

"I see."

Walter nodded and made careful notes. Although he showed no sign, he was pleased. Little things like this could win the case. If the jury believed even one of them, Jeffries was in trouble. Flash could not replace Roscoe, but if they were very lucky, he would do.

When trial resumed the next day, its slow pace grew slower. In place of star witnesses who could supply the evidence directly, Walter and Curtes had to rely on a long string of minor witnesses, each of whom could supply only small bits of the picture. They hoped it would be like an Impressionist painting, a blur close up, but a striking image when seen from afar. They presented a social worker who saw two boys and a girl fully clothed in the House "playing orgy" on the floor; a sales manager for a lighting equipment rental company who testified about receipts for equipment rented (on one occasion) by Leslie Montaigne; two police officers testified about early arrests of House residents on drug charges and the quantity of drugs they possessed.

Driesen fought hard on every witness. He was at his most obnoxious, objecting to every other question on direct examination. He raged about relevance, hearsay, and prejudice. He attacked the witnesses' answers, arguing they were nonresponsive or irrelevant and asked to have them stricken. There were endless sidebar conferences and the jury was shuttled in and out of the courtroom to allow the attorneys more time for legal argument. Driesen made no real dents in the government's evidence but did weaken its impact.

On cross-examination Driesen worked to rebut the government's inferences. The House residents were street-smart, sexually experienced teenagers living in the middle of Hollywood; there were theaters within walking distance that showed nothing but graphic sex, including orgies. The rental company manager admitted that the lighting equipment could have been used for any number of reasons; the police admitted they did not know where the kids obtained their drugs.

Most of the evidence was aimed at tying Jeffries to the video. Curtes presented the testimony of an assistant director who worked on made-for-television movies for Jeffries and described Jeffries's mastery of the technical side of filmmaking. On cross-examination Driesen hammered the assistant director about his status as a mere assistant until the man in his late thirties turned red with anger.

Walter took the testimony of Richard Maddox, an over-the-hill writer-director who taught at the UCLA film school. He was called as an expert on filmmaking; Driesen questioned his credentials and then argued he could not be an expert, since he was only a teacher and no longer worked in "the industry." O'Brien finally found that Maddox was qualified, adding as a loud aside to the jury: "It's up to the ladies and gentlemen of the jury, of course, to decide if it makes any difference."

"Mr. Maddox, have you viewed the video that has been marked as exhibit one for identification?" Walter asked.

"Yes, I have."

"Have you viewed it more than once?"

"Yes. Over twenty times."

"And do you have an opinion, based on your expertise, about the experience and skill of the person who made this video?" Walter asked.

"Objection, compound question," Driesen interjected. "Experience *and* skill. If the witness answers we can't be sure whether he refers to one or both."

Walter seethed. Driesen was not only objecting to everything, he was giving lessons on the law of evidence. Worst of all, he was usually right.

"I'll rephrase the question," Walter said. "Do you have an opinion, Mr. Maddox, concerning the filmmaking experience of the person or persons responsible for this video?"

"I do have an opinion on that," Maddox said.

"And what is it?" Walter asked.

"Well, I should first point out that although this," he said, picking up the videotape in its plastic bag, "is presently in one-half-inch videotape format, it was originally shot on film, probably super sixteen, and then transferred to video."

"Why would anyone do that—shoot on film and then transfer to video?" Walter asked. "Isn't that more expensive?"

"Yes, but the look of the piece, even after transfer to video, is much superior if originally shot on film. The colors are richer, truer, and the light more sculpted. Video tends to look flat and artificially bright. Most network prime-time television shows shoot on film and transfer to tape for this reason."

"I see," Walter said, looking at his notes. "Now, concerning the experience of the person responsible for this film . . ."

"I would say based on the fact it was shot on film, which by the way is very unusual for an adult production of this sort—"

"Objection," Driesen shouted. "The witness is not an expert on adult videos. The answer is also nonresponsive and irrelevant. I move to strike."

"The answer is stricken and the jury will disregard it," O'Brien intoned. "If you could confine yourself to the question asked, Mr. Maddox."

"Sorry," Maddox responded. "Uh, I've forgotten the question."

"Court reporter read back the question," O'Brien ordered.

There was a long delay while the court reporter fished through her tape of shorthand notes and read back the question.

"Right," Maddox said. "Based on the use of film and the production values—the expert lighting, consistent focus and fluid camera work, the editing, the use of music and ambient sound, which by the way was not dubbed—it is my opinion that the maker of this film is someone with years of experience in professional film production, probably in commercial or creative production in New York, Chicago, or Los Angeles."

On cross-examination Driesen made Maddox qualify each of his conclusions.

"You mean it could have been made by someone with foreign experience."

"Yes."

"Or an extremely talented film student."

"That's unlikely."

"But within the realm of possibility."

"Yes."

"And it could have been shot anywhere in the world."

"Yes."

"And you can't say when it was made."

"No."

"In fact, you haven't the faintest idea who did make this video, do you?"

"Not beyond what I have said, no."

Walter was disappointed but there was still plenty to argue to the jury. And Curtes noted that during Maddox's testimony, for the first time in the trial, Jeffries seemed to be paying attention. He listened to every word and wrote notes to Driesen. He frowned and smiled, as if he were taking the critique personally. Walter hoped that the jury noticed too.

On Friday afternoon of the second week of trial, O'Brien finally allowed the prosecution to show the video. Curtes handled the technical arrangements, and he had done it well. They set up three large monitors in the courtroom: one for the jury, one for judge and counsel, one for the audience. All the hardware and cables made the room look like a studio. The courtroom, which had been half-filled for most of the week, was suddenly crowded again. As a technician checked the connections, Walter read to the jury a stipulation worked out with the defense.

"The defendant, Ted Jeffries, and the United States, through their counsel, agree that the video marked as exhibit one for identification depicts a boy of the age of thirteen or fourteen."

Curtes gave a signal and the lights in the courtroom dimmed. Walter pressed the play button on the VCR.

The blank screen flickered once and then snapped clear to show an adolescent boy sleeping beneath a rumpled sheet in a darkened bedroom. A thin slant of sunlight came from a shaded window to the side. The boy stirred and murmured. First a saxophone and then a piano began a quiet melodic riff in the background, a slowly changing cycle of notes that grew gradually louder.

The boy stirred again and kicked off the sheet with one foot. He was nude. The sunlight played against his chest and his midsection, highlighting the dark curly hair at his crotch. The camera pulled back and the blurred vision of a beckoning girl appeared. She pulled off her shirt, revealing full breasts that quivered with her sudden movement. She was older than he, perhaps in her early twenties. She reached a hand out to him.

The vision of the girl faded and the boy moaned. His eyes opened bright and he looked down. The camera followed his look down to a penis that grew dramatically larger. His hand caressed its length until it jutted above his muscled abdomen like the figurehead over the bow of an old sailing ship.

The saxophone sang loudly as the boy swung his legs over the bed

[71]

and then stood, a hand at his member, eyes closed, mouth smiling. The vision of the girl returned. She was nude now as well and she knelt before him, kissing his legs. Behind the blurred image of the girl the boy ran his fist up and down in a steady rhythm. His whole body swayed, his head thrown back, left hand flat against his hip.

The piano and saxophone intertwined now, wilder, following the beat of the hand, cycling faster and hotter. Although the boy's face remained in shadows, his eyes glinted bright and wide. He began to yell, a loud raw cry, and turned into the shaft of sunlight so that when he came the spray caught the sun briefly. Suddenly the screen and sound cut off. The end was so abrupt it seemed as if the boy's cry still echoed in the courtroom.

The courtroom was silent as the lights came up. All eyes turned to the jurors to study their reactions, but they seemed to retreat from scrutiny, looking away, looking down. Walter knew the video had made an impact but he could not tell whether it would help. Jeffries cautiously tracked the courtroom. The reporters at the front scribbled notes and whispered to one another.

"Now seems like a good time to end for the week, let you all beat the traffic for once," O'Brien announced. "'Once more, ladies and gentlemen of the jury, please do not discuss the case with anyone, even among yourselves."

Back in his office Walter set down his wooden tray full of books and papers and was about to sort through his messages when he sensed someone behind him.

"Walter Buris? Hi. I'm John McDaniel and this is Harvey Mitre. We're from the Justice Department, public integrity section."

McDaniel looked like a former football player, with a face crudely formed, square shoulders, and a large gut. Mitre was shorter and thinner, with a sharp cut to his features. Both wore dark blue suits that hung awkwardly on their frames.

"Uh, Walter. We have to talk about these exhibits," Matti said, coming in with Curtes.

"And I want to talk about Flash," Curtes added.

"Uh, gentlemen," McDaniel told Matti and Curtes, "I wonder if you could excuse us."

"No," Walter said. "You can excuse us. We're in trial."

"This is important, Mr. Buris," McDaniel said.

"If it isn't about the trial, it's not important," Walter responded.

McDaniel simply smiled.

"It's a personnel matter. We'd like to keep it confidential," Mitre said. His voice was thin and soft.

[72]

"I trust everybody here implicitly," Walter said.

"It's about you, Mr. Buris," McDaniel said.

"Hey, we'll come back in a while," Curtes said.

Walter put his arm up to protest but said nothing. Matti and Curtes gathered up their materials and left.

Walter sat behind his desk and glared at the two men. They seemed to expect it.

"The Office of Professional Responsibility is a division of main Justice charged with overseeing the ethics and integrity of Justice Department personnel. We are conducting a preliminary inquiry concerning some allegations made about you," Mitre said. It sounded as if he had said the same words many times before.

"What kind of allegations?" Walter asked.

"First we'd like to review some financial matters having to do with expenses submitted for several of your cases," Mitre said.

"No," Walter said.

The two men exchanged stares.

"Perhaps we can take that up at a later date," McDaniel said, and Mitre returned the papers to his briefcase. "Have you ever used a controlled substance, Mr. Buris? Marijuana, speed, LSD, cocaine, heroin?" McDaniel asked.

"I'd like to know who is making the allegations and what they are," Walter asked. He thought of Laura's warning and suddenly remembered Erica Praiz. She worked at an entertainment business law firm. He wondered if they did work for Jeffries's company, Family Entertainment.

"This is just a preliminary inquiry," Mitre said.

"I'd still like to know," Walter insisted.

"As I'm sure you can appreciate, we must keep our sources confidential," McDaniel said, smiling slightly.

"Have you considered who might be making the allegations and why?" Walter demanded.

"We have considered that," Mitre said. "With your cooperation we should be able to wind this up quickly and it won't affect your case."

Walter sighed and looked out the window.

"Sir, there is a question pending," McDaniel said. "About controlled substances."

"I used marijuana and tried cocaine in college and in the two years after college. I have not used any controlled substance since I became an assistant United States attorney," Walter answered.

McDaniel questioned him closely about drug use, but Walter stuck to his story and McDaniel did not offer anything to contradict it. Maybe they were going on secondhand information and hoped to bluff him into an admission, Walter thought. If so they were going to come up empty.

Finally McDaniel and Mitre stood to leave.

"One more thing," Mitre said. "A formality. If you would give us a urine sample." He handed Walter a sealed plastic jar. "We can do it here if you wish or in the men's room. It must be under direct observation, however."

Walter shook his head in disbelief.

"We have enough for a warrant," McDaniel said. "And if you refuse to comply with a warrant you will be terminated. Moreover, the warrant application would not be sealed." Which meant that the information that had brought the men out from Washington would become a matter of public record.

Walter still said nothing.

"Ever since the incident with the assistant in the Southern District of New York we have taken allegations of drug usage extremely seriously," Mitre said. A few years earlier a prosecutor in the U.S. attorney's office in New York had taken cocaine that was evidence in a case to feed his and his girlfriend's drug habits. "Our emphasis though is upon rehabilitation, not punishment," Mitre added.

"If you cooperate we will keep it strictly confidential," McDaniel said.

"You'll let me resign, you mean."

"The Justice Department, responsible for the nation's war on drugs, cannot have prosecutors who use them," Mitre said.

It was a nightmare from the fifties. Walter remembered the old antidrug propaganda films the art house used to play at college about "killer weed." He closed his eyes for a moment, but the dark-suited men did not disappear. Mitre still had his hand out with the jar.

If he were not in trial he would fight back, he thought. He could make things difficult enough that they would have to back off, at least long enough for him to make a graceful exit to private practice. But he was in trial and a refusal would set them off. He knew criminal investigators. Suspects who "cooperated" were treated with respect; the full wrath of the government was reserved for those who stood on their rights. Somehow word of the investigation would get out and he would have to fight it in public. Which was what Jeffries wanted. If Walter became preoccupied with his own problems Jeffries might escape. Realizing that, the decision was easy.

"If you two want to watch me a take a leak, be my guest," Walter said. He led the way to the men's room, holding the jar out for all to see.

NINE

Walter met with Bridewell and Jackson in Bridewell's office early Monday morning. Bridewell sat in one of the side chairs as he always did during personnel matters. Walter supposed he thought it seemed informal. Jackson leaned his haunches on the edge of Bridewell's desk, his arms crossed in front of him. They were friendly, considering. Jackson did most of the talking.

"The OPR have notified us of the basics of their inquiry but nothing more. We have reached an agreement with them that whatever the result, they will withhold action until the end of the trial."

"That's nice of them," Walter said.

"The most important thing is that you stay focused on the case," Jackson said. "Don't get distracted by what's in the paper or anything."

The Saturday *Times* had run a remarkably detailed story on the Justice Department investigation and Walter's drug test.

"You know it's all Jeffries," Walter said. "It's one of his standard tactics."

"You may be right," Jackson said. "In any event, we have to put out a statement." Jackson handed him a press release.

U.S. Attorney Jonathan F. Bridewell said today that he has "one hundred percent confidence" in the work of Asst. U.S. Attorney Walter Buris, who is currently prosecuting the case of *United States* v. *Jeffries*. Bridewell said that Buris would continue to lead the case, which has the office's highest priority.

Walter smiled, thinking of the way coaches of professional teams were fired. Prompted by increasing speculation in the press, the owner would express "total confidence" in the coaching staff—and then a few days later the coach would be, by "mutual agreement," fired.

Walter noticed the release said nothing new and made no sense except as a response to the *Times* story. Bridewell could not even bring himself to mention the allegations. Walter realized his career as a prosecutor was over, no matter how the drug test came back.

"It's fine," he said, handing back the press release.

"Good," Bridewell said. "Now just put this out of your head and nail that SOB. We're all rooting for you."

Walter shook hands with them both and walked back to his office. He sat behind his desk and silently raged. He wanted to scream in protest but he could not. He knew it would sound like every whining defendant he had ever heard at sentencing. Your honor, look at all the other people who do worse things—it's not fair to pick on me. They went on and on about the outrage of unequal justice, as if that required there be no justice at all.

He had known all along what he was doing, he just thought he could get away with it. How could he have been so stupid? He had gone to high school at the end of the sixties and always identified with the student protesters. They were right about Vietnam, about civil rights, about poverty, and about marijuana. He had thought it was just a matter of time before everyone else saw the light. But things had changed. The old men had found new strength and new allies. Marijuana was never legalized; the abortion wars returned, along with executions and on and on until it seemed the sixties were just a fantasy or something he had read about in a history book.

Walter had always tried to avoid the politics of the job. He had been visited by some of the Justice Department's true believers who saw the Jeffries case as part of an assault on pornography, but they had their own agenda and left him alone. They probably had no choice. Thanks to their leader, the federal government was out of money. Despite grand talk about a war on drugs, the office could only prosecute multikilo drug cases; embezzlement cases involving less than six figures went unprosecuted. Lack of federal investigators had made Southern California a haven for white collar crime. It would be a long time before the right-wing promise of a drug-free, smut-free America meant anything, he thought.

But now it meant something. Now the ugliness he remembered from so long ago, the anger of old white men, was coming down on him. He had given five years of his life to the government, sacrificed his material welfare, and then they turned on him. High-level Washington bureaucrats left the government in droves to prostitute their official positions and no one seemed to care. But if a trial-battered prosecutor smoked a little weed they would destroy him.

He wished that Laura would call. When they met in 1981 they were attracted to each other because they clung to the old values. She liked it that he smoked dope and loved rock music and thought the

[76]

Democrats were selling out. Her not calling was deliberate. Even if she had missed it in the paper one of her business friends would have called her to rub in the bad news with soothing words. She did not call because she was tired of his indiscretions. She would see it as more of the same.

In his bitter mood his thoughts spiraled down, ending where they usually did, with his separation from Laura. He traced it back to a Sunday morning years before. He sat in the living room with Laura, watching four-month-old Sara play on the thick white-and-beige carpet. Sara's tiny fingers dug into the fibers, rooting herself for a major lift. Her arms, pudgy extensions with creases for joints like the Michelin man's, quivered with the effort of raising her shoulders off the ground. She pulled her head up abruptly, like the snap and jerk of a power lifter, and she stared, blue eyes wide, taking in the scene with a careful swivel. A crescent of sunlight caught her cheek as she turned toward Walter. She looked like an earthworm, washed out of the ground by a heavy rain, sniffing the fresh air. That was Sara. From the moment she had wrestled her way out of Laura, her eyes were big and roving, intent upon the world, as if afraid it might suddenly disappear.

"What are you thinking about?" Laura had asked him. She sat on the couch, hair still tousled from sleep, long legs folded beneath her.

He hated the question because it made him self-conscious, and he did not like to answer for his thoughts. He had been thinking about going in to work.

"Nothing," he said.

"You always say that."

Walter grunted.

"If we talked more I wouldn't have to ask you," Laura said.

Sara followed the conversation, her ponderous head turning between the two of them like a spectator at a tennis match. Her double chin hid all trace of a neck.

"I was thinking about going in to work a little later," he said.

"Please don't," she replied.

Sara let herself fall on her belly, arms and legs outstretched like a body surfer's. She grasped a set of oversize plastic keys and tried to fit them in her mouth, but they were too big, so she gnawed at them with her gums.

"I'm sorry," he offered.

"That's not good enough, Walter."

Two days earlier Laura had discovered that he was having an affair. The DEA group that had made the case against Roscoe and the others had introduced Walter to a Mexican restaurant on the Eastside, beyond the strange industrial wasteland that surrounded the concrete-lined

Los Angeles River. They would all drive out in the gleaming Audis, BMWs and Mercedeses the agents had seized from drug dealers and eat and drink at El Pescador, where they were served by Maria, a dark beauty in her white smock and short skirt that emphasized her slim muscular legs. When she learned he was a federal lawyer she asked him about immigration papers, and they talked for a long time about her family, most of whom were still back in Mexico. One night after several margaritas Walter asked her out for a walk, and they kissed by the barbed wire fence of a junkyard. He remembered the smell in her black hair of woodsmoke, salsa, and perfume. The next time he came back alone and they went to a motel.

He did not think about it beforehand, but when it happened it felt right. He helped Maria get her green card and she helped him regain his balance. Laura seemed preoccupied with her pregnancy and then the baby, and the stress of his job seemed to push in on him from all sides. There were days when he seemed to fight for every breath. Maria held him in her arms and smoothed his face and told him that he was a good man. She said he would be a much-feared prosecutor and a good father. She said it so sincerely that he believed her. He told her how much he cared for her but he never lied. He never promised her anything.

When the agents found out they made crude jokes about social diseases, but underneath they were impressed. She had turned them all down. Word got around and he gained a reputation in the office as a ladies' man.

Laura found out by calling the office on a Friday night when he had said he was working late on paperwork. He had not tried to deny it, although he could have. He thought it would blow over, but her anger went deeper than he could reach.

"Look, I said it's over and it is," Walter said.

"Until you meet someone else," she responded.

"I didn't mean to hurt you. I don't love you any less."

"That's not good enough, Walter. You don't listen. After that one time before we were married I told you I couldn't take it. I told you about my father and his running around and what it did to Mom and everyone else in the family. You said you understood. You promised."

Walter sighed and looked down at Sara. "Hi there," he said softly and she grinned at him in return, displaying her bright gums. She turned shyly away, burrowing her face in the rug. Despite everything he loved his child desperately.

It all had a lonely sour taste, but Walter did not know how to change it. He had moved out for several weeks and then, promising good behavior, moved back in again, but it was never the same.

There was a knock on the door and Rachel Martin looked in.

"This is not a very good time," he said.

"There's someone here to see you," Rachel replied. "Sharon Brown."

Walter's heart jumped. She was Roscoe's widow. "Why didn't she call?" he asked.

"She did. I saw the messages on your desk the other night when I was reading through the files like you said I could. I thought it might be important, so I called her. She said she had some things to discuss with you, and I asked if she had any papers or records that belonged to her husband relating to his business. She called me back and said she'd found a box of stuff in his closet, including a notebook of Roscoe's. I asked her to come in this morning to see you, with the box."

"She's outside—Mrs. Brown?" Walter asked.

"Yes."

"How does she seem?"

"She seems fine. I don't think she blames you for anything," Rachel said.

"Maybe she should. Bring her back."

Walter had not attended Roscoe's funeral. He was not specially invited and Matti said he would handle it. Walter had satisfied himself with sending flowers from the office. When Sharon Brown first called, trial had just begun, and he was afraid that she might be a distraught victim, wild with grief and anger, a combination he could not handle then. He promised himself he would call when he finished the government's case, or perhaps when they had a verdict. It would be best to call with news of a conviction.

"Glad to meet you," Walter said as Rachel showed her in. "Your husband told me a lot about you."

She was of medium height and broad shouldered, with a soft-featured face dominated by large glasses. She was not at all what he expected.

"He was always talking about you, the big prosecutor," she said.

"Yeah." Walter remembered again the story in the Saturday paper and wondered if she had seen it. She could not think much of him, the big prosecutor who set her husband up to be killed in a drug case, who turned out to be a drug user himself. He knew he should give his condolences but it seemed too little and too late.

"I wanted to see you about a couple things," she said. "I guess you've been real busy."

"We've been in trial. I'm sorry I didn't get back to you sooner," Walter said. "I've been real busy, crazy even, but—I really should have."

"I've got two kids without a father now. I know if he's in the

[79]

military they take care of us. You know, killed in the line of duty. Seems to me it was like that with Roscoe."

He could hear so much in her voice. He remembered all his conversations with Roscoe about her and could see the way they fought and loved each other.

"I agree," Walter replied. "I'll do everything I can. I can't promise you anything, though. The government's rules about these things can be complicated and often rather stupid." He did not want to state the obvious, that informants did not rank high on the government's list of pensioners. And it would depend on how they classified Roscoe's death.

Walter was surprised and relieved when Rachel offered to help her with the federal bureaucracy.

"I appreciate that, Mrs. Martin," Mrs. Brown said. "And I have something for you, Mr. Buris." She pulled out of her bag a green spiral notebook, bulging with receipts, pages covered with small-print notations. "Roscoe always kept a book. Said it was for business. It doesn't mean anything to me, but Mrs. Martin thinks you could maybe use it."

"Thanks," Walter said. He looked at it quickly. It appeared to be a ledger for a drug business: records of appointments, deals, dates, and places for meetings, receipts of gasoline and restaurant bills. It was as if Roscoe were keeping records for reimbursement, or for his taxes.

Mrs. Brown rose to go. "I know you must be busy," she said. "I just have to take care of things, you know."

"I know," Walter said, standing as well. Now he wished she would stay. She was the only person he had met since Roscoe died who had cared about him. "I know Roscoe loved you very much. He was hoping you could get back together," Walter said.

"He was always hoping we could get back together," she said. "He was a good man except for the dope. He couldn't get himself out of that dope business. That's what got him killed."

Walter nodded. In a way that was true.

"I miss him," Walter blurted out.

"We all do. Pray for him some. I think he could use it. Nice to meet you, Mr. Buris."

They shook hands and Rachel led her out of the office. Walter sank back in his chair and took a deep breath. Although he had not done anything he felt better. Talking with Sharon had somehow put everything back in perspective. He remembered why the case mattered so much.

* * *

Flash testified next. He was a classic dirty witness, the kind Walter's criminal procedure professor in law school had called a "criminal on sabbatical." Walter would have to be honest with the jury, let them hear his criminal record and his arrangement with the government.

Walter and Flash had agreed, practically word for word, how Walter would ask and how Flash would answer about his past and his agreement to testify. But from Flash's first few answers in court Walter saw something had happened. Maybe someone had reached him, or maybe it was facing Jeffries in open court. Flash's eyes seemed bright, as if he had taken a little something to help him through the day. He had not dressed down as Walter had advised. He wore an expensive suit Walter had never seen before and subtly tinted glasses that Walter had asked him to lose; his hair was carefully coiffed to hide the small bald spot at the back of his head. He sat erect, hands at either side of the witness stand, a smirk playing at the corner of his mouth.

"Have you ever been convicted of a felony?" Walter asked.

"Yes."

"How many times?"

"Two."

"What for?"

"Commodities."

"Could you be more specific?"

"I had some customers who wanted to buy some things and I knew some people who could sell it. I put them together."

Walter felt the anger rise inside him. Flash was playing games.

"The commodity was cocaine, was it not?" Walter asked.

"We like to call it nose powder."

Walter straightened up from the lectern and took several steps toward the jury.

"You were also convicted of pandering in 1983 and served time in state prison for that offense. Right?" Walter's voice was loud, the tone sharp. He clipped the words for maximum effect. Flash sat back slightly.

"That's right. But it was entrapment. They had these guys that kept—"

"What's pandering?" Walter asked, cutting him off.

"I never could figure that out," Flash said, smiling. He looked around the courtroom for appreciation of his joke. There was no laughter.

"Living off the earnings of a prostitute, does that sound familiar?"

"Yeah."

"Mr. Synes, you were a pimp!" Now Walter was shouting. He knew he was probably overdoing it, but for once he could feel the power in the courtroom surging his way.

"Objection," Driesen said mildly. "Counsel is impeaching his own witness without cause."

"Counsel?" O'Brien asked, looking over his glasses at Walter.

"Sometimes it's the only way to get the truth," Walter said.

"That's not a legal ground," O'Brien retorted.

"Maybe it should be," Walter said. He was mad now and stood motionless by the jury box, waiting for the judge's ruling.

O'Brien peered at him over his glasses for a long moment. "Objection overruled," he said finally.

"You made your living as a pimp, isn't that right?" Walter asked.

"That was a long time ago."

"And you sold drugs."

"A couple times."

For the better part of an hour Walter took Flash through his sordid past. First they discussed his career as a pimp, then a drug dealer, and finally his work at the Youth House. Flash admitted providing cocaine and marijuana to kids at the House on two occasions, one being a birthday party given for Mark and another on Oscar night. Those were the only specific dates Flash had ever been able to recall. Flash insisted that it was all at Jeffries's direction. The harder Walter pushed, the more Flash blamed Jeffries. He described how Jeffries paid him in cash and how he "recruited" kids for the House by passing out cards on the streets of Hollywood. It went well enough until the morning recess.

After the recess the glitter in Flash's eyes returned along with his smirk. When Walter asked about the general level of supervision at the House, Flash managed to say he knew nothing about the videos. When Walter asked him about the incident of Eleana on Jeffries's lap, Flash gave a vague account of Jeffries showing Eleana a picture in a *Penthouse* magazine. In some ways it was worse than nothing. It sounded merely racy and gave Driesen a chance to argue that the government had blown the case up out of a series of essentially innocuous events. Flash's direct testimony ended with a review of his arrangement with the government. In return for truthful testimony, Walter would recommend that state authorities not pursue parole violation charges. But the deal was off and perjury charges could be added if Flash lied. That often impressed jurors who did not know how hard it was to prove that someone lied. The witness could always claim to have been confused, stressed out, or to have suffered a memory loss. Walter knew that Driesen would find a way to point that out on cross-examination. Which he did.

Flash finished his testimony a day later, Driesen having gone easy on him after Walter's harsh direct examination. Walter then read to the jury the stipulation entered into between the government and the defense, which stated that the defendant had in his jacket pocket a glassine envelope containing half of a gram of cocaine when arrested. After reading it Walter turned to O'Brien.

"Your honor, the government rests."

Walter did not like the silence that followed his announcement. It was the same hollow reaction that usually followed the defense's decision to rest without calling the defendant to the stand. Walter had discussed with Matti and Curtes the possibility of calling more witnesses. They had a list of twenty people who could supply one bit or another, but it was all little stuff. It could all be explained. They decided it was better to end with Flash, who at least showed the jury the sort of people Jeffries hired.

That night Walter had just finished dinner—a Lean Cuisine lasagna with a raw carrot and a Dos Equis, when the doorbell rang. He looked out the side window and saw someone he thought was Alec but he could not be sure.

"Who is it?" Walter demanded.

"It's me, Dave," the man responded in a tight, hoarse voice. "I've got the stuff."

Walter smiled. It could only be Alec, doing a classic Cheech and Chong bit that he and his high school friends used to repeat endlessly. Normally he would have played the other part in the bit, that of a stoned apartment dweller, but after what had happened, it no longer seemed funny. He opened the door.

"Hi, Alec."

"Walter my man."

"What's up?" Walter asked, leading him into the house. No one ever just dropped in on him. He used to drop in on people when he first moved to LA but stopped when he saw how uncomfortable it made even his friends. California etiquette required at least a phone call before visiting.

"Oh, man. I just got fucked and I thought, shit. Who can I go see who would commiserate? Had to be someone who got fucked just as bad as me. So—here we are."

"Alec—"

"Don't say it. You're in the middle of trial and don't want to talk about it. All you got to do is join me in a couple." Alec produced a bottle of Sauza Tequila.

Walter shook his head. Alec had been Laura's boyfriend before Walter took up with her. Somehow Laura and Alec had stayed friends and Walter had always liked him. He was a television writer, smart, funny, and dissolute. He treated Walter as if he were a hero and a saint for his work, an attitude so exaggerated that Walter always took it as a put-on, but even so was flattered. Alec had that sort of charm.

"I can't get wasted, Alec."

"I figured that," Alec said. "So this is what I propose. We have two stiff drinks, bang bang. We get blasted for about half an hour, then run around the block three times to get back in shape and bingo, we're refreshed and relaxed, ready for the next day of intolerable stress and ennui."

"Okay."

"I read about you in the paper. What bullshit."

"Yeah," Walter said.

"Revenge of the fascists. They're all over. You ought to see them at the network. They work undercover, all these midwestern shit-for-brains and southern rednecks who've learned to pass for Westside liberal assholes. We go in today for the big meeting," Alec continued. "The show, my show, is up for a midseason replacement. They say they love it. Working-class woman cop in a wheelchair—they say it's new, different, and we've got all the elements. Only maybe she's a little too shrill. They want her tough, but not strident. And the wheelchair's a real downer. And not too working class. You know, like she went to public school but she makes her own pasta. Then they kicked me off the show."

"You got canned?" Walter asked.

"Yup. I wanted to come by to commiserate."

"I think I lost my job too," Walter said.

Alec set up four glasses on the kitchen counter.

"To hell in a handbasket," Alec said, and they drank off one.

"Hey, I got a Ted Jeffries story for you. You'll love this one," Alec said. "You ever heard of Max Studder? He's a big talent agent, handles TV people mostly, very big. Well, couple years ago when Jeffries was looking to get into series and movies of the week, he had to establish relationships with all the big agents. Particularly Studder, since he had some people Jeffries wanted to use. Well, Jeffries didn't give Studder enough respect or something. Anyway, Studder decides hell will freeze over and host the Ice Follies before Jeffries can use any of his clients. Jeffries hears this. Well, Studder is into clothes. At the time he was in his early fifties and had your basic body work done, you know, neck, eyes, all the tucks and rolls, and after all that he really got into clothes. They had to be trendy, but subtle. In other words, expensive.

"And suddenly, everywhere he goes, things are getting spilled on his clothes. He's at Chassen's and shrimp cocktail sauce lands on his cashmere sweater. At Ma Maison a drunk spills a drink down his pants. He goes to the car wash and they spill a milk shake on the driver's seat. I mean this happens everywhere. People start talking about it: the curse of the dry cleaner, you know. Ted's revenge. I mean it's ridiculous. Studder goes to a Dodger game and some bozo three rows up squirts mustard all over him.

"Studder gets tired of it and offers Jeffries a deal—at twice the going rate. Jeffries tells him to take a hike. Then at a fancy Beverly Hills charity affair a valet steps on Studder's wife's dress and rips it in two as she gets out of the car. His secretary is hit by a water balloon walking in to work. Suddenly it's not funny anymore. And Studder's had enough. So, you know what? Jeffries gets everything he wants, at half price. Literally, half price."

"Sounds like Jeffries," Walter said.

"I'm glad I'm not in your shoes."

"Doesn't matter," Walter replied. "I don't care about clothes."

They both laughed.

"Seriously, though, this thing's not worth your career," Alec said.

"What do you mean?" Walter asked.

"He'll do anything. Try to get you disbarred." Alec paused. "Anything."

Walter felt a cold chill rise up his spine. "You work for Family Entertainment, don't you?" he asked.

"Years ago," Alec said. "One of their reality shows—the one where they reenacted famous natural disasters. What a—"

"No. I mean now. But I guess Laura could tell me that, right?"

Alec seemed to slump. "You're a sharp guy, Walter. Look, this is the straight shit. Nobody sent me. I came by because I care about you. This guy is heavy."

Walter stood and pointed at the door.

"He knows where you live," Alec said.

"Fuck you and Ted Jeffries too," Walter replied.

TEN

The next morning Ted Jeffries looked out over the Santa Monica Freeway from the window in Gary Driesen's office. God he loved LA. The bigger, the more crowded, the smoggier, the more dangerous it became, the more he loved it. Everyone bitched and moaned, but except for a few jerks, no one left. This was it, the center of the world's entertainment industry, soon to be the center of world trade, the western entrance to the world's biggest shopping mall, America. He wished the case were over so he could get back out on the street and sell again. The Japanese were looking to buy into Hollywood, and he wanted to be there to show them the way. They just might find entertainment a little tougher than cars.

"About our presentation," Driesen began. "It seems to me we have two viable options. The first, which is probably the safest, is to call a number of character witnesses, say five. Prominent people in the entertainment business and public life who would testify to your integrity and accomplishments. Get at least one major star. We can do that, can't we?"

"Yes," Jeffries said.

"Or—and this is the way I'm leaning—we can just rest. This would send a powerful message to the jury that the prosecution hasn't proven anything. It would be like puncturing the balloon, not that there's a whole lot of air in their case as it is."

Jeffries pulled his chair close to Driesen's. "What about putting on our case? Like you talked about in your opening statement."

"Yes, well, that's why I prefer to defer the opening statement," Driesen said. "At this point there's no benefit to putting on an affirmative case and there are a lot of dangers. They haven't hurt you, Ted. There's nothing in their case I can't deal with at final argument. But as soon as we start putting on witnesses and getting into the facts again, we open it all up. All kinds of things can be brought up on cross-examination, or on rebuttal for that matter. It's a can of worms, Ted."

"You think I can win without it."

[86]

"Absolutely. I think we'll probably win either way, but your chances are much better if you don't introduce new evidence."

"You mean I'll be acquitted."

"On everything except the drug possession. You've all but admitted that."

"I want to be vindicated," Jeffries said. "I want everyone to know that I'm innocent."

"Ted, I'm your lawyer. I worry about the criminal charges, the things that can put you in prison for the rest of your life. Let me take care of those, then you take care of the rest. If anybody can do it, you can."

"Gary, I know that's good legal advice. But I can't wait. Later nobody cares. You have to win when they're paying attention." Jeffries stood and began to pace the office. "You don't know how hard I had to scrape to get to where I am now. And you don't know what it's like to walk into a room and have everybody stop talking and stare at you and you know they're all thinking what a pervert you are. They don't want to shake your hand, they make excuses to leave. And their eyes, they're full of this hate, this acid that eats into you. I can't live with that, Gary. I can't."

"I understand," Driesen said, "but my advice remains the same."

Jeffries sat down again. "I want Mark to testify. And I'm gonna testify," he declared.

"That's out of the question," Driesen responded. "Mark would be a very dangerous witness. For you to take the stand would be senseless. This is not a game, Ted—"

"But it is. You've said so yourself."

"Jesus, Ted. You don't understand. Yes, it's a game, but one of the rules is you never admit it. If anyone catches you playing you get zapped. Like that stunt you pulled with the drug test on Buris. Maybe you thought that would help, get rid of a prosecutor, put them on the defensive. That's going to blow up in our face. They'll never take Buris off the case, and now he's got nothing to lose. He can go crazy and things'll get out of hand. You don't know what you're doing, Ted."

Jeffries laughed. "I can't believe you'd think I had anything to do with that," he said.

Driesen just glowered at him. Jeffries stood up and went to the door. "Charlie!" he yelled out. One of Driesen's associates, Charles Smith, followed him back into the room. Smith was one of several associates who had been working on the case from the beginning.

Jeffries turned to Driesen. "If you refuse, I'll fire you and Charlie will represent me."

"Ted, Charles is two years out of law school. His biggest case was a first-offense drunk driving. Be sensible."

"Charlie has agreed," Jeffries said.

They both looked at Charles. The young lawyer appeared sheepish, but nodded. "If necessary," he said.

"What did you do, offer him a hundred thousand? Tell him your case'd make his career, no matter what?" Driesen asked Jeffries, his face pale with anger.

"It's your choice, Gary," Jeffries replied calmly. "You know me. Once my mind is made up, I don't change it. I just fight."

"How can I get this across to you, Ted. It would be a disaster."

"It's my life, not yours."

Driesen knew he had no choice. Jeffries's decision was an informed one, although monumentally stupid. If Driesen withdrew now, assuming O'Brien let him, he would leave his biggest case under a cloud. There would be endless speculation about it, speculation that Jeffries would manipulate to his advantage. And there was always the chance that Jeffries would change his mind.

"Okay, Ted," Driesen said finally. "We'll put on an affirmative defense. I'll send you a letter memorializing all of my objections so that the record's clear."

"I'm not going to sue you," Jeffries said. "I just want it done my way."

Mark was their first witness. Driesen had hinted all along that at least one of the "victims" would testify for the defense and he made sure that the press knew it would be on Tuesday when the defense opened its case. Before O'Brien took the bench or the jury appeared the room was full of the hushed sounds of anticipation. The regular newspaper reporters and the familiar faces of the television press and their artists filled out the front rows. Lawyers from the federal public defender's and United States attorney's offices filled the back benches. The trial had reached a stage where something was going to happen.

Mark walked in quickly after being called. As in a wedding, all eyes turned back to watch the entrance. He kept his eyes ahead, back straight. Gary Driesen had chosen Mark's clothes—blue blazer, gray slacks—so that he looked neat and clean, but not precocious or monied. Mark took the oath and then, after a glance at the jury, climbed up to the witness stand.

"State your name and spell your last name for the record, please," the court clerk asked.

"Mark Hanson," he said in a thin voice. "H-A-N-S-O-N."

"Good morning, Mark," Driesen began.

"Good morning," he responded, a little too fast.

"Are you nervous, Mark?"

He shrugged. "A little, I guess." He gave a shy smile and ducked his head.

"Most people in that chair are," Judge O'Brien said. The courtroom laughed.

"Just take your time and tell me if you don't understand anything that I or Mr. Buris ask," Driesen instructed.

"Okay."

Driesen took a chronologic approach, leading Mark through his early years in the Midwest, through the story of his running away, and then his arrival at Hollywood House.

"What do you think would have happened to you if you hadn't been taken in by the folks at Hollywood House?" Driesen asked.

The question was objectionable, it called for speculation, but Walter remained quiet and in his seat. The jury wanted to hear everything Mark had to say and would resent objections.

"Probably I would have gotten strung out on drugs. Probably done a lot of chickenhawking. You know, hustling."

"Selling your body for money, you mean."

"Yeah. That's what most kids do on the street."

"I see." Driesen paused to let the point sink in. He wanted the jury to think that Mark was an innocent, thrown out of his home onto the cruel streets of the big city. Driesen knew the story was more complicated.

When Jeffries persuaded Mark to come to the Hollywood House he had been on the streets for two months, had been robbed and beaten, had been chased by the police, but never raped and never arrested. He was skinny and bruised, his teeth were nearly green from lack of brushing, but he was otherwise unharmed. At Jeffries's insistence he called home. He told his mother he was fine but hung up when she started asking questions. His stepfather flew out from the Midwest the next day to take him back, but Jeffries convinced him that, for a while at least, Mark was better off at the House. After that his parents regularly called and wrote letters. It was only after the case broke and his parents found out about the videos that they turned against the boy.

Driesen spent ten minutes asking Mark about life on the streets of Hollywood, about the art of begging from strangers and eating out of Dumpsters, about sleeping in abandoned buildings, shoplifting from stores, and taking drugs. The jury listened carefully. Mark knew what he was talking about.

Next they moved to life at the Hollywood House. Mark, with

Driesen's assistance, painted it in Norman Rockwell style, describing the life of a large rambunctious family in a comfortable old house, a haven from the city, which lurked just beyond the big front door. Mark told of the art and music lessons that Jeffries had arranged, the plays they put on, and the therapy sessions they attended.

"Did you have any particular problems when you were in the House?" Driesen asked.

"I used to drink a lot," Mark said.

"Why did you drink?"

"I guess cuz I had a lot of things I wanted to forget."

"Do you still drink?"

"No."

"What happened?"

"It was Mr. Jeffries. He was the only one who really cared. I remember he took me to a Dodgers game. He didn't say anything at first. We sat with this guy who used to play for the Yankees, I think, and he spent the whole game drinking beer. He was fat and his face was so red it looked like it was going to explode. After the game we sat in the car and Mr. Jeffries asked if I wanted to end up like that. I didn't pay much attention until he asked where I wanted to be left off."

"What did he mean by that?" Driesen asked.

"He wasn't going to take me back to the House. He said I didn't care and he couldn't help anyone who didn't care. He took me to Skid Row where there were all these winos on the sidewalk."

"What happened then?"

"I freaked out, begged him to take me back. We walked around and talked to some of the people. By the time I got back to the car, I don't know, I guess I saw what he meant."

"And that helped you stop drinking."

"Yeah."

"Did you ever see any of the kids use drugs at the House?"

"Yeah. Some."

"Who supplied those drugs?"

"Either they got it on the street or from Roscoe or Flash. They could get anything."

"Did Mr. Jeffries know what was going on with the drugs?"

"No. He would have flipped out if he knew. He hated us using drugs."

After the morning recess Driesen asked about the video.

"While you were at Hollywood House, did you make a movie, Mark?"

"Yeah."

"I'm going to show you an exhibit in this case, a videotape. From the picture on that, do you recognize it, Mark?"

"Yeah, that's the one I did."

"Why did you do it?"

"For the money. And cuz I wanted to be an actor. I still do."

"I see. How much did you get paid?"

"Two hundred bucks."

"Who arranged it?"

"Flash. He knew this guy named Sal, a big greasy Italian guy who made lots of these things. They told me what to do and I did it."

"Did Mr. Jeffries have anything to do with this?"

"No way."

"Did he know about it?"

"No. He would've killed me. He practically did when he found out. I've never seen him so mad, and he gets pretty mad sometimes."

"Did you know of anyone else at the house who made movies like this one?"

"I heard things. I don't know really."

"To your knowledge, did Mr. Jeffries know anything about any of the movies?"

"I know for sure he didn't. He looked out for us."

Walter stared at the faded blue Standard logo on the back of the toilet bowl and thought about throwing up. He took a deep breath and felt the cool of the porcelain against his forehead. One step at a time, he thought.

Mark's testimony had been a rich confection of truth and lies, more truth than lies, but lies at all the critical points. Now Walter had to prove it.

In cross-examination he depended on developing a feeling for the witness and his story. He tried to imagine how the witness spoke in ordinary conversation, what movies he liked, what he ate, and what he wore to bed. If he could see the person behind the witness he would know how to attack. But Mark was elusive. He was like one of those holographic 3-D cards that shifted images when tilted in different directions.

Curtes and Matti told him to take it easy. Mark was a victim and they feared a harsh attack would antagonize the jury. Walter agreed; he planned to take Mark down a road of simple statements until he established a contradiction with other evidence, or his earlier statements to the FBI. He would not confront the boy with these contradictions, but make them the basis of his final argument. Walter just hoped he could use the FBI material. Driesen would object that they were hearsay and the result of intimidation. O'Brien might well agree.

Splashing his face with water in the sink of the men's room, Walter considered another approach. That morning Jackson had told him that his drug test had come back positive for marijuana. He said that Walter would have to have his urine tested twice weekly for the duration of the case. Jackson did not say what might happen then. It hurt more than he expected, but it was also liberating. He had nothing to lose. As he dried his face Walter decided to attack. As long as Mark remained the innocent boy in the jury's eyes, they could not win. He would show the jury the real Mark Hanson.

"Mr. Hanson, was drinking the only significant problem you had while you were at the Hollywood House?" Walter asked Mark after they had exchanged preliminaries.

"Yeah."

"You never had any problems with illegal drugs?"

"No."

"Ever have any problems with other kids at the House?"

"Not really, no."

"What do you mean, not really?"

"Just arguments, the usual hassles."

"Did you seek or receive Mr. Jeffries's assistance in any other problems you may have had?"

"We talked about things."

"But he never did anything for you."

"No."

"I see," Walter said. He raised his voice and spoke clearly. "So you did not seek Mr. Jeffries's assistance when you were arrested, charged, and convicted of ramming a soda bottle up the vagina of an eleven-year-old girl at the grade school on Cedar Avenue near the Hollywood House on September thirteenth of last year?" Walter asked.

Mark leaned forward, his hands clamped on the sides of the witness stand, eyes hard.

"Objection!" Driesen roared, leaping to his feet. "This is outrageous and false cross-examination, your honor. Irrelevant, prejudicial, involving a serious misstatement of the facts, and clearly asked in bad faith. I must move for a mistrial."

O'Brien turned to the jury. "Ladies and gentlemen, it appears that counsel have some matters to discuss outside your presence. I know it is difficult, but please remember that questions by counsel are not evidence. Put out of your minds anything that was not said by a witness and allowed into evidence."

The jury shuffled out to a general low murmur in the courtroom. Walter could hear O'Brien's shoes thumping against the front of the bench. This time he was not impatient, he was mad.

"Mr. Buris," O'Brien began, "I don't know what your game is. Or rather I think I do. And I will not allow it. As we have discussed before, if you have sensitive material to use you will clear it with the court beforehand. I will not have this trial deteriorate into a mud-slinging contest. Is that clear?"

"Yes, your honor."

"Now how is this matter relevant?"

"It contradicts a portion of the witness's testimony on direct examination. It involves a crime of moral turpitude and therefore is proper impeachment under the rules. It also establishes bias because Mr. Jeffries, by his intervention, prevented the incarceration of this witness for a serious crime."

"Your honor, it was a juvenile offense, sexual misconduct," Driesen interjected. "The alleged victim did not wish to testify—"

"After she had been threatened—" Walter interjected.

"Counsel!" O'Brien warned. "We are not going to retry old juvenile cases."

The argument continued for more than an hour. The dispute over asking a witness about prior criminal convictions was a staple of criminal trials. Such convictions could be relevant to credibility, but they could also be meaningless, and courts feared that juries could not distinguish between the two situations. O'Brien finally allowed Walter to ask about the juvenile case without mentioning any particulars of the offense. He ended with a warning for Walter.

"I have my eyes on you, Mr. Buris. Any more nonsense like what you just pulled and I will direct a verdict against the government. That sort of questioning has no place in a federal court."

"Yes, your honor," Walter said. He tried to look chastened but he was secretly pleased. It was a deliberate foul, but now the jury knew a little of the truth about Mark both from the question and Mark's reaction.

To his surprise, Driesen raised no general objections to Walter's questions about Mark's statement to the FBI. Walter saw why when he pressed Mark on it.

"Didn't you tell Agent Matti that there were lots of drugs at the House?" Buris asked Mark, trying for the third time to win an admission on the prior statement.

"Yeah, I said it. But only after he whacked me a couple times," Mark replied. "He didn't like what I was telling him so he took me off behind the house and slammed me up against the wall and said I had to say what he wanted. I said a lot of things after that."

Walter then reviewed with Mark the statement he had given Matti, emphasizing those details Matti could not have known and Mark could not have made up on the spot. Mark became fresh, even rude. He made eyes at the actress from North Hollywood who sat in the front row of the jury box.

Walter ended the cross-examination on a softer note.

"Mark, what did you and the other kids call Mr. Jeffries? What name did you use?"

"Ted."

"Didn't you sometimes call him Dad?"

"Some of the kids did."

"Did you?"

"I don't know. I guess, maybe a couple times."

"He did a lot for you, didn't he?"

"Yeah."

"A lot more than anyone else has."

"Yeah."

"Including your parents."

"Yes."

"So you owe him a lot."

"I guess so."

Walter took up his notes, as if he were finished, then turned back to the witness. "Oh, one other thing. You said you live with a foster family now."

"That's right."

"Why don't you go back home, to your parents?"

"They won't have me."

"No further questions," Walter said.

Rachel Martin lost herself in the case. She spent nearly two weeks in the public library reading everything on Jeffries. The more she read, the more she focused on Leslie Montaigne. Jeffries had not become a force in television until he teamed up with Leslie. After that, Leslie was always present, though always in the background. In the press she was invariably described as Jeffries's "assistant," usually with some diminutive attached. She was variously his "quiet assistant," his "demure assistant" or simply his "girl Friday." Her office was next to his, and in his absence she managed the company. Rachel found a *Daily Variety* piece on Jeffries that quoted an anonymous observer: "People forget that they're a team. Everybody's so preoccupied with Ted that they miss her—then she slips the knife in and it's all over."

Rachel then read Buris's case file. The FBI had gathered a huge archive on Jeffries that contained allegations of murder, fraud, child exploitation, child pornography, drug trafficking, and many lesser criminal endeavors. But it was all second- or thirdhand; all inferences were drawn from ambiguous situations.

She skimmed through it one night, finally leaving Buris's office at two in the morning, her head full of bizarre and disturbing images. When the elevator door opened on the first floor of the courthouse she thought she was dreaming, because swirling across the marble inlaid floor in front of her was a couple dancing to a Viennese waltz. The sound of their tape machine echoed brightly in the stony expanse. The man gave a measured nod to Rachel as she walked by. Then she remembered someone telling her about the Russian émigré couple who danced on their breaks from work.

Then, when Sharon Brown appeared, Rachel spent her days studying Roscoe's notebook. It was largely a record of drug transactions, listing dates, addresses, and amounts. On the back cover she found a list of alphanumeric notations, including one that was labeled "T." Rachel thought she had come to another dead end until she reexamined the original notebook and noticed a faint address near the nota-. tion. From a cross-reference directory at the library she determined it was of a mall in Malibu that contained a video store, a gourmet cheese shop, a Ralph's supermarket, Ernie's Sea Tacos, and the First California Bank of Malibu. On a hunch she called the bank and confirmed they had safe-deposit boxes, but with four digit numbers; the notation had nine. Rachel took the formula to an accountant friend who ran it through a decoding program, with no success. Finally she put it aside. She had a sense that the solution was like a name she knew but could not remember and would elude her until she stopped thinking about it. And that's just the way it worked.

"Walter—you have to see this," Rachel said as she caught up to him returning from trial. She followed him into his office and laid the notebook on his desk. "It's all in code: names, addresses, and amounts," she said, pointing at the notebook.

"Any for Jeffries?" Walter asked.

"Can't tell," Rachel said. "The point is, I broke the code on the back. It took me forever. The first letter is the number position of the alphabet, plus three. He had a thing about threes. See B, that translates to a five, then the next number is a dummy. Every odd-numbered digit is just a marker—"

A knock sounded at the door.

"Come in," Walter said.

Curtes and Dan Matti entered.

"Rachel," Walter said. "Bottom line."

"Bottom line," Rachel responded. "This note gives the number for a safe-deposit box at the First California Bank of Malibu, a mile from Jeffries's beach house. I think it's where he keeps everything. It's why we didn't find anything at his house or office. I called the bank. One of the numbers goes to one of their big boxes. It could have film, videos, everything."

"Or it could be a figment of your imagination," Matti said.

"Wait a minute," Walter said. He went over to his files and started digging.

"I have an affidavit for a search warrant," Rachel said, offering it to Walter.

Matti took the papers from her and flipped through them. "You don't have the authority to do this," Matti said.

"Let me see," Curtes asked. Curtes looked it over. "This code thing—don't you think that's a little farfetched? I mean, do you do a lot of code work for the county probation department? And even if you got this right, I don't see any probable cause. It could belong to anyone and contain anything."

"Yes!" Walter shouted, waving a sheet of yellow paper. "I can't believe I never followed up on this. The first night we talked, Roscoe said something about a security box where Jeffries kept lots of stuff. He made it sound like it was in Jeffries's house. You know, a safe. I remember he said something about him having to put things there, but it was really vague." Walter turned to Rachel. "I'll draft a paragraph. Dan, you can swear to the thing. And call this bank, see if they're still open. Curtes, see what magistrate's on duty tonight. Tell him we're going to need him. We'll plan on a search first thing tomorrow—before the bank opens for business."

Curtes and Matti looked skeptical.

"You never know," Walter said. "Maybe we finally got lucky."

ELEVEN

Driving west toward the Pacific, Walter beat his index fingers on the steering wheel and remembered when he first came to the city. It was nearly dawn when they had passed through downtown, Walter driving the van, the rest of the band sprawled asleep. When the van emerged from the tunnel at the freeway's end in Santa Monica he had yelled at the bright blue of the ocean, the wide expanse of beach, and the dramatic bluffs. Wiping sleep from their eyes the others had spilled out onto the sand and whooped at the crashing waves. He never forgot the light of that morning, the way the air, still full of mist, seemed to sparkle from the inside, promising untold glories when it finally cleared.

They had all been sure that in a few years the moment would be immortalized by their fame. At the Pacific's edge all hopes might be realized. He was older and gloomier now, but the land still took his breath away. As he emerged from the tunnel at the end of the freeway he looked out on the empty beach and the sea beyond and lifted off the accelerator for a moment. It would be wonderful to lie there on the sand, listen to the waves and feel the sun, he thought.

He was late, though, and he hurried on, gunning the Toyota until its four-cylinder engine whined. It was like Christmas morning when he was a kid but did not have to wait for his parents to come downstairs. Roscoe, he was sure now, had kept something in reserve. He might have told if Walter had known enough to press him, but maybe he forgot, or maybe it was his trump card, something to hold over them all. They knew Jeffries made at least four sex films, maybe as many as eight. If Roscoe had copies in the safe deposit box, they could reopen the government's case-in-chief. Driesen would scream and O'Brien would roar, but it would happen and Jeffries would be convicted.

On the other hand it might be nothing and Walter was taking time out from trial to supervise a simple search. A series of phone conversations with bank officials that night had convinced him that he had no choice, however. Only when Walter threatened the bank president with indictment for obstruction of justice did he agree not to notify the box holder before the search. The bank seemed especially sensitive about the box they planned to open. Walter sensed they were getting hot.

The bank was in a small stand-alone building at the edge of a mall in Malibu. The parking lot was nearly empty, but a group of cars clustered around the bank entrance. To one side were two OGV's, official government vehicles, next to a deep black BMW and white Saab Turbo. Dan Matti, his partner Whitney Young, and Rachel Martin stood on the sidewalk outside the bank's front door.

"They wouldn't let us in until you got here," Matti announced as Walter got out of his car. "They have their counsel here. A real prick."

Walter knocked on the door. Cupping his eyes against the glass to block the glare, Walter saw two business-suited men inside, conferring at a desk. One spoke briefly on the phone, then put it down. Finally the older and shorter of the two came to the door. He unlocked it, came outside, and relocked it.

"Stuart More, associate counsel for the savings and loan association," he said, putting out his hand.

"Walter Buris, assistant United States attorney."

More's handshake was vague and perfunctory.

"I have a few questions about this document," More said, waving the search warrant in the sunlight. "First, I see that it authorizes only agents of the FBI to search."

"Or any other federal law enforcement agency," Walter pointed out.

"That's boilerplate. I'm not letting this, this probation person in without explicit authorization from a judicial official," he said, pointing at Rachel.

"Fine. The FBI agents can handle it."

"The order also seems lacking in particularity. You don't know what you are looking for."

"The magistrate signed it," Walter said. "The box holder can litigate the validity later. That's the way it works."

"It's hard to believe we can't even get in front of a judge before you all barge in here," More protested. "It's a terrific abuse of governmental power and an invasion of privacy."

"Let us in or we'll kick the fucking door down," Walter said. He said it calmly but with great satisfaction, knowing that More would be as shocked as if Walter had dropped his pants. It would probably inspire a long letter of complaint to Bridewell, the state bar, and various elected officials, but so what.

"In the practice of law, courtesy is the first rule," More said smarmily.

"Dan, why don't you get out the shotguns," Walter suggested.

Matti nodded and headed for his car.

"Wait," More said. "It appears I do not have any choice in this matter. I would like the record to reflect that I am opening the bank door and will be opening the safe deposit-box under coercion and duress."

Walter smiled. He loved it when lawyers made pronouncements "for the record," as if there was some great stenographer in the sky taking everything down.

They started with the big box, the one that belonged to Family Entertainment. Walter always opened the biggest one at Christmas first.

"Nothing inside," Matti declared.

Walter felt the weight of the case upon him again.

"When was this last opened?" Walter asked More.

"We cannot say. The privacy of the customer under the Privacy of Financial Records Act—"

"When was it last opened?" Walter demanded.

"Chuck, let me see the ledger," More said to the young, sandy-haired man beside him. More studied the book, holding it close to his chest. "It has not been opened since you called the bank late yesterday afternoon."

"What about before then?"

"I cannot say and you have no right to know."

"Okay, open the other box, the one in Jeffries's name," Walter told Matti.

Matti turned the key and pulled the long gray box from the wall, carefully laying it on the table. There was nothing beneath the lid, but when he tipped it up from the end Walter heard something slide down.

Matti reached in and produced a California driver's license.

"California DL number N9914859 in the name of Thomas E. DeWit, 5219 Holly Oak Drive, Hollywood." Matti held it up to the light. "It's a fake. This says he was seventeen but he couldn't have been more than fifteen when he got it. Probably one of Ted's favors."

Matti reached into the box again and pulled out a man's gold ring with a blue stone. His hands seemed to tremble as he held it up, trying to make out the inscription. " 'To T, with all my love, L.' " He quickly put it down on the table.

"So what do you think? What's this stuff doing in Ted Jeffries's safe-deposit box?" Walter asked.

"Tommy's dead," Rachel replied.

[99]

Matti and Walter turned around.

"I'm not going to wait out there when I'm the one got us here in the first place," she said."Tommy's things are there because he's dead and Ted wanted something to remember him by. Leslie would have cleared it out except she didn't know about this box. She only had access to the other one. Wonder what she'd think if she saw it. That ring's from her."

"You certainly have a lively imagination," Matti remarked.

"How would Roscoe know about it then?"

"He probably put the stuff there. He used to be a signatory too," Rachel said.

"I don't know. It doesn't make a whole lot of sense," Walter said. "And it sure as hell doesn't prove anything." He did not like to think that Roscoe had anything to do with Tommy's disappearance. Roscoe had always maintained that Tommy just took off, the way runaway kids were wont to do. "Why don't you finish up here, Dan. Check it all for prints, then bring it back to the office."

Rachel Martin followed him out to the parking lot. She walked with him to his car, rushing to keep up with his long strides.

"Leslie Montaigne cleared out the big box the day before yesterday. Took a big bag of stuff out of it," Rachel said.

"How do you know?" Walter asked.

"I got here early and talked to the younger guy. He's the one in charge of the safe-deposit area. I told him I'd keep it confidential."

"How'd she get into the box?"

"She and Ted are the signatories on the big one. The little one was Roscoe's. He probably opened it when he was doing some business at the bank for Ted."

"Shit," Walter said.

"You know what happened, don't you?" Rachel asked.

"No."

"Someone leaked that we had the notebook. It's just whoever got told didn't know about, or forgot about, the other box."

"Someone leaked it?" Walter asked. The idea was absurd.

"Can we sit in your car for a minute?" she asked.

He unlocked it and they got in.

"Two nights ago I was in the office late," Rachel began. "This was just after we got Roscoe's notebook. I was reading the file and I went to make some copies and I heard Curtes on the phone to Gary Driesen. I heard him say 'Gary' and they talked about the case. Curtes said we had just gotten something and might be letting them see it. My impression was that he wanted something out of Driesen. I'm sure they were talking about the notebook."

[100]

"I find that hard to believe," Walter said.

"You saw the way Curtes reacted to my search warrant. Matti too."

"That was just a turf battle," Walter said. "They don't like you showing them up."

"Curtes told you about the internal Justice Department memo the IRS found in the Family Entertainment files, didn't he?" Rachel asked.

"No."

"I told him about it two weeks ago. The IRS as part of their tax investigation went through the company files and found one of your progress reports to main Justice. I told Curtes about it, and he said he'd look into it."

"Doesn't make sense. And why wouldn't the IRS call me? It's probably just the usual bureaucratic screwup," Walter said. Nevertheless, it left a nasty taste in his mouth.

Back in court Driesen was presenting character witnesses. Although they were usually a waste of time—encomiums from friends or family who knew nothing of the facts of a case usually carried little weight—the Jeffries case was different. Based largely on circumstantial evidence the government was asking the jury to believe the defendant capable of child exploitation. Evidence of good character from reputable, sincere members of the community might raise serious doubts in their minds. Driesen had started with a list of fourteen such witnesses, but under pressure from O'Brien cut it to four.

Walter came in at the midmorning recess. Curtes, who had been covering for the morning, was organizing his folders at counsel table.

"Go okay?" Walter asked.

"Yeah," Curtes replied. "More of the same drivel. What about you? We come up with anything?"

"Nothing that'll make a difference."

"That's unfortunate."

"Uh, Paul, did you tell anybody about Roscoe's notebook?" Walter asked.

"What do you mean?"

"Maybe we should talk about this later." The courtroom was filling up again.

"What's up, Walter?"

Walter heard a strain in Curtes's voice.

"Did you talk to Driesen Monday night? On the phone?" Walter asked.

"I might have."

"Did you mention Roscoe's notebook?"

"I'd like to know what this is about," Curtes said.

"Leslie Montaigne cleared out the big safe-deposit box Tuesday morning. Quite a coincidence."

"I talk to Gary occasionally. Just touching base," Curtes said. "I never mentioned the notebook. Why would I?"

"I'm just asking," Walter said. "Did Rachel Martin tell you about a Justice Department memo that turned up—"

"Hey, Walter, I don't like the tone of this. I discount everything that bitch says about ninety percent so I wouldn't know what she said. But if it's that IRS thing she was going on about I checked it out and it could have come from a hundred different places. They had so many people on that investigation, there's no telling who had copies."

"Okay."

"Wait. You think I'm leaking stuff to them?" Curtes asked, nodding at Driesen and Jeffries.

"We'll talk about it later."

"No," said Curtes. "Now."

"All please rise," the clerk intoned. "This honorable court is again in session."

Judge O'Brien conferred for a moment with his clerk, who stood before him, back to the lawyers.

"I just had to know," Walter said quietly.

"So? So am I cleared?" Curtes demanded in a loud whisper.

"We'll talk later."

"You clear me or I'll walk out of here right now," Curtes said in a speaking voice, putting his finger in Walter's face and pointing to the door.

"Don't do this, Paul."

"You're telling me not to be upset?"

"Gentlemen?" O'Brien inquired from the bench. "Are we ready to proceed?"

Walter and Curtes looked up to see that all eyes in the courtroom were upon them.

"Yes, your honor," Walter said.

As Driesen called his next witness Walter wondered about Curtes. Before he had become a prosecutor Walter had prided himself on his ability to spot a lie based on simple observation. But in a business where the lie was an art form, where police lied their way into the trust of criminals and criminals lied for their living, personal impressions were dangerous. The fumbling, contradictory witness might be battling stage fright to tell the truth, and the clear-spoken police officer might be spinning a grandiose falsehood. Walter tried to confine himself to the logic of situations and coherent stories about human nature.

Curtes was an ambitious prosecutor; his career depended on convicting Jeffries. He could not be bought. Blackmail was unlikely. Although the pattern was suspicious, it did not yet prove anything, let alone point to Curtes. Rachel probably misheard or misunderstood the phone conversation she overheard. The business about the Justice Department memo was probably a bureaucratic oversight from start to finish. Although how did it get there in the first place? As always, there were more questions than answers.

Gary Driesen called Arnold K. Sybeck, former regional director of the Child Protective Division of the state's Department of Health and Human Resources, currently president of Child Services, Inc., a private nonprofit organization dedicated to the "health and welfare of California's youth," as his expert witness. Driesen worried about Sybeck. After hours of witness preparation Sybeck still spoke in jargon.

"Based on my education, which includes two graduate degrees, my experience of twenty-three years in the field, and my own human experience as a human being," Sybeck declaimed, "I believe that the Hollywood House was extremely functional in an affirmative, life-positive fashion, providing a structured but nonoppressive nurturing environment for runaway and throwaway youths."

Curtes's cross-examination of Sybeck proved frustrating. Sybeck played the cocky professional witness, trying to anticipate and repel Curtes's every move. As a result, he answered his own questions and rarely addressed those put to him by the prosecutor. Asked about his experience with runaways Sybeck took ten minutes to defend his salary, his work as a regional director with the state, and his opinions as a consultant. When Sybeck left the stand O'Brien quickly called an end to the day's session, as if afraid the witness might return.

Whatever momentum the defense lost with Sybeck they regained the next day when Edgar Wines took the witness stand. A short man with a ruddy, thickly jowled face, Wines seemed dangerously constricted by his tie and jacket. He stared straight at Driesen, too nervous to look at the jury. At first he spoke softly, far from the microphone, so his words were a whisper in the large courtroom. Then he hunched closer and the microphone rang and crackled. Suzie, his daughter, had run away to Hollywood at the age of fourteen and ended up at the Hollywood House.

"I don't know, I—I guess it was my fault," Wines said, looking down, his voice thick.

"Just take your time," Driesen said.

Wines coughed loudly. "I grounded her because she was out late. We had a curfew and she kept breaking it. She was going to a new

[103]

school and hanging out with the wrong kids. The next morning when we got up, well, we didn't know anything was wrong for a while because she sleeps late, you know. So I was at work when my supervisor says I have a call. I'm not supposed to get calls at work unless it's really important. It was my wife, she said that Suzie was gone. We knew she was gone because of the stuff she had taken, and she left the back window open. But the police said they couldn't even report her missing for two days."

"What did you do, Mr. Wines?"

"We went crazy. We called all her friends' houses and figured out that she had probably gone to Los Angeles. She—she looked a lot older than fourteen. She was mature for her age, I mean she wasn't really, but she looked it. But she didn't know what she was doing. I was just going crazy. I went to Hollywood, cuz that's where the police said kids go and—it was like hell. I mean the kids you see there and what they do—"

Driesen took Wines through his five days of searching in Hollywood, which culminated in a call to his motel room from the Hollywood House.

"So I rushed over there and they told me she was in the rec room upstairs. I went up and she was playing Ping-Pong with another girl, just like she did at home, laughing, you know, listening to the radio real loud."

"Did you have occasion to meet Mr. Jeffries at that time?" Driesen asked.

"Yeah. I guess he had heard about me looking all over for my kid because he got one of the pictures I was giving out and when he found Suzie at a McDonald's or something he talked her into coming to the Hollywood House."

It was all hearsay, but Walter did not object. He wanted Wines off the stand as soon as possible.

"Suzie was different after that. The place really turned her around. She stopped cutting classes and now she's taking college prep courses. We're real proud of her."

"When you were at Hollywood House did you gain any impression of how the other youths at the House regarded Mr. Jeffries?" Driesen asked.

"Yeah. He came in after I got Suzie. The other kids—they're teenagers, you know, and kind of tough, so they didn't like run up and hug him or anything—but as soon as they came in they all like crowded round and had something they wanted to tell him. And he listened to each of them, you could tell he really cared. It was like a teacher at school, you know, that you really respect."

Wines saw no evidence of any drug use or sexual exploitation.

On cross-examination Walter limited himself to establishing how little Wines saw of the House and Jeffries. He could not make the real point, that Suzie Wines was the last person who would know anything of Ted Jeffries's dark side because Suzie was, by California standards, homely, and she had frantic parents. Jeffries was attracted to the beautiful and the abandoned.

The trial dragged on. Each night after court Curtes and Walter prepared for the next day's witnesses in their own offices, speaking to each other only to divide the work. Dan Matti shuttled between them if any more communication was required. By the time Walter got home he was so tired that if he had not eaten at the office he simply did not bother. Sometimes he ate a slice of bread while he watched the late news in bed. He awoke in the morning with crumbs embedded in his skin.

Driesen saved his celebrity witness for last. Now in his early sixties, Geoff Baxter had been the star host of one game show or another for nearly thirty years. Although he had long since moved out of prime time, his TV-Q—the rating for public identification and appeal—remained higher than the leads in most prime-time shows. He was tall and well tanned, his dark hair thinning in a small but graceful concession to age. His selling feature was his smile, a great midwestern, gosh-darn open-toothed gusher of such spontaneity and energy that it was almost impossible to resist. When he unleashed it upon an audience they laughed and cheered on cue.

As Geoff Baxter strolled down the aisle toward the witness stand on Friday the mood in the courtroom lightened. He was a familiar face; he seemed an old friend who had stopped by unexpectedly. Nearly everyone in the courtroom, from Judge O'Brien who in private spoke disparagingly of the "twinklies" from the entertainment business who dominated the city's social life, to the trial-weary jurors, to the reporters in the front row, studied Baxter to compare his real-life image with what they remembered from their living rooms. They wanted to be able to say what he was "really like" when their friends asked.

Baxter reminded Walter of Ronald Reagan, the way he issued platitudes that, driven by the force of his presence, sent waves of good will throughout the room. What he actually said about Ted Jeffries was patently unbelievable, the sort of exercise in superlatives normally restricted to awards dinners and descriptions of upcoming productions on talk shows.

Walter asked Baxter a single question: "Would your opinion of Theodore Jeffries change if you learned that he gave children cocaine and marijuana and exploited them for sexual purposes?" It was a 'When did you stop beating your wife?' question. Any affirmative response showed that Baxter had little to say on the essential allegations of the case; a negative response confirmed the witness's bias.

Baxter answered that it would change his opinion if "those things were true." He paused a moment and delivered his last words in a booming voice, his eyes raking the jury. "But the Ted Jeffries I know would never, ever do such things, could not even imagine this kind of thing. I know that as surely as I am sitting here."

After Baxter left the stand, Driesen dropped his bombshell. "Your honor, when we resume tomorrow, Mr. Jeffries will take the witness stand."

TWELVE

Sitting on the witness stand was like being onstage, Jeffries thought. He perched high above the crowd, the center of attention. The stabbing in his gut brought back his days on the street when he lived by fear and the adrenaline it created.

He had prepared carefully. He watched videos of the TV news reports of his arrest and indictment. He went through a day of mock direct and cross-examination by Driesen and his team, then spent the night in a critique of his performance via videotape. He worked on his expression in the mirror. He wanted to project both outraged innocence and respect for the legal process. The jury had to believe he was innocent but not that he thought himself above it all.

Leslie helped him pick out his clothes. They agreed on a dark, conservatively tailored suit that he had not yet worn during the trial, one that looked respectable, almost dull. He skipped his weekly haircut, knowing that if his hair was not quite right he would look more vulnerable, more sympathetic.

"State your name for the record, spelling your last name," the clerk intoned.

"Theodore Henry Jeffries. J-E-F-F-R-I-E-S."

"Mr. Jeffries, what is your occupation?" Driesen began.

"I am a television producer and distributor."

"Do you also devote substantial amounts of your time and energy to charitable enterprises?"

"Yes, I do."

"Do you have any connection to the Hollywood House that has been mentioned frequently in this trial?"

"Yes. I am its founder, major financial supporter, and president of the board of trustees."

"Mr. Jeffries, have you ever, in connection with the Hollywood House or in any other context ever provided or assisted in the provision of any illegal drug to any person under the age of eighteen?"

"No."

"Before March of this year did you have any knowledge of, or involvement in, any activity, including the making of a film or video, that involved the sexual activity or sexual display of persons under the age of eighteen?"

"No."

"Are you guilty of any of the charges in this case?"

"No."

The problem was where to go from here. Jeffries had discussed with Driesen the possibility of ending the direct examination with the simple denials and leaving the details to cross-examination, but they agreed that did not give Jeffries enough chance to present himself as a person. So Driesen led his client through a capsule version of his life story: from runaway sleeping on Venice Beach, to messenger, to crew person, to producer and syndicator. As he usually did, Jeffries made it sound as if he had arrived in the city as a lost and innocent teenager, when in fact he was in his midtwenties and had spent nine years fending for himself in cities across the country before he made it to LA. He gave a sanitized version of his encounter with the pimp from Santa Monica Boulevard to explain his interest in runaway children. Told this way, though, the story lacked punch. He was better when he talked about founding Hollywood House.

"Did you ever become aware that residents of the House were using drugs?" Driesen asked finally.

"Yes, I did. I only learned for sure after this case started, but I had some suspicions beginning about this time last year."

"What caused those suspicions?"

"I've been around a lot of people who used drugs. You can see it in their eyes; with marijuana they get red, with cocaine kind of bright and glazed at the same time. You can tell from how they talk, the kind of excuses they make. One or two of the kids were using."

"Did you have any idea where they were getting the drugs?"

"At first I thought they were getting them on the street. During the day the kids are pretty much free to come and go. Finally I began to suspect my staff, but that was just about a day or two before the police busted in."

"Did anything happen to make you suspect any particular individual?"

"Yeah, Roscoe said he and Flash—"

Walter leapt to his feet. "Objection, hearsay."

After lengthy argument O'Brien sustained the objection, but the damage was done.

"Did you ever become aware that any of the children in the House were involved in pornographic movies?" Driesen asked.

"Not until this case started."

O'Brien turned to the jury. "Ladies and gentlemen, I have another matter calendared for this afternoon, so I think we will break now," O'Brien announced. "But before we go, Mr. Jeffries—"

"Yes?"

Jeffries's bright and quizzical response brought laughter from the spectators and several of the jury.

"Why do you think the government has brought this case against you?" the judge asked.

"I'm a prominent figure. I'm easy to blame."

"You mean because you're rich and famous?"

"Yes. We live in an age, your honor, when anyone in the public eye is target for all kinds of abuse and accusations. And since I am politically active as well, in what many would consider liberal causes, that makes me a particular target."

"It wasn't because some of the youths at the House used drugs?" the judge asked.

"No, they don't care about that. There are kids using drugs all over the place."

"And you don't think it had anything to do with sexually explicit tapes involving young people who resided at the House?"

"Well, that's what got their attention," Jeffries said. "They knew that would play. In my business it's called high concept—something you can sell in one sentence. That makes it easy to promote. Sex is always high concept. For example, the highest-rated TV movie of all time was about teenage prostitutes. With a sex theme you can get people excited and still get away with it as long as you say it's wrong. It's bread and circuses, a way of distracting the public from the real problems of the country."

"Thank you, Mr. Jeffries," O'Brien said. "This case will be in recess until nine-thirty tomorrow morning."

Walter watched Driesen's jaw tighten with anger. O'Brien had a talent for sticking the knife in smoothly, but Jeffries still did not seem to realize what had happened. He was grinning broadly, watching the jury leave, as if he were on a talk show, waiting for the end of a commercial break.

Back in his office Walter entertained a variety of suggestions for the next day's cross-examination. Curtes had prepared a ten-page memorandum on the subject, which he supplemented with fifteen pages of notes made during Jeffries's direct testimony. Dan Matti spent nearly an hour with Walter sharing his ideas. Several of the other prosecutors in the office dropped by to hear the discussion and offer their own words of wisdom, usually adding a story of a particularly satisfying cross they had done. Even Rollie Jackson poked his head in and offered moral support.

Although the mood was jovial, even hilarious, Walter sensed desperation. By taking the stand Jeffries had given the government a second chance, but no one thought Walter could take advantage. They all just hoped.

Walter left early, hoping to get home in time for a daylight ride on his motorcycle. It was the best way he knew to clear his head. In law school he had bought a brilliant red-orange Kawasaki 550 with swept-back fairing and road-racing seat from his friend Sam Wu after Sam took a spill on the Harbor Freeway and his wife had made him choose between her and the bike. The machine scared Walter—it went even faster than it looked—but that was the point. The machine stripped away the nonsense and reduced everything to a matter of life and death.

Although it was nearly seven by the time he fired up the bike, the day was still bright, the air sparkling with sun and particulate. He rode over the lane dividers between long rows of cars, feeling their small bumps beneath his wheels, his eyes wide for sudden lane changes. Traffic thinned as he climbed the long broad highway up through Glendale to the mountains that lurked behind the haze.

He turned onto the Angeles Crest Highway, a road that wound up and through the arid mountains north of the city. He concentrated on his riding, leaning from side to side with the sweeps of the road, drifting from center line to road's edge, seeking the fastest line. The bike's high scream filled his ears; its vibration entered deep into his hands and arms. Down the straights he accelerated into top gear, the road coming up at him as it did in the movies, jerky and wild. It was his warp drive, where matter turned crazy and his brain had to accelerate to separate the irrelevant from the deadly.

He took successive S-turns in a quick rhythm: lean over, up; over, up; and again. He did not ride enough to be really good, but he had a feel for it. Coming off a crest down a long incline he twisted the throttle open until the engine reached full cry. A long sweeping left-hander stretched out in front of him. He geared down and braked smoothly, setting himself for the turn. Then an old red Chevy appeared from around the curve. Going too fast, it wallowed across the center line, heading straight for him. Walter pushed hard to the right and slipped by the huge machine, feeling the vacuum of its wake. He leaned back to make the curve, but the bike fought for a straight line and carried him to the edge of the road, where sand covered the tarmac. The handlebars went soft in his hands as the front wheel began to

[110]

skid. For a long moment he froze. Any sudden move would send him off the side of the mountain.

He thought of Laura, and Sara, and the case. Would anyone miss him if he went? Maybe they would after all.

Inches from the pavement's edge, the tires caught the hard surface again and Walter rode out the curve, the bike slowing gradually.

He turned around and rode carefully out of the mountains, high on the thrill of survival. Coming around the last bend the city appeared before him, a vast, vaguely feminine mass hidden in a wrapping of pink and orange gauze. He stopped and gazed out over the city, his heart still pumping hard; having vanquished death, he would come down out of the mountains with new strength. He would take on the city's worst, he would be the people's champion and defeat the forces of evil, which had kept so many in horror and fear.

Jeffries had scared him as he had scared everyone else. It was not a question of running away or giving in, but of playing it safe. In the back of his mind Walter had worried about consequences, and that gave Jeffries the edge. Jeffries never played it safe. Walter had to follow his instincts. From now on he would push as hard as he could, regardless.

Walter expected the first day of cross-examination to be slow, and it was. Jeffries fought even the simplest points.

"Didn't you have primary responsibility for the supervision of the children at the House?" Walter asked.

"No."

"Who did?"

"The staff and the director."

"But you supervised the staff and director."

"No."

"Didn't you, as chairman of the board of the Hollywood Youth House supervise the actions of the professional staff and the director of the House?"

"No, I did not," he responded.

"Then who did?"

"The board of directors of the House, a body comprised of fifteen people."

"Of which you were the chairman."

"That is correct. I had, however, only one vote."

But Jeffries also knew when to stop. Just when Walter thought he could turn Jeffries's nitpicking against him, Jeffries became expansive.

"Isn't it true, Mr. Jeffries, that over the four years of its existence, you were the single most important person in the organization and running of the Hollywood House?" Walter asked.

"Yes, I think that's true," Jeffries said. "And like anyone in a leadership position, I have to take responsibility for those underneath me. That's why the failings of the people who worked for me hurt so much."

He showed a sense of humor. He said he thought television should be like chewing gum—"sweet and juicy from the first bite and then spit out when you can't stand it anymore." By the end of the morning Walter had only managed to emphasize Jeffries's close involvement with the House. Jeffries was as good as Walter expected, yet Walter remained hopeful. As Jeffries became more relaxed he played more to the audience, forgetting about the prosecutor. Walter saw that Jeffries considered him a lightweight.

Walter began the afternoon on the topic of drugs.

"We earlier spoke about the interview you gave to *Rolling Stone* magazine, Mr. Jeffries."

"Yes."

"In that article, and in your testimony, you said you are against intoxicants generally."

"Yes, that's right."

"And you made sure that all of the kids at the House received some form of drug and alcohol counseling."

"Yes, that's right."

"As I understand it, you do not use drugs."

"I have an occasional glass of wine. That's about it."

"Yet on March fifteenth of this year you had in your jacket pocket a bindle of cocaine."

"I already explained that. I don't know how it got there."

"You suspect that someone at your office or on the set which you visited that day put it there," Walter suggested.

"That's the best I can figure."

"You know that people who work for you use illegal drugs?"

"I don't know for sure, but I know it's everywhere. There's probably someone in this room who has used an illegal drug during the last month." Jeffries fixed his gaze on Walter.

Walter tried to cross-examine Jeffries about statements he had made in an interview four years earlier that suggested he sold marijuana when he first came to Los Angeles, but O'Brien sustained Driesen's objection.

By midafternoon the atmosphere in the courtroom was heavy with boredom. Walter took Jeffries over a variety of details of the layout and operation of the Hollywood House that did not seem to prove anything. Jeffries slid back in his chair. He glanced carefully over to the jury box, trying to make eye contact. Meanwhile O'Brien's feet made a muffled thumping against the bench. Walter knew it was time to make his move.

"You have testified as to your substantial experience in a variety of filmmaking," Walter said.

"Is that a question?" Jeffries responded.

"Yes. Did you so testify?"

"I did, I think."

"You are familiar with the term 'high production values'?" Walter asked.

"Yes. It means a film that is technically proficient. Good camera work, sound, editing, that kind of thing."

"Did the video shown here last week have high production values?"

"I guess so. For what it was."

"Would it meet your standards for acceptable professional quality lighting?"

"Yes."

"Camera work?"

"Yes."

"Sound?"

"The ambient sound was a little muffled. Otherwise it was fine."

"Editing?"

"Yeah."

"And what about its content? In your professional opinion do you believe it achieved its aims?"

Driesen stood. "Objection, irrelevant and calls for speculation. The witness is not a movie critic."

"Your honor, the witness's opinions go to the essence of credibility and the basic issues in the case." Walter's response was purposefully vague; he did not want to give away the point he would try to make.

"Overruled. You may answer, Mr. Jeffries," O'Brien said.

"I don't know what the aim of the film was," Jeffries replied. "I didn't make it."

"From watching it, what do you suppose its purpose was?" Walter asked.

"To show a teenage boy masturbating."

"Yes. Did this strike you as an informational work, something that was trying to, say, explain adolescent sexuality?"

"Could have been. Except it didn't say anything about it making you go blind."

Many in the courtroom laughed. Walter smiled. Jeffries was forgetting his real audience.

"Was the depiction of masturbation a positive one, in your professional opinion?"

"Objection," Driesen cried.

"Overruled," snapped O'Brien.

"Your honor, the government is—"

"Overruled."

Walter saw that Driesen was trying to warn his client but O'Brien would not allow it. It didn't matter; Jeffries paid no attention to his lawyer.

"Was the film a positive depiction of the sexual act?" Walter asked.

"Yes, it was," Jeffries replied.

"Would you say that it was also a respectful depiction?"

"I don't know what you mean."

"I mean, if the actor in that movie were an adult friend of yours, would you feel embarrassed or ashamed for him?"

"No. As long as he got paid." There was laughter, but a little less.

"Because there's nothing wrong with the act depicted, is there?"

"No."

"And nothing wrong with depicting it as long as it is consensual, is there?"

"No. It's part of life, something that everyone does."

"In fact, the sexual act can be beautiful," Walter said.

"Yes, it can." Then Jeffries hastily added, "Of course it has to be consenting adults."

"Of course," replied Walter.

Jeffries sat up, waiting for the next question. Walter saw that he understood now how his testimony would be taken and was anxious to repair the damage.

"Your honor, I believe this might be a good stopping point for today," Walter said.

"Court will be in recess until nine-thirty tomorrow morning," O'Brien said.

Ted Jeffries started his third day on the stand mad at the world. Driesen had told him to calm down, that anger was dangerous in the courtroom. He could see that, but how was he supposed to feel? Buris's cross-examination had been a typical right-wing sleaze attack, hinting that because he held progressive views on sex, because he was not terrified of ordinary bodily functions, that he must be guilty of child exploitation. He raged at the way Buris had made it seem that mere proximity with drugs made you a drug pusher and that anyone who would want to help kids must have a secret and ugly motive.

The political slant of the case was coming clearer every day. Why wouldn't Driesen expose the fraud? He was a pawn in a political game. With domestic policy in a shambles in the wake of the Reagan Revolution and no attacks on Third World dictators in the offing, the administration needed a symbolic target. Who better than a Hollywood producer and Democratic fund-raiser with a reputation for enjoying the good life? They would make him the symbol of a decadent nation's excesses. He was red meat set out for the fascists.

He saw them in the courtroom, men in white polyester shirts, dark ties and jackets, ladies in print dresses, all straight out of K mart, holding Bibles in their laps, staring at him with eyes of blind rage. They shouted scripture at him about little children when he came in and out of the courthouse. He would hate to see the twisted monsters they were breeding. They were the same screamers who had the networks on the run. They shrieked, and everyone in Jewish liberal Hollywood panicked as if it were Iran under Khomeini. It was time to spit in their faces, to stand up and send them back to the red-dirt, soul-parched South where they belonged. That was what the country did to Hitler; McCarthy reigned supreme until someone finally had the courage to call his bluff. Soon he would be able to do that. For now he had to be satisfied with little things, like the prosecutor being under investigation for smoking grass. It was so typical—the hypocrisy of the self-righteous. He took a deep breath and exhaled slowly.

"Mr. Jeffries. Did you know an individual by the name of Roscoe Brown?" Buris asked.

"Yes. He was on the staff of the Hollywood House."

"At one point you were pretty good friends with Mr. Brown, were you not?" Walter asked.

"No. It was a professional relationship. He was a former—or I should say he *said* he was a former drug dealer. He knew the streets. I thought he would be a valuable role model for the kids. I was wrong."

"What was his nickname?"

"I don't know."

"You never heard anyone call him Santa Claus?"

"I don't remember."

"Did you ever tell *Rolling Stone* magazine that he was called Santa Claus because of a phrase from the poem 'The Night Before Christmas'? 'And placing a finger to his nose, up the chimney he rose,' " Walter quoted.

"Yeah, I remember that."

"His nickname referred to cocaine, did it not?"

"Yes."

"Roscoe Brown didn't know anything about making movies, did he?"

"The only thing he knew anything about was drugs."

"What about Andrew Synes, the man called Flash?"

"Flash might have known some people in the porn business."

"You knew that Flash was a pimp when you hired him, didn't you?"

"No I did not."

"You knew he had a criminal record."

"I don't recall. But it wouldn't have disqualified him. Most of the kids in the House have been in trouble with the law too."

"You're a bachelor, aren't you, Mr. Jeffries?"

"Yes."

"Never been married."

"No."

"But for romance, you prefer young women, do you not?"

Driesen objected, but after brief argument O'Brien allowed the question.

"I don't think that's true," Jeffries replied.

"How about for sexual satisfaction? Isn't it true, Mr. Jeffries, that you have a reputation for being seen out with actresses aged eighteen and nineteen?"

"If I do I imagine that's the product of their press agents. In Hollywood, actresses stay very young for a long time."

The audience and several of the jury laughed appreciatively.

"Mr. Jeffries, you also have a reputation for giving some of the best parties in Hollywood, do you not?"

"I do give the best parties in Hollywood."

"You get quite involved with the planning, don't you?"

"Generally, yes."

"You decide the guest list."

"Yes."

"And the food. To the extent of tasting everything that is served."

"I try to do that."

"And you make sure there is plenty to drink."

"Yes."

"You want your guests to have a good time."

"I thought that was the point. Although some parties you go to, you wonder." Jeffries said this with a smile and swung his expression toward the jury to share the joke with them. The laughter was warm and appreciative.

"You also serve illegal drugs at your parties, don't you?" Buris asked in a matter-of-fact tone.

"I do not."

"So guests at your parties would not find cigarette boxes filled with powerful marijuana cigarettes."

"No."

"Marijuana is widely available at your parties, though, isn't it?"

"No. The people who come to my parties are successful people in the entertainment business. They are law-abiding citizens."

"You've never seen or smelled marijuana at one of your parties?"

"Not that I can recall."

"But that's right—marijuana's out of fashion these days," Buris said lightly. "Cocaine is the drug of choice in the entertainment business, isn't it?"

"That's what I read in the paper."

"You have no firsthand knowledge?"

"I know some people who have had problems with cocaine. That's true in almost all sectors of society today."

Gary Driesen snapped his pencil in two; he had broken three since his client had taken the stand. Jeffries had insisted that Driesen object as little as possible, saying he wanted to handle it himself. So far Buris had done no major damage, but Driesen worried about the cumulative effect. Two days of innuendo and character assassination, even if there was nothing behind it, could take a toll, especially without an immediate, vigorous response from counsel. Yet an objection might anger Jeffries, and Driesen feared his client's anger more than anything.

"Isn't it true, Mr. Jeffries, that at several of your parties, including last year's birthday party, guests found sugar bowls full of cocaine and prerolled dollar bills set out for their partying?"

"That's a lie. A total lie."

"It didn't happen?"

"Not that I know of."

"But it might have happened?"

"I often invite two or three hundred guests. I have a party director, staff, caterers, waitresses. I'm not aware of everything."

Walter nodded.

"I resent your insinuations," Jeffries added.

Walter suppressed a smile but looked up at Jeffries curiously. Jeffries's jaw was set at an angle, his mouth hard. He wanted a chance to fight back, and Walter would give it to him.

"Your house in Beverly Hills has an extensive garden area in the rear, does it not?"

"It has a nice backyard."

"Several wooded acres, isn't that right, with a particularly secluded section known as the Cherry Orchard."

"Yes."

"So named because that is the place where you have liaisons with your young romantic interests."

"No!"

"There are no cherry trees there."

"No. It's just always been called that." Jeffries's voice grew louder. "People say things about me because they always enjoy tearing down anyone who has something they want. You can stand here all day repeating other people's dirty rumors and wishful thoughts. It doesn't prove anything. It's all lies."

"You often show your guests movies in the screening room in your house."

"Yes."

"Sometimes sexually explicit ones," Walter suggested.

Driesen stood now, an arm raised. "Your honor, I've tried to be patient with all this, but counsel seems determined to trade in the most scurrilous and patently false sort of character assassination totally unrelated to the case—"

"Is this an objection, Mr. Driesen?" O'Brien asked.

"Yes—on relevance and prejudice grounds," Driesen said.

"It goes to motive and intent," Walter argued.

"Objection overruled. Mr. Jeffries, answer the question. Do you ever show your guests sexually explicit movies?"

"Most movies today would fit that description," Jeffries replied.

"Movies that graphically depict the act of sexual intercourse, men with clearly erect penises, various acts of oral sexuality and male ejaculation? Have you ever shown movies like that to your guests?"

"No."

"Ever?"

"There may have been an occasion—for a bachelor's party or some such thing."

"Any time with a mixed audience of men and women?"

"Not that I recall."

"But it might have happened?"

"Not that I recall."

"Of all the youths who were residents at the Hollywood House you were closest to Eleana Torelli and Mark Hanson, isn't that right?"

"I don't know what you mean by that," Jeffries said flatly.

"You spent more time with them than any of the others."

"I think they spent longer at the House than any others."

"Which means you saw them more than any others, right?"

"I guess so."

"Mr. Jeffries, I wonder if you'd look at exhibit ten in evidence," Walter said.

Curtes held up a large chart that had pictures of those who had resided at the House.

"You recognize these pictures as belonging to House residents?"

"Yes."

"If you wanted a photogenic boy and girl out of this group, you'd pick Mark and Eleana, wouldn't you?" Walter followed Jeffries's eyes over the chart. Mark and Eleana appeared striking in their beauty.

"Depends what I was looking for."

"How about attractiveness?"

"Maybe."

"Now, as I understand it—correct me if I am wrong, Mr. Jeffries—you had absolutely no knowledge of the filming or production of any sexually explicit film or video involving any minor who resided at the House until after formal charges were brought in this case."

"That's right," he said.

"Yet you had one of these films, in video form, in your possession at the time of your arrest. In the glove compartment of your automobile, which you were driving, alone. Isn't that true?"

"I'd like to renew the objection to this I've made previously," Driesen said.

"Overruled," O'Brien ruled. He then turned to the jury. "Ladies and gentlemen, what counsel is now asking about is a matter that goes only to the credibility of this witness—that is, whether the witness should be believed in some, or any, aspect of his testimony. It is what is called in the law impeachment. You should not consider this as direct evidence of guilt or innocence."

It was one of the strange fictions of the law of evidence that damaging material could be brought up to show that a witness was lying but not to show, at least directly, that the defendant was guilty. The distinction escaped many judges; Walter was sure it was lost on the jury. Once they heard that a video had been found in Jeffries's car, they would want to see it. He just hoped O'Brien would let them.

"Answer the question, Mr. Jeffries," O'Brien said.

"I was not aware that any videotape was in my car on the day I was arrested," Jeffries said. "And I was not aware of the contents of the videotape until my attorney showed it to me a few months ago."

Walter paused, holding his chin in his hand. Throughout his cross-examination he had wandered from the lectern, though never more than two arms' lengths away. Now he moved deeper into the well of the court.

"So, as I understand it, although you had cocaine in your pocket and a graphic video of child sex performers from your Hollywood

House in your car on the day you were arrested, you had no prior knowledge of either item," Walter said.

"That's right. Someone else must have put them there," Jeffries replied.

"Someone else must have put them there," Walter repeated. "I have no more questions."

As Walter left the courtroom he was surrounded by reporters seeking quotes. Lately he had abandoned his constant "no comments" and answered particularly tempting questions.

"Will you show the video?"

Walter said nothing.

"Do you think you hurt Jeffries on the stand?"

"You'd have to ask Mr. Jeffries or Mr. Driesen that. Isn't it time for their daily press conference?" Walter quipped.

"Do you plan to call anyone in rebuttal?"

"Yes."

"Who are you going to call? Any surprise witnesses?"

"If I told you it wouldn't be a surprise," Walter said, trying to give his statement an air of mystery.

In fact, he could not think of anyone who mattered. There was only the second video.

THIRTEEN

Friday night was Sara's sixth birthday party, and though Walter felt like nothing but a shower and going to bed, he was expected. Sara had requested an adult dinner "with the whole family."

Driving out of downtown Walter kicked himself because he had not bought Sara a present; he had asked Laura to get something for him. It was one of the things his father always did that he had vowed to do differently. He resolved to make it up to Sara somehow.

Traffic on the Westside was tangled and anxious. It was always more crowded there, especially on the weekend. The center of money and glitter, its streets were full of silvery European sedans, low sports cars with fat tires, and streamlined Japanese cars that curved like the female form. Everything here seemed new, from the glass-faced buildings to the minimalls done in geometric shapes and bold colors. North of these busy streets were the hills where the monied lived along winding streets behind security gates and lush landscaping.

When he finally neared Laura's building he began looking for a parking spot, first circling her block and then widening his search until he covered a three-block radius. He finally grabbed one by waiting for the exit of a Rabbit packed with teenagers headed out for the night.

Laura lived in a condominium in a new slab-sided stucco building, cheaply built but expensive. She moved in six months after they had separated and he always took it personally. He knew that Laura was not like that though. She just had no patience for real estate.

She had given him the outside key, so he let himself in the high-barred gate and took the elevator to the third-floor apartment.

"Daddy's here," Sara yelled after he rang. Her voice sang through the door, followed by her quick footsteps. She flung it open, out of breath, hair across her face. She brushed it away.

"Hi, Dad."

She looked too grown up to be his daughter. He remembered when she begged to wear tights to her preschool and he had to stretch them over her diapers. They never lasted more than a day. He remembered coming in the front door at night and Sara running the length of the dining room and living room to greet him, so that when he knelt down to take her embrace she nearly knocked him over. She would wrap her small arms around his neck and hug him tight. Now she stood at the door, tall and slim, in a black-and-red dress covered with sparkles, her hair pulled back and tied with a bow, smiling shyly. He kissed her on the forehead.

"Hi, beautiful. Happy birthday."

Laura appeared in the hallway and kissed him on the cheek. "Hi, Walter," she said. She looked older as well, the delicate tracery of lines at the corners of her eyes more noticeable. She still had the quiet look and slim body that made him pause. She wore a short white dress he did not recognize. "Things going okay?" she asked.

"Yeah," Walter replied. "In fact, today they went pretty well."

"Great. You must be almost finished."

"Another week or two. Depends what we do for rebuttal mostly. I was cross-examining Jeffries today—"

Laura raised her hand. "You remember Rick, don't you?" Walter was surprised to see Laura's boyfriend; he had thought it was a family party, but then he realized that to Sara this was family. He knew far stranger arrangements—like the married couple who liked to double-date with their lovers. Their biggest problem was deciding who would go home with whom, they said.

"Ted Jeffries is a tough cookie," Rick said. "You better watch out for him." Rick was shorter and thinner than Walter, with dark curly hair and modest good looks. He was a vice president of business affairs at a studio but wanted to be a producer.

"Okay," Walter said.

" 'Course you know that better than I do I guess. I've never met anyone who really had animal magnetism—except him. You walk into his office and he's there and—boom—it's like this electrical field, drawing you in or pushing you away, depending on his mood. AC/DC, you know? What do you want to drink, Walter? We have white wine, Perrier, fruit juice. What'll you have?"

Walter hesitated. Wine gave him a headache, but he wanted something. Otherwise he would soon be watching the time and feeling sorry for himself. "Any beer?" he asked.

"You know, I think there's some from the last time you were here. I'll get it. Sit down. The ladies are making dinner."

"Great."

He sat on the low white sofa in the living room, the one that looked comfortable but left him sprawling without support. With a small Navajo rug on one wall and a selection of old framed movie posters the room had a semblance of warmth and personality. The cottage cheese ceiling was barely noticeable. Soft New Age music played on the stereo. Walter smiled, thinking what trash they would have considered it ten years earlier. Then they would have played something loud and had to shout to be heard.

"I guess you must be pretty tired," Rick said, handing him a glass of beer.

"Yeah. I try not to think about it."

"Know what you mean."

The beer was warm and tasteless. It had been a long time since he had drunk American. Rick sipped a glass of Perrier.

"What's new?" Walter asked.

"We've been looking at houses," Rick said. "Laura and I."

"Oh."

"She's having a good year. And nowadays you just can't get a better investment than real estate, you know. Although the prices . . . We went to look at a place last weekend. Dumpy little place off of Robertson south of Olympic. *South* of Olympic. Three bedrooms, two and a half baths. No style, no charm. You know what they wanted?"

"No."

"Four hundred big ones. And our agent said it was underpriced."

"Wow." Walter hated to talk about Los Angeles real estate, especially with people on the Westside. With prices so high it was really a conversation about selling out, except no one even acknowledged the concept anymore. Somehow it was understood that you did whatever it took to buy a house, as if it were required for survival. Especially if you had kids.

At dinner he sat next to Sara, who was working hard on her table manners. The peas kept slipping off her fork and she patiently chased them around her plate until she captured them again.

"How's dance class?" Walter asked.

"It's over for the summer."

"Right."

"Sara's in a soccer league," Laura said.

"That's great."

"I scored a goal last week," Sara said.

"Fantastic."

"We're going to Disneyland tomorrow with Katie and Jennifer," Sara said. Katie and Jennifer were her best friends. "Mom says I can go on any ride I want."

"Sounds great," Walter said. "I'm sorry I can't go. I'm really busy with this trial." Walter felt guilty all over again. He could take the day off if he worked night and day Sunday, but he was tired and hated Disneyland.

"I know, Dad," Sara said cheerfully. "You should put in jail all the bad people who paint things on walls and buildings. They keep doing it on the wall of our school and it's so gross. I think they should go to jail for ever and ever and ever if they won't stop it."

"You know forever's a long time."

"Longer than you've been alive?"

Walter smiled. "Yes. Even longer than that."

After dinner Sara attacked the mound of presents on the coffee table, soon strewing the floor with a gaudy mess of games, clothes, dolls, books, and crumpled wrapping paper. She had nearly finished when she opened a small box that contained nothing but a small envelope.

"It's for you, Dad," Sara said.

Written in a large hand on the outside of the envelope were the words "For Sara's Dad."

Walter held the envelope to the light. Inside appeared to be a piece of paper with a single line typed on it. He opened it carefully.

LEAVE TED'S KIDS ALONE, it read. Also in the envelope was a photograph.

"What is it, Dad?" Sara asked.

Laura leaned over and Walter showed her the note. She blanched.

"Who gave you that present?" Walter asked Sara.

"I dunno," she said.

"I brought it," Rick said. "Somebody left it with my secretary. I figured it was somebody in the office or something."

Walter showed him the note, now holding it by the edges.

"Oh God," Rick said.

"Daddy, what is it?" Sara wailed. "I want to see."

"Actually it was for me. A note about my work," Walter said.

"Then it shouldn't have my name on it," she protested.

"You're right," Walter said.

"Can we have the cake now?" she asked.

"Sure," Laura said.

Walter carefully dropped the wrapping paper, box, envelope and note in a grocery bag to keep as evidence. After singing "Happy Birthday" he went to Laura's bedroom and took out the photograph. Then he called Dan Matti at home.

"The photograph is in color, taken with a telephoto lens from across the street of Sara's school," Walter said. "It shows her playing with two other girls that are leaving. There is a red circle and crosshairs which intersect at approximately her left temple."

"Jesus, Walter," said Matti. "I'll get somebody over there right away."

"Thanks. Now I want your professional opinion. Is this for real?"

"You mean, would he do it? No. He's too smart for that. He's got too much to lose and nothing to gain. But I wonder why it's coming now. I mean the trial's practically over. Unless there's something going on we don't know about."

Walter waited in the living room as Laura put Sara to bed. Rick had already left, explaining that it had been a long week. Walter let his head drop on the couch and forced his eyes shut. He could not go crazy about it. That was what Jeffries wanted.

"Tired?" Laura asked as she came in.

"Yeah. Uh, Rick left. Said he'd call you or you could call him. I told him he could stay if he wanted."

Laura nodded in a way that said she did not want to talk about it.

"He doesn't spend the night?" Walter asked.

"That's none of your business," said Laura. "Unless you have a concern for Sara."

"No," Walter said.

"You know Sara's going to my mother's for two weeks starting Monday."

"Oh, thank God. Why don't you go with her?"

"Because of that note? I'm not running away, Walter. Besides, you said it wasn't serious."

"Probably. It would only hurt him if anything actually happened. But there'll be some agents coming over—just a precaution. And I could stay if you want. Sleep on the couch."

Laura shook her head slowly and grabbed a tissue. She blew her nose loudly.

"You have a cold?" Walter asked.

"Just my allergies. The Santa Anas have been blowing again."

"Why don't you take a bath? I can do the dishes and then we can talk," he suggested.

Laura smiled, one side of her mouth curling up.

"What?" Walter asked.

"Just you," Laura said. "Anytime anybody's sick you love to play doctor. I used to look forward to it. You always took such good care of me. Sara too. Now I have to deal with it when she throws up. You really don't think it's anything—that note?"

"I'm sure," he said. "I'm just sorry it ruined your evening."

"It's not your fault."

"I miss you, you know. Do you miss me?"

"Would it matter if I did?" she asked.

Walter sighed. "I'll check on Sara," he said.

She was already asleep, curled up under her sheet, her special blanket clutched to her cheek. Her favorite tape of the *Nutcracker* played softly on her portable cassette player. He noticed that she had a picture of him on her dresser.

"I'm going," Walter said, leaning in the kitchen doorway. Laura was doing the dishes. "I talked to the FBI and they're going to keep an eye on the building. The local police too."

"Great. Just what we need."

"It's probably nothing but—"

"Okay, Walter. I don't want to hear about it. Thanks for coming."

"Yeah." He lingered in the doorway.

"Oh—how's it going with that internal investigation thing?" Laura asked.

"The, uh, test came back positive, so I'm fired, as soon as I finish the trial. Twice a week I have to go down to the probation office to pee in a bottle and mingle with all the other hypes and lowlifes. It builds character, I guess."

"I'm sorry, Walter."

"But you're not surprised," he said.

She pulled her hands from the soap suds and looked at him. "You're not very careful."

Walter rearranged the magnets on the refrigerator. They were all shaped like different kinds of fruit. "Maybe now you can see why I want this guy so much," he said.

"He seems dangerous," she agreed.

"But you still don't think it's worth it."

"It's not that, Walter," she said, drying her hands. "He obviously ought to be in jail where he can't hurt anyone. But that's not what you're trying to do—not really. You're trying to show what a bad person he is, like he deserves something. I don't know if I believe in that. I mean, who does? You make things hard for yourself."

Walter nodded. "I'll call," he said.

Driving back he felt his guts tighten into a single complex knot. He tried to calm himself down. Jeffries was playing the litigator's game of making everything personal. If you could make the opposing lawyer stay later at the office, come in more on the weekend, if you could get his wife annoyed, his kids upset, make him lose sleep, then he might weaken. He might, consciously or unconsciously, fail to bring a motion or make an argument, hoping to avoid more conflict. If there was a chance of settlement, he would not hang tough. Jeffries just played the game more viciously than most.

*　　*　　*

Ted Jeffries arrived fashionably late for the dinner party at the Beales. He was looking forward to a night out. He needed to forget his troubles. Overall his testimony had gone well, but it had not been the decisive triumph that he expected. And looming over all was Mark's report that Eleana had disappeared.

Mark had called in a panic that afternoon to say that Eleana had packed up her stuff and run off. Mark was sure she was headed for the FBI, and he wanted to take action. Jeffries calmed him down. First they had to find her.

"But it's gonna be like Tommy, I know it is," Mark said.

"No," said Jeffries. But he was not sure. She had been slipping away from him for a long time. If she was really gone, he would have to do something, and that would be hard. She got to him in the soft place that no one else could find. It was always a mistake to care that way, but he could not help it. He hoped that she was coming to see him. Maybe she just needed to talk.

Otherwise, all was going according to plan. Leslie was keeping the pressure on the government, and he knew that with enough time they would crack. Somebody would do something stupid and they could turn the tables, putting the blame where it belonged.

Jeffries made a grand entrance, impressing the group with his exuberance. He worked the room for about half an hour and then slipped away to inspect the place cards at the dinner table. Although he knew his hostess, Teri Beale, had probably spent days agonizing over the placements, Jeffries had his own ideas of good company. He decided that he preferred the company of the young Christi Beale to that of Eileen Crouse, the diet queen, and switched their cards. Christi was fifteen years old, with blond hair, bright blue eyes, and a woman's body. She had always liked "Uncle" Ted. He knew how to make her laugh and took seriously her show business aspirations, a contrast to her parents, who wanted her to work harder at school so she could become a doctor or lawyer.

Her parents, Teri and Bill Beale, were giving the party to show their support for Jeffries. The Beales needed him because Bill distributed Jeffries's shows overseas and Leslie had recently discovered serious discrepancies in their accounts. Bill was skimming the receipts, costing Jeffries's company several million a year.

At dinner Jeffries talked to Christi about school and her boyfriend, Dave. He laughed at her jokes and asked about her acting plans. As she sipped her wine she was thrilled by his tales of the trial.

"I can't believe that you're, like, here," she said.

"Never let the bastards get you down," he replied, smiling.

Christi was a Southern California girl, more interested in boys, fashion, and glamour than school. She had tried marijuana once, but didn't like it. She hinted that she and Dave fooled around. That was when Jeffries felt the glow begin. He squeezed her hand once beneath the table and she blushed.

He did not know why but there was an age for girls when they were special. Some time in their teens, after their bodies matured, but when their beings were still fresh—not innocent, but curious, open—when they smelled to him of life and hope. They smelled of morning. Christi was like that.

He leaned across to her and said quietly, "Do you want to go for a drive after dinner?"

"That'd be great. But I better ask my mom," Christi said.

"Why not your father?"

"He always says no. Mom's a soft touch."

"Let me take care of it."

"Okay."

Jeffries found Bill in the kitchen, where he was supervising the preparation of coffee.

"Hey, Bill. Great party. Just what I needed to take my mind off things."

"I'm really glad, Ted. You need it."

"Yeah. Hey. You mind if I take Christi out for a drive? I'll have her back in a little bit."

"Oh, well—hold on a second, let me talk to Teri. Just—hold on."

Jeffries watched Bill and Teri confer in the dining room. Teri kept shaking her head. They came back together.

"Ted, I hope you understand," Teri began, "but it's a school night and we'd like Christi to get to bed."

"I see."

"She's just a kid, you know," Bill said, awkwardly.

"And what with the trial and everything," Jeffries suggested.

"No, no," Bill said. "It has nothing to do with that."

"It's just late," Teri said. "And she's kind of young. That's all."

"I see," Jeffries responded, his voice cold.

"Ted, see it from our perspective," Bill said.

Jeffries nodded. "Well, like I said, it was a fine evening."

"You have to go now? I was sort of hoping we might talk," Bill said.

"I really don't have time. And, to be frank, there's not much to talk about."

"Ted, we go back a long way."

Jeffries nodded but said nothing. Bill looked at Teri, desperate. She looked away.

"I think there were some accounting mistakes. . . . In fact I know there were," Bill offered.

"I'm sure Leslie would like to hear about it," Jeffries said. He moved toward the door.

"Ted—look. You can take Christi out," Bill said. "We don't want to make a big thing about it. Just, have her back in a little while. Okay? You understand."

"Sure, Bill."

Teri gave her husband a hard look, her bottom lip quivering.

Jeffries caught Christi's eye and nodded his head toward the door.

"It was a great party," Jeffries said, putting a hand on Bill's shoulder. "And Bill—I'll have Leslie send out the renewal papers in the morning. I'm sure it was just a mistake."

"I appreciate that. Drive safely," Bill said with a nervous laugh.

Jeffries started up the BMW and felt a surge of irritation at Leslie. After days of her nagging he had finally relented and garaged the Jaguar, the Ferrari, and the Shelby Mustang for the duration of the trial. Leslie had leased him a garden variety BMW, arguing it was less conspicuous and looked better if the press saw him drive to court, even though he usually arrived in Driesen's Mercedes. She thought it would stop him from speeding.

On a night like this, though, when the city threw off its tawny cover to reveal a deep black sky, when the sparkling lights above and below glittered against the night in strange rivalry, when the air held the desert's cool bite, on such a night, at the wheel with a girl by his side, he had to fly.

Christi was willing, she cheered as the car stormed up the canyon toward Mulholland. He took Mulholland northwest toward the coast. The road was clear of traffic and dry; Jeffries knew it well. Many times he had raced on the road that wound along the hilltops from the city out to the beach. Car wrecks littered the hillsides below, marking where drivers had lost their way; it was an unforgiving road. He pushed the engine past 5,000 rpm in third, his hand on the gearshift for a quick move into fourth as he steered out of an easy curve when he caught a flash of black and white by the roadside. By the time he recognized it as an LAPD patrol car he was long past. He kicked himself for not demanding that the dealer install the radar detector before he took delivery. The red lights flashed in his mirror and the siren sounded in his ears.

"Aren't you going to stop?" Christi asked.

For a moment he debated. He could outrun the patrol car, but if there was a helicopter or another unit nearby, the odds were against him. And it was a bad time to take chances. But that just meant it would be more fun.

"No," he said with a smile. "Hang on."

He braked hard around a sixty-degree turn and then pushed the pedal to the floor. On the long straight he reached a hundred and was far ahead of the police car, but still in sight. He had to find a place to hide. He tried to remember the back roads and driveways ahead. A quarter mile up, just past Coldwater Canyon, he switched off the lights and threw the car down a driveway barred by a long chain. The chain snapped with a harsh clang as the car broke through it. Christi shouted and hid her face in her hands. Ted let the car cross the drive and coast down a dirt trail he remembered from years before when a real estate agent had shown him the property.

"It's okay," he said, finally stopping the car in a wooded grove. The ticking of the cooling engine and the crickets were the only sounds. "They'll think we went down Coldwater," Jeffries explained.

"Wow," Christi said.

"Now don't tell your parents."

"I won't," she said quickly.

He could not take his eyes from her legs, which stretched long and smooth beneath her short dress.

They got out of the car and he led her to the crest of the hill and showed her the ruins of the home of a silent movie star whose name he forgot. She was delighted at the outlines of the pool, which overlooked the city. She took the hand that he offered and he kissed her softly. He wondered for a moment if she would talk, but decided it did not matter.

They sat beneath a towering eucalyptus and played for a while. Jeffries warmed her with his gentle hands and then showed her what he wanted. She was awkward at first, but enthusiastic. She wanted to please.

He spread his legs wide as she bobbed up and down upon his length. At the end of each stroke the tip bulged out her cheek like a chaw of tobacco. He ran his hands up her chest to handle her full, firm breasts, their nipples stiff. He watched the way she worked with hands and mouth, intent.

"Longer and deeper," he said. "That's a girl. Now bring it faster. Faster."

The charge was starting, like an electric current. No matter what they did to him, he would come back stronger. He thought again of Eleana, and her delicate touch. There was always such a sadness in her eyes that he wanted to hold her. He wondered where she was.

Reaching the final moment he imagined himself a running back with the football tucked under his arm, on a blood-and-gold afternoon, a wonder of strength and speed. He lengthened his stride as the goal line neared and then, after an agony of struggle, broke through.

"Catch it now, it's precious. Oh. Yeah!"

She tried, but gagged and pulled away. The last spurts landed on her cheek, in her hair, and in big drops on her thin blouse. She coughed hard, trying to catch her breath.

"I'm sorry. I—went down the wrong way. Please—"

"Don't worry about it. It was nice," Jeffries said.

"Was it? Dave says—"

"Dave doesn't know what he's talking about." He smoothed the wetness in her hair, smiling at the thought of her walking in the door to her waiting parents, smelling of his come.

They lay back and gazed up into the hazy night sky. Sometimes life could be very good.

FOURTEEN

When Walter reached home Friday night he was too wired to think of bed. After checking again with Matti, he sat at the kitchen table and flipped through the mail while listening to his phone messages. He stopped the machine after the third one.

"Mr. Buris, this is Eleana. Remember me? I have to talk to you. I'm at this place, Buddy's Restaurant, it's off the 10 Freeway. Bye."

She did not say when she called or leave a phone number for the restaurant. Her faith that he would be able to find the place, that he would drop everything on a Friday night and drive out to see her, that he would even listen to his messages, seemed extraordinary. He knew, though, that it was less faith than despair, a feeling that nothing would probably work, so everything was equally likely.

He actually knew the place. Buddy's was an old truck stop southeast of downtown he had discovered when he was doing an interstate transportation of stolen property case involving electronics goods taken off the docks in San Pedro and shipped east. Tucked in among huge warehouses, with a large parking lot full of tractor-trailer trucks, it was a large, rough-hewn place. Without traffic it was about a twenty-minute drive from his house.

He got there a little after midnight. Walking in from the parking lot he saw her at a table by the window. It reminded him of an Edward Hopper painting, the way she sat by herself under the bright light that spilled out into the darkness. She was drinking soda from a glass and reading a battered paperback. When Walter entered she hastily put the book away and lit a cigarette.

"Hi," he said.

"Hi," she replied. "Took you a while."

"I was out. You're lucky I got the message at all."

"Have a good time?"

"Huh?"

"You said you were out."

"Oh, yeah. It was my daughter's birthday."

Walter noticed the duffel bag beneath Eleana's seat.

"How long have you been here?" he asked.

"A while."

"It's not a great place to hang out. Some of these truckers could get the wrong idea."

She shrugged. Walter ordered a coffee.

"So. What's up? You going somewhere?" Walter asked.

"I just had to get out of that creepy place. It's all Wonder Bread and Jesus. Every night I wait for them to come out, like that guy in *Friday the 13th*. It's the normal people you gotta watch out for. Like whenever they get somebody for some really twisted killing they always have the neighbors on the news saying, 'Well, he seemed like a nice guy. Very quiet.' "

"You have a place to stay?"

"I got some friends," she said.

"What did you want to talk about?" he asked.

"Can we get out of here? I've been here so long I know all the roaches by their first names."

Walter laughed.

"What are you laughing about?"

"That was funny—about the roaches."

Eleana smiled. "There was one cute little one named Mario. He wanted to be a famous dancer but all the others ignored him because they said roaches can't be dancers. But he could move, you know."

Walter smiled and led her to his car.

"Where to?" he asked.

"Anywhere, just don't make me decide," she said.

Walter shrugged and started the car. By the time they reached downtown she was asleep, her head resting on her arm against the door jamb. The air played with her hair, tossing it across her face and then pulling it back. She looked different asleep, softer and younger. He saw how she might have been.

"Where are we?" she said when he stopped the car by his house.

"Elysian Heights. I didn't know where you wanted to go and it seemed like you needed a place to sleep. There's a motel down the street—I can give you some money. And then tomorrow we can talk."

"Where do you live?"

"That house up there. With the yellow light." Walter pointed.

"Can I see it?"

Walter hesitated. After months of avoiding his questions why would she suddenly come to see him? She could be doing it for Jeffries as part of a setup. But then why threaten Sara? Maybe they knew

Eleana was coming. He looked over the street and saw no unfamiliar cars. He felt her watching him.

"Come on," he said. Eleana picked up her duffel and followed him up the walk to the house.

"Nice place," she said, looking around. She turned the television on to MTV, then poked through the kitchen, looking in the refrigerator and kitchen cabinets, going through the broom closet.

"What are you doing?" Walter asked.

"It's one of my weird things, so don't make a big deal, okay? I have to make sure nobody's hiding."

She went through the rest of the small house, opening closets and drawers, looking under beds and furniture. When she returned to the kitchen she took a cup of coffee from Walter.

"It's great," she said. "Real funky. I like old places. They make you feel like people belong in them." She looked around nervously, gnawing on a fingernail. Her fingertips were blunt and raw from the practice.

Walter hesitated again. He probably should take her straight back to San Bernardino. But if she had come on her own, it was an opportunity that would not be repeated. He remembered his new resolve.

"You can stay in Sara's room," he said. "I'll show you."

She used the bathroom first and came out wearing a worn T-shirt that ended just below the curve of her rear. The shape of her breasts was clear beneath the thin fabric.

"Good night," she said.

"See you in the a.m.," he replied. It's what he always said to Sara before he turned out the light.

He slept late in the morning, awakening to strange sounds. At first he thought it was an animal outside, but it seemed to be coming from inside, a soft moaning sound, rhythmic but irregular. After standing at the door he recognized it as Eleana, in her bedroom. She gave out a low gasp and then there was silence. A few minutes later he heard her get up, go to the bathroom, and walk down to the kitchen, singing to herself.

She sat at the kitchen table in her T-shirt, reading the paper, one leg doubled up in front revealing red bikini underwear.

"Sleep well?" he asked.

"Yeah. They used to come wake me up and I hate that. I like to get up on my own."

"I thought maybe you had a bad dream or something."

"You mean, just now? Sorry, I guess I was kind of loud. That's how I wake up, you know. You ever do that?"

"Uh—sometimes," he said.

"I bet you do it a lot. Most guys do."

"What do you want for breakfast?" he asked.

"One of those big man's breakfasts, you know, bacon and eggs and hash browns and lots of toast, a Danish. Coffee. Orange juice."

"There's cereal in the cabinet," Walter said pointing, "and bowls over there."

"Great," she muttered.

"What did you want to talk to me about?" Walter asked after she finished her second bowl of Rice Krispies heavily sprinkled with sugar.

"You should lay off Ted."

"It's a little late for that."

"But you should."

She seemed edgy again, looking around the room and then down at her bowl.

"Why? Why should we lay off Ted Jeffries?" Walter asked.

"Because he never did anything."

"He fed you kids drugs and put you in porno movies."

"Gimme a fucking break. Even if that's true—and you can't prove it—that's shit compared to the other shit I've seen. That all the other kids have seen. You don't know shit. I bet you did drugs when you were my age."

Walter shrugged.

"And you've got dirty magazines in your closet. Same thing as our movies except ours are better. It's art, it's just ahead of its time."

"That's Ted speaking."

"It's true."

"Ted Jeffries had Roscoe Brown killed. He's threatened my wife and child. I think he may have killed Tommy."

"You're full of it."

"Does he know you're here?"

"No way."

"Did you ever sleep with him?"

"Ted? Are you kidding? You know how old he is?"

"Did you ever sleep with him?"

"No!"

"Okay. You told the people you were staying with that you were going somewhere, didn't you?"

"I left them a note."

"I'll call and tell them where you are."

"No." The word came out high-pitched and strained. "Please, Mr. Buris."

"You can call me Walter if you want."

"Please."

She looked much younger then.

"You have to call them and tell them you're fine and you don't want to tell them where you are," Walter said. "Or I'll drive you back."

"You can be a real motherfucking cocksucker, you know that?"

Walter shrugged and pointed at the phone.

Later they sat outside in the small backyard, moving their chairs to catch the morning sun. The night's chill still held close to the ground and in the stone wall that bordered one side of the yard.

She had retreated into herself after the phone call, and Walter sensed that unless he made a move she would leave. He was convinced she had come on her own, because of something about the case. She wanted his help, but did not yet trust him. Somehow he had to get her to open up.

"You know, I never planned to go to law school," Walter began. "When I got out of college I thought about being lots of things but never a lawyer. That was too dull. I did different things and then I managed a rock band for a while. That's how I got to LA. Came here to make it big. I was going to be another Brian Epstein. Do you know who he was?"

"Yeah."

"I bet you don't."

"He was the fucking manager of the Beatles. And you probably think they were just the greatest."

"Well—I don't know. Their stuff was pretty good. Don't listen to it much now though. Too cute. Anyway, I managed this band for a couple years till the lead singer got a record deal and the band split up."

"Were they any good?" Eleana asked.

"Yeah. Kind of an Allman Brothers sound, rock but with a Southern feel. You know their stuff?"

"Twin lead guitars—Dickie Betts and Duane Allman. Big album *Brothers and Sisters*. Big hit, 'Jessica.' Great guitar work."

"Who do you like now?"

"Nobody."

"Come on, you must still listen. If you're into music, you never give it up."

She shrugged. "Ted used to take us to all the clubs. Me, Mark, Tommy, some of the others. We'd just walk in, you know, they all knew Ted. He couldn't buy anything, everything was free. Sometimes we went backstage to see the musicians. I met Bob Dylan once."

"Really." Walter was impressed.

"Except for Ted, none of us had anybody that gave a shit about us, ever."

[136]

"I met your mother," Walter said. "I could see why you might run away."

"How was she?" Eleana asked after a long pause.

"She seemed okay." Walter remembered their conversation at the restaurant in Covina, where his questions about Eleana were met with her mother's questions about the trial. She hoped it would be sensational so she could sell her own life story to the movies. She would tell how she had been victimized by men and attacked by her own daughter. Evil was all around, she said.

"Do you like your folks?" Eleana asked.

"Sure. I don't see them too much. They're divorced, but each of them comes out maybe once a year or I go back to see them. They live in Florida."

Eleana nodded and went inside.

After a lunch of tuna fish sandwiches Eleana turned on the television and found a horror movie just starting on cable. Walter moved to the kitchen table where he began a chart of exhibits and witnesses for rebuttal from a master list of potential evidence in the case Curtes had compiled. He found it hard to concentrate, wondering what it meant that Eleana was sitting in the next room.

She watched the movie, rapt, a pillow clutched to her chest.

After the movie Eleana switched to MTV and told Walter about all the new groups and their videos, who she liked, who she didn't. She knew the music scene better than Walter ever had.

"So, you want to go out tonight?" Walter asked. "We could see a movie or go hear some music."

"I dunno," she replied, sneaking a look at him before she turned back to the television. "David Bowie. His old stuff was pretty good, you know, *Aladdin Sane*, *Diamond Dogs*. 'Rebel, Rebel' is one of my favorite songs of all time, but this is so K mart."

"I don't see how you know those records. They were made before you were born."

"Ted let me make tapes of all his records. He had everything. After you guys kicked us out of the House somebody ripped them off. I'd like to kill whoever did it."

"We could go out and get a bite to eat," Walter suggested.

She started in on Michael Jackson, whose video was playing. She sat close to Walter on the couch, leaning his way so that her shoulder was warm against his side.

"Are you going to testify for me?" he asked.

"Mark told me he'd kill me personally if I did," she replied without looking at him.

"When was that?"

"He said it a couple of times. Once last week. I told him to fuck off. Did you know he likes to hurt little kids?"

"Yes. I don't blame you for being scared," Walter said.

She shook her head. "I don't get scared anymore. I got over that a long time ago. I just want it to be fucking over. I mean you should just fucking lay off. You don't know what you're doing. You don't have a fucking clue."

"I'll make you a deal," Walter said. "If we can talk, I mean really talk, then I won't bug you about testifying. You tell the truth, I tell the truth, that's it. Just between you and me."

Eleana shrugged. Walter took it for a yes.

He ordered a pizza from a local restaurant and picked up some beer and soda to go with it. They sat in the kitchen, listening to the Rolling Stones's *Sticky Fingers* album, their faces turning red from the pizza, which they loaded with red pepper.

"You know what the worst thing about being in trial is?" Walter asked. "You have to talk all the time and you never get to say anything—you never get to say what's really on your mind. Then after a while you get so you can't talk about anything anyway, because you're so wired on the trial. It used to drive Laura—that's my wife—it used to drive her crazy."

Eleana nodded.

"Maybe it's like that for you. You've forgotten how to talk," Walter suggested.

"I can talk," she replied.

"I mean really talk," he said. "So it counts."

She stood up and walked into the living room in a way that was a statement in itself. He followed and sat opposite her in front of the fireplace he never used.

"I was never scared when I was at the House," she said. "I was there more than two years, and I was never scared. You gotta understand about that. You were safe there. I mean, like, all that drug shit you scream about, it's not like kids were ODing all over the place like on the street. Because when you're on the street, you gotta do something. To keep your head straight, you know. Everybody's after your body and you gotta eat and you don't have anyplace and nobody gives a shit, so you get fucked up. At the House there was this thing about getting clean. The first thing you have to do when you get there is take a shower. They give you this stinky soap and make sure you get really clean. Then they give you these clothes like pajamas—you can't have your old clothes back for a week. It was a trip after being on the street. Ted said you had to clear out all the poisons. They basically locked you in the back of the House for two weeks 'til you were clean. But after that it was up to you. He said we had to decide for ourselves, you know. I mean that's what growing up is about."

"Did you get drugs from anyone while you were there?" Walter asked.

"I got some grass from Roscoe once."

"Did other people?"

"Sure. Roscoe, and Flash, and the other kids—everybody had shit."

"Did you like Roscoe?"

"Oh, yeah. Next to Ted, he was the one everybody liked. He really looked out for you."

"And got you drugs."

"So?"

"You were too young."

Eleana laughed.

"I never really understood how Roscoe got involved with Jeffries," Walter said.

Eleana shrugged. "They got along pretty good. Roscoe made Ted laugh, I don't know. I mean if Ted liked you, you were friends, you know. He was just like that. It's almost like you didn't have any choice. I mean you did, but it didn't work like that.

"The kids liked Roscoe, especially the guys because he played sports and stuff with them and he told these incredible stories. Mark said it was like going to the movies listening to Roscoe tell stories. Most of them he made up."

"Eleana. What did Roscoe think about everything that happened there?"

"I don't know. I guess there were things he didn't like. But you can't really argue with Ted."

"Were you happy there?" Walter asked.

"We did great things. Sometimes we'd have a dance. We'd put on music real loud and dance or we'd invite people in off the street. We were like a family, you know. If somebody was really down there'd always be someone to make them feel better. You have any dance music?"

"Look over in the tapes. I made some dance tapes a couple years ago."

Eleana found a tape and slotted it into the cassette deck. Walter recognized the simple refrain of an old Foreigner song.

"I love this stuff. It's loud, obnoxious, and stupid—but it gets you going," Walter said.

Eleana turned it up until it filled every space in the room.

"All the kids were into heavy metal," she yelled over the din.

She danced, her hair flying while Lou Gramm's high-pitched wail

[139]

seemed to taunt her. She was graceful and quick, a contrast to the heavy pounding music.

They danced through the Lynyrd Skynyrd and Rolling Stones portion of the tape until Walter turned down the music.

"Don't want to blast out the neighbors," he said. He flopped down on the couch. She sat on the floor opposite him.

"Where's your wife?" Eleana asked.

"Oh, we're separated. As soon as the trial's over I guess we'll get divorced."

"So why do you wear that?" she asked, pointing to his wedding band.

"Because we're still married. I tried taking it off once but it just didn't feel right. Do you think that's weird?"

"I don't know."

"We have a kid, a little girl, Sara. It's funny what things you miss, because you never think you will until they're gone. I mean I don't miss diapers or getting up all night, but when she was little, about two or three, she'd get up really early, when it was still dark, and you'd hear these little footsteps, she had feet pajamas and they made this soft kind of shuffling sound on the wood floor as she came down the hallway and then she'd stand by the bed until I hauled her in and she'd snuggle close and go back to sleep. Of course by that time I was wide awake and thinking about everything I had to do that day so I never got back to sleep, but I still miss it." He looked at her. "Am I talking too much?"

"Nah," she said.

"When I was about your age my parents got divorced and I told myself I'd never get married and if I did I wouldn't have kids and if I did I'd never *ever* get divorced. But you don't want to hear about my problems."

"It's okay. When I turned tricks all the johns told me their problems after I sucked them off. It was like they were on a talk show or something. 'Course then they'd want a freebie. You know, like we were supposed to be in love or something." She yawned. "I'm tired. See you in the morning."

After she left he put on some Philip Glass—he found the music sad and restful—and tried to think beyond the trial. It was a fantasy that he occasionally indulged. Perhaps he could find some quiet firm that did important work where he could investigate and negotiate settlements. They would hire him for his trial experience but he would avoid the courtroom. He would try to put things back together instead of blast them apart.

He could buy a house in the hills and every night he could go out the sliding doors onto his porch and smoke a little sinsemilla and look out over a bejeweled city. He would live in relative anonymity, without pressure, going to work every day and living for his nights and weekends. He would live alone, but Sara and Laura would visit. He would take up a hobby like woodworking or fixing old cars. It might be lonely sometimes, but he would not have to hurt anyone.

He went to bed shortly after midnight. He had drifted below the first layer of sleep when he heard sharp sounds coming from somewhere in the house. His first thought was that Sara must be sick again. Then he realized it was Eleana. It was a strange thumping, sometimes heavy and muffled, other times sharp and lighter sounding. A voice, strained and quiet, moaned at irregular intervals.

He pushed himself out of bed and turned on the hallway light. Eleana stood nude at the other end of the hall, hair wild, her eyes wide. She paced up and down, bare feet heavy on the floor, her arms flailing, fists hitting the walls.

"He's gonna kill him. He's gonna do it." She held her right hand out toward Walter, index finger pointing at him, thumb up. "Boom. Boom."

She stopped suddenly then, as if she had seen something.

"No, don't do it!" she screamed. She put her hands to her ears and began to spin, crashing into walls.

"Eleana! Eleana," Walter said, but she paid no attention. He tried to take her in his arms but she fought him, her body all bone and sharp edges. He held her tight until he felt her relax.

"Eleana, it's me, Walter Buris. I think you had a bad dream."

He tried to catch her eyes, but they skittered away. She moaned.

"Come on, it was just a bad dream." He led her back to her room. With one hand she clung to the front of his pajama shirt. He noticed that her hand was bloody where she had ripped the knuckles with her teeth.

He put her beneath the covers of her bed, her slim legs sliding neatly beneath the sheets, but she would not let go of his arm. He sat on the edge of the bed, waiting for her to loosen her grip, but her eyes remained full of terror and her hand held firm.

"Okay," he said finally. "I'll stay with you." He slipped beside her beneath the covers and she moved close, so that he felt the softness of a breast against his chest and her knee against his leg. She brushed her hair out of her face and looked at him expectantly. He smoothed her hair and she laid her head in the hollow of his shoulder.

He held her, his arms going easily around her narrow back, until her breathing slowed and her body became heavy against his. She turned over and he felt her pubis dig into his thigh. He wanted to brush the dark hair from her face and taste her mouth and ease the terrible aching. He knew she would not mind, but he kept himself still. The way she slept curled against him reminded him of a kitten nestled against its mother.

Sleep came finally in the early morning but it was thin and nervous, full of his problems. When he awoke, the bed was empty and he had a moment of terror wondering what had happened the night before until he heard her rattling dishes in the kitchen. He rolled over and tried her method for starting the day, hoping it would clear away the frustration that gripped him still. Although he fought it, her face kept coming back to him until he found release. He threw back the sheets and waited a moment to catch his breath. It was as if he were sixteen again.

"Did you take care of it?" she asked cheerfully when he shuffled into the kitchen. "It kept poking me all night long."

"What do you mean?"

Eleana laughed at his embarrassment.

"Now you're really in trouble," she teased. "You just slept with a sixteen-year-old."

"Please." He sank down into a chair. She seemed different, more relaxed. She trusted him.

"You grind your teeth," she said.

"No I don't."

"Yes you do. You get them all tight like this." She demonstrated gritting her teeth.

"Sorry," he said.

"It's okay. At least you don't snore. I hate it when guys snore." She poured herself a cup of coffee. "Ted snores," she said.

Walter looked at her, interested.

"But if I'm gonna tell you bad shit about me you gotta say bad things about you too."

Walter smiled. "We used to play a game like that at college. I think it was called truth or something. But I don't have any interesting secrets."

"They said in the papers that you used drugs."

Walter sighed. "I smoke marijuana. Occasionally. Somehow Jeffries found out about it and they made me take a test and after the trial I'm getting fired."

"What's the worst thing you ever did?"

"I don't know. I wasn't a very good husband. I could be a better father. There's lots of things I've done wrong. Probably a lot I don't have any idea about."

"I slept with him a couple times, maybe more, I don't know,"

Eleana said. "It was no big deal. I slept with guys a lot older than him. It made him happy."

"But how did you feel about it?" Walter asked.

"Like I said, it was fine. I mean, it wasn't great, it wasn't horrible. It was fine."

After breakfast they drove out to Topanga on his motorcycle. She had not wanted to leave the house until he showed her how the helmets would cover their faces. She clung tight to him on the freeway and along the narrow canyon road that wound through the shaded bottom-land and by the ramshackle cabins that were for Walter the last vestige of the sixties in LA. They took another road up into the hills, past the new houses with redwood siding, emerging finally in the state park that overlooked the region.

"This is one of my favorite places," he said as he pulled off his helmet. To the north and east lay high open hills, close-shaven and tawny with summer grasses, their easy flow interrupted by dark green clumps of oak trees. Rounded, with deep crevices cut by runoff, the hills looked like sand mountains that had been smoothed over by the sea. Eleana followed as Walter climbed a broad dirt path westward, toward the ridge that overlooked the Pacific. It was still early and they met only one other, a runner wearing earphones who barely nodded as he passed, intent upon his own exertion.

They rested beneath a live oak at the top and Eleana told him about her time at the House. She began by talking about drugs. It was as if she had known all along what she would tell him, for the stories seemed well rehearsed.

"We used to play Monopoly with a joint in Community Chest. By the end of the game everyone was laughing so much nobody cared where you landed," Eleana said. "Ted hated that because he always wanted to win. He yelled and screamed if he thought no one else really cared."

He asked her about the movies. There were four in all, she said, made secretly the year before. Eleana, Tommy, Mark, and another girl, Tina, who was older and did not live at the House appeared in them. She described their making and defended them.

"They're beautiful and you're full of shit if you think any different," she said.

"I want you to testify," Walter said. "If you do we can provide protection. You don't have to go back to San Bernardino. We can give you a new name and a new identity. Some money to get started. We can send you to college."

Eleana nodded.

"But you have to testify," Walter added.

"I can't," she said.

"I'm just asking you to say what happened. It's up to the jury—and the judge—to decide what they do with it. If Ted's convicted, you can tell the judge he shouldn't go to prison. If you've already testified, that'll make a difference."

Eleana said nothing for a long time. Walter watched a squirrel run up the trunk of the tree.

"I won't say anything about the sex stuff," she finally declared. "If you ask me I'll say I don't know anything about it."

"Eleana, if you take the stand you have to tell the truth."

"I don't have to do anything."

Walter nodded. He would take it one step at a time. He had seen experienced agents do the same thing with their informants. They had to get used to the idea gradually.

He asked her about Tommy but she just shook her head. He ended up telling stories about growing up in eastern suburbia and his first year in LA managing the band. Eleana was a good listener.

On the ride back he made his plan.

FIFTEEN

"In nearly twenty years of the practice of law I have never seen such high-handed and outrageous conduct from the government as I have witnessed this morning," Gary Driesen said. His voice was loud and harsh.

The courtroom was thick with dark-suited litigators who had gathered for the Monday morning calendar of civil motions—the motions to dismiss, for summary judgment, for a more definite statement, for sanctions—and all the other legal miscellany that make up the paper battles of civil lawsuits. They came two and three to a side, bearing enormous black briefbags stenciled with the names of their firms in small gold type. They tried to act casually, as if they came to court every morning, although their usual practice was in high-priced offices far from the courthouse. Driesen's tone caught their attention.

In the front row of the spectators' section sat two reporters who had learned something was up. Three deputy marshals sat near the defense table, obvious in their blue jackets, gray slacks, and their attention to Ted Jeffries who, in his polo shirt and dark pants, looked as if he had been snatched off a golf course.

"The government gave no notice of this motion unless you can call a telephone call at nine last night saying 'be there' notice," Driesen complained. "Eight months after indictment and after nearly a month of trial, counsel all of a sudden decides that bail must be revoked and my client must be detained in jail. On an emergency basis. Why? I submit, your honor, that it is a purely tactical move by the government to gain an advantage by poisoning the atmosphere of trial and making our defense more difficult. It is a desperate attempt to get jail time out of a case that is disintegrating before their eyes. I am not one to easily accuse the government of bad faith. I was a prosecutor once and I know how easily that accusation comes to the lips of defense attorneys." Driesen paused and stared at Walter. "But I do now.

"Although in this motion the government accuses my client of some of the most heinous offenses imaginable, it offers no proof, only the rankest sort of double hearsay and twisted innuendo. This motion should be denied without further argument."

Driesen threw his papers on counsel table and sat down.

Walter ignored Driesen's accusations. "As I stated before," he began quietly, "the government brings this motion for pretrial detention based on danger to the community, specifically the threat of further obstruction of justice by this defendant during the course of this proceeding, a ground specifically recognized by the Bail Reform Act of 1984. It is not a motion brought lightly. During the course of this legal proceeding, the government's key witness was assassinated shortly after this court ruled that he could testify at trial. I personally received a threat from an associate of the defendant. And the note and photograph delivered to my daughter's birthday party speak for themselves. My daughter is six years old and now is in federal protection. The government will be calling further witnesses in its rebuttal case. We have made a strong showing, your honor, that the lives of these witnesses, the lives of my family and justice itself remain vulnerable as long as this defendant remains free. I ask that he be remanded to custody immediately."

"Your honor, may we approach the bench?" Driesen asked.

"Counsel, there is no jury present."

"It is a sensitive matter, your honor."

"Very well."

They gathered at the side of the judge's bench, Driesen taking the spot closest to the judge.

"Your honor, I have a hard time believing this myself, but I have to conclude that this whole motion is a ploy by the government to force my client to plead guilty," Driesen said. "Talks concerning disposition have begun again and have reached a delicate stage. Either the government is totally incompetent or it hopes to force the issue."

"I don't know what Mr. Driesen is talking about," Walter responded. "We are in the middle of a trial seeking conviction on all counts."

"My plea discussions have been with Mr. Curtes," Driesen said.

"Mr. Curtes has no authority to make any offers," Walter said angrily.

"He says it comes from the front office," Driesen said. He turned to Walter. "Maybe you should talk to your own people."

"I'll take the motion under submission," O'Brien said. "Please remain in the courtroom."

When the judge returned ten minutes later, his expression was somber. "Counsel, I have read and considered the motion and accompanying papers. I have heard and carefully considered the arguments presented. While I am extremely reluctant to grant a motion such as this in the middle of trial and while the burden of proof is high, I find that the government has shown by clear and convincing evidence that the defendant presents a danger to the integrity of the justice system and should be detained for the remainder of the case. I do not expect the case to last longer than a week or two more and counsel must realize that a conviction will bring a prison sentence. Defendant is ordered remanded forthwith. Mr. Driesen, you may of course take this upstairs if you wish." Upstairs sat the Ninth Circuit Court of Appeals, which could hear appeals from denials of bail. "Clerk, please call the civil calendar."

Walter found Paul Curtes in his office, reading the *Daily Journal*, the local legal newspaper. Curtes liked to keep up on the legal community and the latest appellate cases.

"Paul. What's happening?" Walter asked as he sat down.

Curtes lowered the paper.

"Oh, hi Walter. Not much. We should probably talk about rebuttal. I had some ideas."

"What's this about a plea offer?" Walter asked.

"Who told you?"

Walter just sat back. From now on he was going to push everyone to the limit.

Curtes tried to fold his paper but it seemed to resist his efforts. Finally he met Walter's gaze.

"It was Jackson's idea," Curtes said. "A plea to the 841, distribution to minors, with a five-year lid. It's the best we're likely to do. Rollie wanted me to do it discreetly. So I talked to Gary about it. I was a little surprised, but he says they're interested. They haven't committed but we haven't committed either. I think Jeffries's testimony didn't go as well as they hoped."

"You're a shit," Walter said.

"No, Walter. You are. I'm counsel of record on this case too. I'm not going to see my reputation and the good name of this office go down because you're taking it all personally. This would be a good deal and you know it."

"Why do you think Jackson cares?" Walter asked.

"It's good for the office."

"You know that Bridewell is up for a federal judgeship."

"Yeah. But this doesn't have anything to do with that."

Walter nodded. "I got Jeffries detained this morning." He tossed Curtes a copy of the declaration he had filed. Curtes read it carefully, his face growing pale.

"Jesus—" Curtes said. "Are you getting protection?"

Walter nodded.

"Somebody ought to blow him away," Curtes said. "Save us all a lot of trouble."

There was something about what Curtes said that made Walter pause, or maybe it was the way he said it. Suddenly it was obvious.

"He threatened you," Walter said.

Curtes went through a curious series of gestures: a shrug of his shoulders, a look out the window, a final smoothing of his newspaper. He took a candy bar from a desk drawer, then put it back.

"He threatened you. Or was it your wife?" Walter asked.

"She called me up screaming. She's taking two Valium a night," he said softly.

"You should have said something."

"She was so upset about it she could hardly talk. She begged me to get off the case. I talked to Matti about it and he said it was just Jeffries's style, something to keep us off guard, but he called the local police for them to keep an eye on our house. And basically that's it. Of course it didn't affect my conduct on the case in any way."

Walter looked at him, puzzled. "Why didn't you tell me?"

"I should have. I guess I just wasn't thinking straight."

"It doesn't sound like you," Walter said.

"It's what happened."

"It just seems to me that if it happened the way you said, you would have told somebody in the office. You would have made an official report. You wouldn't just forget about it, not someone who did that to your wife. You never would have recommended the plea. Unless of course they had something on you. Do they have something on you?"

"Absolutely not," Curtes said. "What could they have on me? That I like junk food?"

"I used to think I was pretty clean myself," Walter said.

Curtes stared at him, but Walter simply waited. Finally Curtes stood up and shut the office door. When he began speaking he avoided Walter's eyes.

"About two years ago we were having kind of a bad time, Jessica wanted kids, I didn't. I got involved with someone. A . . . guy. Jessica found out I was having an affair but she didn't know anything else. She'd leave me if she did. She has a thing about that. She can't even stand to go to West Hollywood. Somebody found out I guess, and—the letter said I should cooperate."

"Do you still have it?"

Curtes shook his head. "I burned it. Walter, I didn't do anything. I didn't tell them about the safe-deposit box. Rachel hadn't even figured that out when she heard me on the phone."

Walter nodded. "We'll talk about rebuttal later."

"This can't get out," Curtes said.

An hour later Jonathan Bridewell appeared in Walter's doorway. "I thought we ought to talk," he said.

Walter gestured for him to have a seat.

"Rollie's just been bringing me up-to-date. He hadn't told me about the plea discussions. I understand he didn't tell you either."

"No."

"Rollie's a good man, but sometimes he takes too much on himself. He's always had a thing about this case, you know."

"Yeah."

"He thinks an acquittal could cost me a judgeship."

"It could," Walter noted.

"I doubt it. And I don't practice law that way. You have to look out for yourself, only a fool doesn't, but in the end you do what's right. In this job that's the whole point." He waited for a response but Walter gave none. "I want you to know it's still your case, Walter, and nothing—I mean nothing—gets done without your approval. You've done a terrific job. It's a nasty, ugly business that's gotten very personal and you haven't yielded. We all respect that. The case will not plead without your agreement. I want that clear."

"Okay."

"So let's talk about it," Bridewell said. "Do you really think you'll do better with the jury?"

"I don't know," Walter said.

"I'm concerned that you're taking this personally. That's a mistake, even if you win. I've done it a few times myself. We're supposed to be advocates, not participants."

"That's not the way Jeffries sees it," Walter said.

"All the more reason," Bridewell said. He stood up. "It's your decision, Walter. Just keep me informed."

Walter took Eleana through her direct testimony in his living room that night. Although she shifted constantly in her chair, biting her knuckles and fingernails and tossing her hair, her words were direct and powerful.

"How old are you, Eleana?"

"I'm nearly seventeen."

"How old were you when you left home?"

"I was almost fourteen."

"Why did you leave home?"

"I ran away because my mom's boyfriend raped me and she didn't care."

"Where did you go?"

"My mom lived in San Diego. I went up to Hollywood."

"What did you do there?"

"Just hung out."

"Where did you stay at night?"

"Different places. Sometimes hotels, sometimes there'd be a place where nobody was living."

"You lived on the street."

"That's right."

"How long did you do that?"

"About nine months."

"What did you do for money?"

"Different things. What I had to."

"Can you be more specific?"

"I pulled some dates. You know, tricks."

"You were a prostitute."

"I did that some."

"Tell us about how you met Ted Jeffries."

"Okay. I was on Sunset Boulevard, around La Brea, there are a bunch of motels around there. And I was hanging out with my friends and this guy pulls up in a Jaguar. I thought it was somebody looking for a date. But he started telling us about this place—"

"The Hollywood Youth House?"

"Right. But nobody else was listening except me. I was feeling really down and so I said what the fuck."

"How long did you stay at the Hollywood House?"

"More than two years. Till March when you assholes kicked us out on the street."

Walter decided to ignore the outburst. She might swear at him in his living room but she would not do it in federal court.

"When you were on the street did you use drugs?" he asked.

"Sure."

"What drugs did you use?"

"Whatever there was. Pot, coke, acid once. Speed—but I didn't like that. Downers. Probably some other stuff."

"What was the policy on drugs at the Hollywood House?"

"You weren't supposed to do any."

"Did you do drugs while you were there?"

"Sure."

"Did the other kids?"

"Yeah, but you're getting this all fucked up. I mean, there were rules and there were rules. Nobody gave a shit about smoking grass, and if you snorted a little, you could get by on that too. But Dad was real strict about rock, he didn't want anybody freebasing or smoking coke. He kicked you out if you did that."

"You called Ted 'Dad'?"

"Yeah. Or Big Daddy. Roscoe was Little Daddy."

"Was Ted Jeffries aware of the drug use in the House?"

"He knew everything."

"Do you know Mark Hanson?"

"Yeah."

"Do you know anything about a film he made while he was at the House?"

"I told you, I'm not talking about this."

"You don't have to talk about yourself, Eleana," Walter urged. "Just what you know about Mark's film. It's already in evidence, everybody's seen it."

"I'm not talking about it. If you ask me, I'm gonna lie."

"I'm just asking you to tell the truth," Walter said. "You can tell the jury you didn't think there was anything wrong with it. It's up to them."

"No way. They're a bunch of perverts, just like you. You think just because somebody's young they can't decide anything, do anything. I'm not talking about it and you ask me about it one more fucking time and I'm outa here."

In a simple blue and white print dress, her hair pulled back, hands in her lap, Eleana could have been a schoolgirl on the witness stand. She held herself stiff and concentrated on Walter's questions as he asked them, trying to answer directly and formally. He wished she would relax, she could even swear, just so the jury heard the sound of her real voice. Even so they were enthralled and seemed to perch forward in their seats, as if trying to gain an early hearing of her words. Meanwhile Driesen made no objections but took notes and occasionally leaned over to listen to comments from Jeffries.

Cross-examination began after lunch.

"Miss Torelli, my name is Gary Driesen and I am the lawyer for Ted Jeffries," Driesen said, standing at counsel table.

"Hi," she replied.

"I wonder if I might call you Eleana. Is that okay?"

"It's what everybody else does," she quipped and laughter broke throughout the courtroom.

Walter's heart sank. With a single question Driesen had broken the ice and established a rapport with Eleana.

"Fine," Driesen said. "Eleana, did Ted Jeffries ever speak to you about your use of drugs or alcohol?"

"He said I drank too much."

"Did you?"

"I guess. I also used to do coke."

"And did Mr. Jeffries ever do anything about that?"

"He got me into a program."

"A drug treatment program?"

"Right."

"Did he help anyone else at the House with substance abuse problems?"

"Yeah. He made sure everybody got help. Most of the kids came in pretty strung out."

"What was his philosophy about drug use after you received counseling?"

"He didn't like it but he said it was up to us. He knew that we'd do whatever we wanted to, so he wanted to know what we were doing. He figured that if he was a real narc about it we'd just go back out on the street and that would be worse."

"Did his efforts help you?"

"Yeah."

Driesen paused briefly behind the lectern but now stepped closer to Eleana, his chin in one hand, as if deep in thought. "Did Ted Jeffries care about the kids in the Hollywood House?" he asked.

"Oh, yeah. We were his family. He talked to us about what was going on, gave us advice, showed us things. He gave us birthday parties and stuff. Last summer, there was this really tough black girl, Shari, who came in, but she wouldn't say anything, just got into fights a lot, and ripped off everybody's stuff. Everybody wanted to kick her out but Ted wouldn't, I don't know why. Anyway, I guess he found out it was her birthday because he arranged this whole surprise birthday party over at his place and gets everyone over there and then when Shari comes in and we all said surprise, it was like someone hit her over the head or something. She couldn't believe it. She started crying. She must have cried for about an hour. She was different after that. See, just about everybody there was there because nobody ever cared about them. Except for Ted."

"I see," said Driesen. "Now, Eleana, this is important. When you were at the Hollywood House, did you appear in any movies or videos?"

"No, I didn't," Eleana answered.

Walter felt a pain in his middle.

"To your knowledge, did any other young person at the House participate in any way in a film or video while there?"

"No, they didn't."

"To your knowledge, was Ted Jeffries sexually involved with any resident of the House?"

"No. He wouldn't do that."

"No further questions, your honor."

As Walter approached the lectern for his redirect examination he considered his options. He could try to impeach Eleana on the sex charges, hoping that she would recant under pressure, but that was unlikely. And she might turn on him for breaking his promise. If he limited himself to minor clarifications of her testimony her denial would stand, but if they showed the second video the jury would see the truth. That one piece of evidence would put the whole case into perspective.

On redirect Walter tried to restore the original mood of Eleana's testimony. He needed something new. He needed a story as good as the surprise birthday party which Driesen had elicited. He could think of only one possibility.

"Did Ted Jeffries ever see you or anyone else take drugs?" Walter asked.

"I don't think so," Eleana said.

"What kinds of things did he do with you?"

"We talked, he took us places. He played ball with the guys. Sometimes we played games, charades, and stuff like that."

"Did you ever play Monopoly with him?"

"Uh, yeah, a couple times."

"Did you have special rules?"

"No. Except there was a joint on Community Chest so if you landed there you had to smoke it with everybody."

"By a joint you mean marijuana."

"Yeah."

"Did Ted smoke marijuana with you when he played with you?"

"Yeah. He didn't want to. He didn't think it was good for your lungs and it made everybody too silly but that was the rules, so he did."

Walter sat down.

"Great job," Curtes said, patting him on the back.

Walter nodded. The worst thing he could pin on Jeffries was something he figured shouldn't even be against the law.

As court ended for the day Gary Driesen allowed himself a moment of self-congratulation. Without notice, without any prior statements to use for impeachment, with an unpredictable and apparently devastating witness, he had turned the case around. When he had stood up to begin the cross, everyone in the courtroom believed the slim, pretty girl had sent Ted Jeffries to prison. But by breaking all of the rules of cross-examination, by asking open-ended questions and letting Eleana go where she would, he had put a different twist on it. She really cared for Jeffries and that came across. Overall, her testimony hurt, but not as much as it could have.

He still thought the plea was the best option and the cross-examination had given Jeffries a plausible basis for it. He could argue he never gave the kids drugs but he was not strict enough about supervision at the House. That was a mistake in judgment, but not in morals. Even O'Brien, who could be a tough sentencer, would see that.

After court he had only a few minutes with Jeffries in lockup before they took him down to Terminal Island. Driesen wanted to talk about the plea, but saw that Jeffries was wearing his secret smile, the one that appeared before he shared a story or juicy insight. It was just the hint of a curl at the edge of his mouth and a way he had of leaning forward.

"Tell you something about that girl," he said, motioning for Driesen to come closer.

"You mean Eleana?" Driesen asked.

He nodded. "Best blow job I ever had. Knew how to do it right, very smooth, but with lots of enthusiasm. You ever had one like that? Can you imagine looking down and seeing that face sucking you off?"

Jeffries roared with laughter at Driesen's shocked expression.

"I have to see the press," Driesen said. "You think about that offer. We should decide tomorrow."

Jeffries was still laughing as Driesen escaped into the open corridor of the courthouse.

SIXTEEN

Rachel Martin continued her search for the house in the hills but only because she did not want to tell Buris that it was hopeless. The way he threw himself into the case, even after it turned bad, reminded her of herself at a younger age. He showed the same desperate stubbornness that she developed after her divorce, the same bitter refusal to acknowledge defeat. In the end it was usually a mistake.

After Eleana's testimony she called in for her phone messages and returned them in order. The last was from a Helen Meyers. She knew no one by that name but she often got calls from strangers.

"Hi, this is Rachel Martin with county probation. You called."

"Yes, hello, Mrs. Martin. You might remember that we had the nicest chat over tea several weeks ago."

"I'm afraid I don't," Rachel replied, trying to catch what was familiar about the clear, proper voice.

"You were looking for a certain house."

"Do you live in the Hollywood hills?"

"Yes."

"Now I remember—we talked politics, sure."

"I think I may have your house."

"Really." Rachel was doubtful. More likely Helen was feeling lonely. "What's the address?"

"It's 532 South Hillaway."

"That's not on my list," Rachel said.

"I think it's your house," Helen replied.

"Look, I appreciate your time, but I really don't—"

"You have to believe, dear."

Rachel was too tired to argue. "Okay," she said. "I'll meet you tomorrow at ten."

"Fine dear. Don't be late, because I play bridge after lunch. We have a regular game on Wednesdays."

"I'll be there."

The next morning Rachel drove Helen through the hills around her neighborhood until they reached a bend in a road about a quarter of a mile from Helen's house. They stopped and Helen pointed out an undistinguished tract house that sat high on a bluff two hundred yards away. Rachel checked the address against her list.

"You know, Helen, I really appreciate your efforts, but this can't be the place," Rachel said, trying to keep the frustration out of her voice. "You can see there's no garage and there's no record of an upgrade in the electrical service and we know they had to do that for what they used the house for."

"There might be a garage in back. You can't see where the driveway goes," Helen said pointing. She handed her binoculars to Rachel.

"I guess. You can't tell from the aerial photos I have either," Rachel said. She also realized that Jeffries could have had someone change the electrical service without a permit. In fact, knowing him, that would be the way he would do it. He knew plenty of skilled electricians in his business who would do it for him, no questions asked.

"Who lives there?" Rachel asked.

"An Iranian family."

"When did they move in?"

"Four months ago. It has a pool and a view of the signs you said. See?" Helen pointed out the landmarks. "It was a friend of a friend who told me about it. Most of the people up here just move in and move out, but there are some of us who have been here from the beginning and we all know each other. We keep an eye out. Mrs. Simpson who lives on Hickory Court below—she spoke to Connie who lives up the street and she's the one who said she noticed the moving trucks even though there weren't any For Rent or For Sale signs. I called everyone and asked them about people moving in and out because I thought from what you said that they would at least have to rent the house. Don't worry, I didn't tell any of them what it was really about and—"

"If a family moved in, I don't see the point. Jeffries would never rent his private studio to a family."

"Dear, we should follow everything through to its natural conclusion, that's what my Harry always said," Helen responded.

"Then we have to get inside."

"Leave it to me," Helen said, opening the car door.

"Here," Rachel said. "Take this—it's a Polaroid. Do you know how to use it?"

"I think so."

"And be careful."

Helen smiled and walked slowly toward the long row of stairs that led from the street to the front door, carrying the camera carefully in her left hand. She spoke briefly to a man who answered the door and disappeared inside. She did not reappear for nearly an hour.

"My goodness, what awful taste some people have," Helen said when she finally returned.

"Well—was it the house? Tell me about the tile."

"Let's have a cup of tea and I can tell you all about it. He seemed like a nice enough man, I have to say that—"

"Helen. I want to hear about the tile."

"My goodness, you sound like Harry. He was such an impatient man. We had the worst fights about, you know, before we got married. And afterward too. But I suppose most men are like that. They need women to slow them down. It's not good for you to rush around so much."

Rachel groaned and started the car. If Helen had found anything she would have said so. Her comments were just a way of extending the adventure.

"He seemed like a very nice man," Helen began as they sat in her living room, waiting for the tea to steep. "I didn't quite catch his name. I'm not very good with names, especially foreign ones. Hareef or something. Anyway, I explained that this was the house where I grew up and I just wanted to see it one more time."

"Where you grew up? That house is thirty years old—at the most," Rachel said.

Helen laughed. "Yes, but in Los Angeles no one has any sense of time. I'm not sure he entirely understood me anyway. I said a lot of things about my husband and showed him pictures of my children. His family is away and he seemed lonely. He showed me pictures of them, down to the cousins and grandchildren."

"Did you see the pool?"

"Certainly."

"Did you take pictures?"

"I had a little trouble with the camera. But you can see for yourself."

Helen spread out four Polaroid pictures on the table. Rachel compared them with the blowups from the second video. They matched perfectly.

"Oh my God," said Rachel. "We found it."

Over the weekend Leslie drove down to see Jeffries at Terminal Island. She was surprised at how pleasant the place appeared. Set on a small peninsula that stuck out into Los Angeles Harbor, its walls were surrounded by green grass; seagulls whirled in clear blue skies. Inside, though, it was all hard surfaces, loud and ugly.

She gave the prison guards the fresh shirts and suits she had brought for Jeffries. They took them away and a female guard ran a metal detector carefully over her body. She stood very still and tried to put herself in another place mentally. She was afraid there would be a body search but there was not.

He was waiting in the interview room.

"You look good," Leslie said.

Jeffries gave her a hard look.

"Are you getting enough fresh fruits and vegetables?" she asked.

"I'd do anything for those kids," he said. "Why would they turn on me?"

"They probably threatened her," Leslie said.

"When she came to us she had lice in her hair. We nearly had to cut it off."

"Try not to think about it. Pretty soon the jury will find you innocent and you'll be out of here."

"You don't fool me," Jeffries said, his voice suddenly bitter. "This is what you've been waiting for. You've got me out of the way now. You did this."

"You know that's not true." When Jeffries really felt the pressure he became paranoid. It had been a long time since she saw that side of him. "You just leave it up to Gary and me. I'm planning the biggest birthday party you've ever had and you're going to be there."

"You stole from the studio and now you're stealing from me," Jeffries said coldly.

"I take what's owed me and no more."

They sat in silence for several minutes. When Jeffries broke the silence he was calm again. "I think I'll plead," he said. "I wanted vindication, but that's impossible now. No matter what happens there'll be a taint. If I just plead to the drug thing and do my time I can start over. Lots of people go to jail nowadays, it's not such a big thing. I can write a book or something."

"I don't know, Ted—"

"I just don't want to turn out like Nixon, you know, always whining about being innocent, always fighting the past. I'm too young for that."

"I'll support you no matter what. You know that," Leslie said.

It grated on Walter, the idea that it all might come down to a legal ruling. It might all depend on O'Brien's decision on whether to allow the jury to see the second video. Walter was not a great fan of the law of evidence. A finely nuanced set of rules designed to produce justice overall, it often could not account for what really mattered. For Walter the issue was simple. If the jury saw the video they would see the truth. If it was kept from them they might be fooled. Yet he knew the odds were against him. The tape was sensational and would be admissible only for a limited purpose. It was just the sort of thing the Ninth Circuit Court of Appeals liked to reverse on, and O'Brien hated to be reversed.

Most of the videotape was blank. It had either been erased or was an imperfect "dupe," a copy made by a malfunctioning video recorder. Near the end of the tape, picture and sound appeared suddenly out of the black-and-white static. To the sound of loud rock music, an adolescent boy and girl dove off a diving board in quick succession. The camera followed the arc of their leaps from the light blue sky into a greenish blue pool. The boy, Tommy DeWit, wore a bright red bathing suit. The girl, Eleana, wore a bikini bottom and nothing else.

The video cut to the two of them kissing in the shallow water of the pool. The bright sunshine seemed to catch their eyes. Tommy pulled back and laughed, a light, infectious sound.

They kissed again, more deeply, almost angrily, and the camera traveled down from their faces along their smooth bodies. Now they were naked. Her hand reached down and pulled at his erection. She hugged the boy and he lifted her out of the pool, the water dripping off them in sparkling drops. She guided him inside her as he pressed her against a wall, her legs wrapped around his waist. Their movements became frantic, almost violent. Lines cut deep around Tommy's eyes and mouth, as if he were in pain. Then the tape went blank.

"Counsel, I have considered your arguments carefully on the second video and find that it is not admissible for the reasons set out by the defense," the judge announced, looking at Walter. "You may present evidence about its discovery but may not show it. I am further, Mr. Buris, going to disallow most of your proposed rebuttal witnesses. There will be no accounts of parties given by Mr. Jeffries nor of his private collection of erotica. These are matters quite collateral for impeachment purposes and smack of trying to reopen the government's case-in-chief. We should be able to wrap this case up by the end of the week. Clerk, bring in the jury."

That afternoon Dan Matti's partner, Whitney Young, testified about finding the second video in the trunk of Jeffries's car along with a number of other videotapes that contained more innocent material. On cross-examination Driesen emphasized the FBI's failure to do any fingerprint analysis on the exterior of the videocassette.

At the end of the day Gary Driesen asked Walter to join him in the rear corridor, which ran between the courtrooms and the judges' chambers.

"My client is willing to plead according to your offer," Driesen said. "As long as there's no restriction on when he's eligible for parole."

"You're kidding," Walter replied.

"No. I must say I was a little surprised, but he seems to think this gives him the best opportunity to get his life back in order. He does not want it to drag on and on."

"You realize I did not authorize the offer."

"Yeah, Curtes explained the whole thing to me. Walter, look. We've both stared down the barrel of the gun on this thing and no one's blinked. It's time to get sensible. No big wins, but no big losses either. And, let's be honest, Walter. You're not gonna get anything better out of the jury. In fact, I wouldn't be pushing this deal myself except Ted wants it."

"I'll think about it," Walter said.

"I need to know, Walter."

"Tomorrow," he replied.

Walter returned to the courtroom, now empty except for Matti, who stood at counsel table, sorting through files. Walter sat on the front bench in the courtroom and closed his eyes. Fatigue settled around him like a cloud, soft and damp.

Eleana's testimony had changed the feel of the case. Since she took the stand several prosecutors in the office had told Walter they admired the way he was handling the case. Walter took that to mean it was okay to accept the plea. Rollie Jackson reported that main Justice in Washington approved. Even Curtes favored the deal. He had gone from snacks of potato chips and Twinkies to a bottle of Maalox, which he carried in his jacket pocket and nipped at during court recesses.

"What's up?" Matti asked finally.

"You mind taking a walk?" Walter asked. "I feel like I gotta get out of here."

They left the building and crossed Los Angeles Street to the Civic Center mall. They sat on a bench beneath the looming shadow of the Triforium, a strange two-story, three-legged structure used to broadcast music at lunch hour. It was part of the city's cultural affairs program, a monument to the days when the city was anxious to prove its cultural maturity. The bench faced east, leaving the sun hard on their backs. The horizon was a smudge of bourbon above a tan city.

"I haven't asked for your advice very much," Walter began. "I want to know whether I should take this plea or not. Everybody else says yes, except Rachel Martin, and even she says she'll understand if we do."

"How nice of her."

"She says she's found the house in the hills."

"You've got to be kidding," Matti said, turning toward him in surprise.

"No. She showed me some pictures this morning. We'd be doing the search now except that Eleana's disappeared."

"Oh great," Matti said.

"Your guys are already looking for her. She probably just got restless. Anyway, what do you think?"

"I think it's up to you, hot shot. We're fucked if we do and fucked if we don't. So who the fuck cares?"

"You can be so helpful, Dan. Just the model of the intelligent, insightful FBI agent."

"Fuck you."

"I'm the one who'll lose the case, not you."

Matti laughed. "I got a buddy who's pretty high up in the Bureau in Washington. Apparently my future's all decided except they don't know if I'm going to Tulsa or Lubbock. They'll make me the special agent in charge so it'll look like a promotion."

"Could be worse," Walter said.

"Try telling that to my boys. Or my wife. It took me ten years to get back to LA after I joined the Bureau. And even if it wasn't for them—I'm a field agent, Walter. I like the action. Being a SAC means sitting behind a desk going over reports. I'd die of boredom."

"You could quit."

"That'd be worse."

"Tell me something, Dan. How'd you get on this case? You told me you volunteered but I could never see why. And you're this star investigator, why work on a case where you're not in charge?"

Matti shrugged. "It's a long and boring story."

"I'd like to hear it," Walter said.

"Too boring."

Walter saw that Matti was not going to answer the question. "So what do you think about the plea?" he asked again.

"Take it. We gave it our best shot. Between Roscoe and the way O'Brien screwed us, we don't have much left."

"Yeah," Walter said.

"Except you're not going to," Matti said. "You don't listen to anybody."

"Well, I've enjoyed working with you too," Walter said.

"I gotta go," Matti announced. He nodded at Walter, then stepped quickly across the plaza, headed for the parking lot on the other side of the freeway.

The light was low and hard, still strong on Walter's face when he stood up. Over on Spring Street, next to City Hall, a line of white trailers signaled a movie production. Walter liked to watch the shoots that frequently used the downtown locales. Crew members sat nearby in folding chairs and talked with the high-booted off-duty motorcycle cops who provided security. One day Walter had passed Robert De Niro and Robert Duvall on the sidewalk. In their wide-lapeled suits and fedoras from the thirties, they looked just like movie characters.

On the other side of City Hall groups of homeless sprawled on the lawn. Men sat in groups of twos and threes; one family was laid out on a blanket under a tree. Every so often when the city administration got fed up the police came by and cleared them out, but within a few days they were back. Skid Row was only two blocks away.

Walter wondered what held him back. Roscoe would not have cared, not as long as Jeffries was out of the child rescue business. Walter wondered why he still cared, why he felt the need to settle accounts, even if it didn't do any good. He went home and went to bed, his mind still in conflict.

The phone's harsh jangle woke him early the next morning.

"Yeah?" he answered groggily.

"Hi, Walter, this is Rachel Martin. Have you seen today's paper?" Her voice sounded clear and bright.

"What time is it?" Walter asked.

"I guess you haven't. It's in the Metro section and it's about the case."

"Mm."

"The headline reads, 'Jeffries Case May Still End in Plea.' Listen to this. 'Sources close to the federal criminal case involving Hollywood producer Ted Jeffries indicate that the producer may soon plead guilty in an arrangement that would permit the judge to sentence him to up to five years in prison.' You didn't leak it, did you?" Rachel asked.

"No," said Walter.

"Then it must have been Jeffries. It's what he did before," Rachel said. "Except this time he wants it to happen. The story's slanted so that it looks like a good deal for us. They're serious, Walter. What do you think—maybe we should stop beating our heads against the wall."

"Mm," he said, noncommittal.

"You know how I feel about the House, Walter. But even that's not going to really change things."

"Yeah."

"So we gonna take the plea?"

"You ever see the movie *Cool Hand Luke*?" Walter asked. "One of Paul Newman's big pictures?"

"A long time ago," she replied.

"Remember that scene when Paul Newman fights the tough guy in the prison, George Kennedy? All the prisoners go outside and make a big circle and they and guards watch while Kennedy beats the shit out of Newman. Kennedy keeps knocking him down but Newman ends up winning because he won't quit."

"This isn't the movies, Walter."

"Sometimes it feels like it," he replied.

Later in the morning Walter wrote up the press release and Bridewell approved it without comment:

> Contrary to recent reports, there will be no plea bargain in the case of *United States* v. *Theodore Henry Jeffries*, the United States attorney's office announced today. The government seeks, and will be satisfied, with nothing less than conviction on all counts.

SEVENTEEN

Final arguments began on a Tuesday morning in August, when summer was at full strength. The ocean mists of June and early July had vanished, and the Santa Anas, the hot desert winds, had temporarily subsided. Rachel thought of it as smog season.

In that season the days opened clear and bright, but by noon a thick white haze masked the mountains and distant views. Trapped beneath an inversion layer, the city cooked in its own juices. The air that stung the eyes and soured the stomach seemed to glitter with particulate. In early evening, as the sun made its dramatic exit over the Pacific, the city seemed to sigh with relief. But at sunrise it began again.

Rachel Martin hated it because there was no telling how long it would last or how bad it would get. As she walked from the Olvera Street parking lot to the courthouse she tried not to breathe deeply.

She felt better sitting in the back of Judge O'Brien's courtroom, waiting for final arguments to begin. She still wondered at the difference from the state courts just across the street. The room was bigger and brighter, and more serious somehow, than any of the courtrooms on the state side. The state courts were forbidding only in their bureaucracy and chaos. At least in federal court there was a sense of drama.

O'Brien appeared on the bench and all in the courtroom stood.

"Be seated," O'Brien said abruptly. "In the case of *United States* versus *Jeffries*, let the record show that counsel and the defendant are present, as is the jury." He turned toward the jury. "Now, ladies and gentlemen, is the time for final argument. This is the opportunity for the lawyers to present arguments about the evidence that has been received in this matter. What they say is not evidence in the case. You have already heard all of the evidence in this case. The arguments are presented only to assist you in evaluating that evidence. The government will go first."

To Walter it seemed as if the case were suddenly hurrying to an end. The last witness to testify had been Leslie Montaigne, called by Driesen in surrebuttal. She testified that she saw someone put something in the trunk of Jeffries's car as he left work the day he was arrested. On cross-examination she said she had never told the police or FBI because she knew they were "out to get him."

Then they had spent two days arguing over jury instructions. Driesen and his associates had custom-drafted instructions on conspiracy, the testimony of informants, on circumstantial evidence, on impeachment and the testimony of defendants, all interpreting the law in the light most favorable to the defendant. Curtes argued for the instructions proposed by the government, supporting his positions with memoranda of law drafted during breaks and at night. The instructions could be critical; they represented the rules of the game. Or they might be irrelevant; the jury might resolve the case based on which witness they liked, what piece of evidence they believed, or their impression of the defendant.

O'Brien had listened to the legal arguments with his characteristic casual attention, peering over his reading glasses, asking pointed questions, urging counsel to move on when the argument became repetitive. When he heard something significant the judge would look up and ask, "What's your best case on that?"

After the lawyer fumbled through his papers to find a case citation, O'Brien wrote it down and sent a law clerk back to his chambers for it. Then he read the case while the lawyer continued, urging him not to stop. "Go ahead, I hear you," he said as he scanned a volume of the federal reporter. As the day wore on, the law books on his bench piled higher.

Walter listened impatiently. He did not share Curtes's appreciation for legal craftsmanship, nor Driesen's skill at manipulating precedent. Instead he sat drumming his fingers on the table, pondering the dour judicial portraits on the wall. He also worried about Eleana. The FBI had begun a search for her, but Walter wondered how much effort they were putting into it. Matti thought she had just taken off "the way kids do" and would reappear when the trial was over. He seemed more concerned that Rachel Martin had drafted an affidavit for a search warrant on the House. Matti insisted that as case agent he should sign the affidavit and the FBI should conduct the search. Walter decided not to worry about it until Eleana turned up. He wanted to be sure she was safe before they made any move.

Finally it was Walter's chance to sum up the case for the government.

"Your honor, ladies and gentlemen of the jury," he said, leaning over the lectern. "Nearly a month ago I stood here and told you that this case was about betrayal. Now I think you can see what I meant.

"A few things should be quite clear, because the evidence concerning them is clear. They are undisputed facts. During the period charged in the indictment a number of young people, most of them in their teens, resided at the Hollywood Youth House here in Los Angeles. During their residence at the House they were supplied and they used, frequently, a variety of controlled substances, including marijuana and cocaine. During this period a fourteen-year-old boy, Mark, appeared in a movie. The movie, made with technical skill and sophistication, shows him masturbating. The movie was made for the sexual satisfactions of others.

"All the evidence, the government submits, points to the defendant as the one responsible for these actions—for the drugs the kids at the House used and for this movie." Walter held up the videotape. "In a few minutes I will go through that evidence in detail with you. But first, I want to talk about something that the government does not have to prove, but which you may think important.

"Why would a man like Ted Jeffries, a wealthy, successful, self-made man, an apparently well-adjusted individual with a good reputation in the community, do such terrible things?"

Walter looked into the face of each of the jurors as he paused for effect. They were familiar to him by now, but he had no more idea of what they thought than when they were selected. Mrs. Thompson, the former schoolteacher, had her head cocked in a friendly way, but that could be personal and not related to the case. The would-be actress looked at him blankly. In the back row Mr. Martinez had his arms firmly crossed. Walter hoped that he was just cold.

"Mr. Jeffries is, by profession, a producer of entertainments. That means two things. He likes to be in charge—and he wants to be liked. He's always had a soft spot for runaway kids. He told you why, he spent some time on the street himself. That's admirable. And he helped some of those young people. Suzie Wines, for example. You remember what her father told you.

"Unfortunately, as you also heard, not all the young people who spent time at the House fared so well. Many of these kids used drugs while they were there. For these kids who had seen so much of the worst of this city, drugs were like candy—if it was there they were going to take it. And Ted Jeffries made sure it was available. He hired pushers to work at the House to ensure a liberal supply. He wanted the kids to have drugs because he wanted them to like him. And he knew that as long as there were drugs, they would stay. For Ted Jeffries, drugs were the poison apples that kept the children under his spell."

Walter paused again.

"Ted Jeffries likes to be in charge. We all know what drugs can do to adults. Think of what they can do to kids. Think about how much control the person has who supplies those drugs.

"The movies were just the same. These kids came to Hollywood to be in the movies. That's why everyone runs away to Los Angeles. And so he put them in the movies. He took their youth, their innocence, their most private acts and preserved them for all eternity for the titillation of himself and his friends. That's Ted Jeffries, being in charge, entertaining others."

It had been his toughest argument to prepare. It was a case with the heart missing. The one witness, the one piece of evidence he needed to rave about in front of the jury, was missing. Over the weekend the *Los Angeles Times* had published a guest editorial by a local law professor about the case and the "contemporary commitment to crime fighting by morals prosecutions." The author, Duncan J. Hynes, argued that Jeffries was being treated as a heinous criminal for doing things to teenagers that most adults enjoyed—and that the teens were more "experienced" than most people twenty years older. Walter threw it down, furious. He put on some early Rolling Stones and decided to be a hypocrite. He would act as if the allegations were the essence of evil. He would scream as if giving drugs to street-roughened kids and putting them in adult movies were capital offenses. He told himself it was truer than anything Driesen would say.

Walter spoke for nearly two hours. By the end of that time he had covered all the evidence and still had the jurors' attention. A number of them were leaning his way. He noticed heads tilted forward and small nods as he made his points. But he did not want to push it. The engineer in the back row had twice looked up at the clock in the last five minutes and the pace of shifting in chairs had increased.

"Now you may want to know more," Walter said. "You may wish for more evidence. I wish to know more, I wish for more evidence, but this is not a perfect world. We never know everything. We have to decide on what we do know. And, I would submit, the government has provided more than enough evidence of what happened here.

"You have an important job ahead of you, ladies and gentlemen, and that is the job of bringing this man to justice," Walter declared, pointing at Jeffries. "This manipulator, this user of the young, he wants to use you too. He wants you to believe that no one, certainly no one who looks like him and is as important as him, could do such things. Don't be fooled.

"This is a man who takes in the battered and bruised, who feeds them, clothes them, gives them shelter and aid, and then does this."

Walter held up a blowup from the first video, showing Mark in the last moments of his rite, his erection thrust before the camera. Driesen had gone wild when he saw the blowups but O'Brien had allowed their use.

"He professes to be antidrug but when arrested he has this"—Walter waved the glassine envelope containing the cocaine exhibit—"in his jacket pocket. He says he doesn't know anything about sexually explicit videos made with underage actors—but one was in his car."

Walter paused.

"He says he is innocent, totally, absolutely innocent and this whole case has arisen because some former employees of his, in conjunction with the entire federal government, from the Federal Bureau of Investigation to the United States attorney's office, conspired against him."

Walter took a last long pause.

"Ladies and gentlemen—don't be fooled as Mark and Eleana and all the other young people at the House were fooled. Judge not words, but deeds. Judge what Ted Jeffries did to those who trusted him. Do that, I submit, and you will find him guilty beyond a reasonable doubt of every charge in that indictment."

Walter sat down still charged with the fury of his talk. Sweat soaked through the armpits of his jacket, and his shirt stuck to his back, although the courtroom remained cool.

When Buris sat down, Driesen knew the case was his for the taking. The jurors were disturbed and confused. They wanted something solid they could grasp and he would give it to them.

Some lawyers did not think that final arguments made much difference. Driesen considered final argument the most important part of trial because that was when he could reach out and touch the jurors.

He had a system for preparing his argument. He instructed his secretary that he would see no one and take no calls. He settled in his rocking chair with a hand-held dictating machine and reviewed the stack of three-by-five note cards on which he had listed the main points he needed to make. He dictated an argument, had it transcribed, edited it, and reduced it once again to note cards. Then he committed it to memory. A final argument had to come from the heart and the head, not pieces of paper. Finally, he went home and gave the argument, from start to finish, to his wife, Edie. She had great common sense and told him what needed changing. She also gave him the encouragement he needed to sustain him in court.

Jeffries's incarceration had made the process smoother. Driesen found he could devote his hours out of court to work, instead of negotiating with Jeffries about strategy. Although Jeffries's instincts were good, he hated compromise, and Driesen had had to marshal all his persuasive strength to win a simple argument. Now Jeffries had to call from jail and Driesen did not always take the calls.

Driesen stood to begin his closing argument after the lunch break, which meant he did not have to face the fury Buris had whipped up but had to battle physiology. Following a meal most of the body's blood went to the digestive tract, making mental work difficult. He would have to work patiently and repeat himself often.

"The prosecutor in his argument spent a lot of time talking about his impression of the man charged in this case, Ted Jeffries. The prosecutor called him a lot of names. By implication, the prosecutor called him a witch. Remember that bit about the poisoned apples? Ted Jeffries is a witch, a warlock," Driesen began.

"Let me suggest, ladies and gentlemen, that in this case the government is engaged in an old-fashioned witch hunt. Cynically manipulating the wrongs done to a few young people, the government has whipped up a frenzy against an attractive scapegoat. If we're going to be consumed with moral righteousness, who better to attack than a rich, liberal Hollywood producer? As an officer of the court it pains me to say it, but that is what this case is about."

Ted Jeffries liked it. Driesen spoke calmly, but with an edge. He put the case back on the government where it belonged. And Driesen spoke the truth. People said Ted Jeffries did not know the difference between truth and lies, but he did. He believed in using the truth as much as possible. There were just more truths than most people recognized.

Sitting in the courtroom Jeffries felt like a gopher emerging from its hole to sniff the air and feel the sun. Freedom was all around him. Everyone in the room except him could get up and go to the bathroom. At the end of the day they would all get in their cars and drive home. They would not go back to chains and a van with wire-mesh windows filled with coarse-mouthed bitter men. They did not eat a bologna and processed cheese sandwich made with Wonder Bread for lunch. They did not get excited at the prospect of a piece of soggy lettuce caught between the cheese and the bread. They did not have to listen to the guards and prisoners tell dirty jokes and the same stories over and over. They did not have to watch another inmate relieve himself on the toilet in the cell, hear him grunt with the effort, and then smell the result. They did not have to listen to the constant din, the rattling of metal on metal, shoes on concrete, blasting radios and shouts.

Yet he could take it. He had lived through worse. What made him want to scream was the helplessness. His life lay in the hands of his lawyer and twelve strangers and now there was nothing, absolutely nothing he could do to make a difference. He would have liked to give the final argument himself. He knew he could do it. But he did not want to take any chances. As bad as things were, he could see how they might be much worse.

"The prosecutor, Mr. Buris, spent a lot more time calling my client names than he did reviewing the evidence," Driesen continued. "That is probably because the evidence in this case of Ted Jeffries's involvement in any of the crimes charged is very thin. This is a case rich in innuendo but poor in facts.

"Take the drug charges. Mr. Jeffries is supposed to have engaged in a conspiracy to distribute drugs to youths at the Hollywood House. What kind of evidence would you expect to prove a charge like that? Maybe the testimony of an undercover police officer? Sorry, we don't have that here. Maybe tapes from a wiretap? No, nothing like that. Perhaps the testimony of agents who could report, based on surveillance, about meetings between members of the conspiracy? Nope. At least we should have a substantial quantity of drugs confiscated. We see that on the news every day. They lay it out on a table with the guns and the money." He paused. "But not here.

"What *do* we have? We have only the testimony of Andrew Synes, otherwise known as Flash, who allegedly participated in this drug ring. In order to convict Ted Jeffries on *any* of the drug distribution charges you must believe the word of this pimp-turned-drug pusher, who is getting out of his own criminal charges in return for his testimony in this case. In a little while I will talk about the beyond-a-reasonable-doubt standard, but surely, the word of someone like Flash is hopelessly inadequate to convict on charges such as these.

"Now you might be tempted, ladies and gentlemen, to rest your decision on the drug charges on the testimony of Eleana Torelli. She said there were drugs around and Mr. Jeffries knew that. But the judge will instruct you that mere knowledge is not enough for conviction. Mr. Jeffries must have been actively involved, he must have done something to get the drugs to the youths. He must have paid for them, arranged for their purchase, physically given them out or something of the kind. Just to know about them is not enough.

"And on the sex charges, the evidence is even thinner than on the drugs," Driesen continued. "We know that hundreds, thousands of people could have made these films, including the defendant. He knew one actor, Mark. That's all the direct evidence the government presented.

"Now I'm not going to play games with you. There are a lot of mysteries in this case, including who made the films. And I'll be honest with you. Ladies and gentlemen, we don't know who made them. The government put out a lot of hints here, but, I would submit, they don't know either. They have suggested and no doubt will suggest that it's up to Mr. Jeffries to provide a better explanation for these things than they have.

"But it's the *government's* job to prove who is guilty. It is up to the government, the FBI, and all the other agencies, with all of their resources, all your tax money, to produce the evidence. You heard Mr. Buris—he wishes he had more. I bet he does. But don't let that fool you. It's not your fault he came up short. And it's not Mr. Jeffries's fault. It was the government of the United States of America that decided, for one reason or another, not to do undercover buys, not to do extensive surveillance, not to conduct latent fingerprint analysis. They're the ones charged with investigating—and proving, beyond a reasonable doubt—criminal activity. Mr. Jeffries makes TV shows."

Driesen rubbed his chin and took several paces away from the lectern, head down, parallel to the jury box. He looked up at the jurors.

"If you have any doubts about what I have said, I'd ask you to think about this. If Ted Jeffries did half the things of which he is accused, what would his victims think of him? Wouldn't they be clamoring to testify against him? None of them live at the House anymore, you heard that. All are now beyond Ted Jeffries's influence. So who did we hear from? First, we heard from Mark, the main "victim" in this case, who testified *for* Ted Jeffries. And then, very late in the day, in its rebuttal case, the government put on Eleana, who, I would submit, gave testimony very favorable to Mr. Jeffries. Think about these two young people and their attitude toward the man who saved them from the street. Listen to them, if you listen to no one else."

Driesen caught the eyes of the jurors who would look at him. Almost all did.

"I won't stand here and tell you that Ted Jeffries is perfect. He has made some serious mistakes and he's admitted that to you. He took responsibility for some runaway kids and, while they were in the House which he founded, some unfortunate things happened. He knows he should have had stricter supervision. He knows he made some terrible mistakes in hiring. But those things aren't crimes. Ted Jeffries put his money, his time, and his reputation on the line helping hundreds of kids get off the street. Ladies and gentlemen, that is not a crime. You must acquit Ted Jeffries of all charges."

Walter had hoped to give his rebuttal argument the next day, but Driesen finished by midafternoon and O'Brien was impatient.

Walter was tired when he approached the lectern. Perhaps it was a mistake to take both of the arguments, he thought. He knew Curtes thought so. Usually he could depend on his adrenaline to conquer fatigue—it was a kind of borrowing from future energy—but standing before the jury he felt drained. His legs wobbled beneath him and his throat was scratched and dry. The jurors slouched in their seats and glanced frequently at the clock on the rear wall of the courtroom.

The rebuttal argument was the prosecutor's chance to put aside legal niceties and roar about the defendant's essential evil. In rebuttal he could shed his mild-mannered public servant demeanor and flash the sharp steel of outrage. The jury was not yet ready for that, though, and neither was Walter. They would have to build up to it.

Walter brushed his hand back through his hair and leaned heavily on the lectern. "Defense counsel talked a lot about the beyond-a-reasonable-doubt standard. It is a high standard of proof for the government to shoulder and we do so proudly. But Judge O'Brien will instruct you that beyond a reasonable doubt does not mean beyond all doubt because nothing is beyond all doubt."

The jurors seemed distant. He could not catch their eyes, even when they looked in his direction.

"Every person who has ever been convicted of a crime in this country, every single one since we became the United States of America, has been convicted beyond a reasonable doubt."

As he spoke Walter felt himself drift away until he was listening to himself, like a spectator in the courtroom. The words came without any thought, as if in a dream, and he was terrified that they would suddenly stop, leaving him speechless and confused. He paused and considered his options. His chances of winning over the jury at this stage with a brilliant argument were slim and the risks of trying too hard were substantial. He decided to be short, hitting only the most obvious facts one more time. He closed by talking about Eleana.

"She came to the Hollywood House hungry for friendship, for love, and Ted Jeffries seemed generous with affection. He hurt her, again and again, but she always forgave him because she needed his love so badly. When you saw her on the witness stand you saw her trying, desperately, to break the connection. I wonder if you noticed her fingers— the way she bites her fingernails. They're raw, sometimes they bleed. Consider Mark, who needed Ted Jeffries even worse, who would do anything for the man he calls Dad.

"Mr. Driesen asked you where the victims in this case were—why you didn't hear from them. But you did. You heard them. And if you listen carefully enough, you can hear their real story. Can we really expect these children, who have seen things many of us could not even imagine, can we expect these kids to act the way we think we would, given what they experienced? These kids who hurt so much they don't even know they hurt?

"It's up to you, ladies and gentlemen. Only you can stop the pain." Walter sat down.

For the rest of the afternoon, O'Brien instructed the jury on the law. The instructions, and the way O'Brien gave them, with a careful, rolling cadence, reminded Walter of the prayers he heard when he was a choirboy. He remembered the way the minister stood in front of the altar before communion, white-robed arms outstretched and intoned, "And now let us pray for the whole state of Christ's church."

By evening the case was in the jury's hands. The prosecution team gathered in his office, too hyped to go home but too tired to talk. Matti's partner, Whitney Young, produced a bottle of cheap champagne and, though it seemed inappropriate, they passed it around, drinking the sweet bubbly liquid from Styrofoam coffee cups. At least they had survived.

Walter sat in his chair and tried to respond when spoken to, but managed no more than monosyllabic responses. Rollie Jackson came by and wanted a full briefing; Curtes and Matti gave a glowing account of Walter's performance. Matti started a pool on when the jury would come back with a verdict. Walter noticed that no bets were placed on what the verdict would be.

"Walter?" Rachel Martin tapped him on the shoulder. He turned back from the window and saw that everyone else had left.

"Yeah?" he asked.

"You were great today," she said. "A regular Clarence Darrow."

"Wrong side. Darrow was a defense attorney."

"Anyway, look what I found." She laid a copy of a deed in front of him. "The house belongs to Leslie Montaigne. Let's do the search."

"Eleana told me a little about the house," Walter said. "She and Mark knew where it was. She wouldn't tell me. I don't think she was protecting anybody. She was scared."

"So now's the perfect time. Jeffries is in jail, she's nowhere to be found," Rachel argued. "And anyway, she's on the other side. She doesn't want to be saved."

"Mm."

"You don't know people like her, Walter, not like I do. They have a good side, one that makes you see the way they could have been. But that's not the way they are. She lied for him in court. You don't owe her anything."

"I'll think about it," he said.

EIGHTEEN

By Thursday Walter had cleaned his office twice, returned all the calls he had received over the last weeks, and caught up on office gossip. He tried not to think about the case, but the harder he tried the more it dominated his thoughts, like a jingle that played over and over in his head. He felt more wired with every passing minute.

At first he was optimistic. The arguments had gone well enough and the jurors had chosen Mrs. Thompson, the former schoolteacher, as foreperson. From the beginning Walter had thought her among the strongest supporters of the government. But after three days without a verdict he changed his mind. A quick verdict usually went for the prosecution; extended deliberations meant a strong defense contingent on the jury. He knew it might mean nothing; with a trial this long deliberations could easily take a week or more. But the hard feeling in his gut remained.

He called Laura and said he wanted to talk. Over the weekend they met for brunch at a Westside deli that was crowded and noisy, but the service was good and they could sit as long as they wanted.

"I drew up a separation agreement," Walter said, sliding the piece of paper across to Laura. "It divides our assets equally and provides for joint custody of Sara. She'll stay with you except some weekends and vacations until she's nine, and then we'll switch unless she decides she wants to stay with you."

"Don't you think we ought to discuss this?" she asked.

"Sure. If there's something you want different."

"No. I guess it's just, after all this time I thought we'd have something to talk about. Even if it was an argument."

"Yeah. Well, I don't think so," Walter said. "You just don't care about me anymore. Uh—as far as that note's concerned, I think the danger's passed, but I still want you to be careful. There are a couple things I need to follow through on and you never know."

"I wish you could just give it a rest."

"Me too."

On Monday the jury came back with a question about conspiracy. Judge O'Brien discussed it with Curtes and Driesen and reread the conspiracy instruction to the jury, adding a slight elaboration to which the lawyers had agreed. The jury retired for more deliberations. Based on the question, Walter thought it would be a few more days before they had a verdict, if they ever did. He hated to even think about a hung jury.

The next morning at 11:15 Walter's office phone rang with its peculiar muted buzz. He expected it to be an agent with whom he had been trading calls about an old case. Instead it was Judge O'Brien's court clerk.

"Mr. Buris? We have a verdict. If you could come down right away."

"Sure—"

The clerk hung up before Walter could say anything more. Walter found Curtes and told his secretary to call the agents. They rushed out to catch an elevator going down.

O'Brien was in the middle of a civil suit against the City of Long Beach involving a police shooting that left a burglary suspect paralyzed from the chest down. Walter and Curtes waited in the back of the courtroom for Driesen to arrive. Jeffries sat in the front row with marshals on either side. Driesen finally walked in at 12:17.

"All right. Call in the jury," O'Brien instructed his clerk after the attorneys had taken their places at counsel tables.

Walter hated taking a verdict. He even hated taking a verdict for someone else. The announcement of the verdict was pure ritual with no purpose but the heightening of tension. It could be done with a simple statement, but instead the law insisted upon a process more formal than a coronation.

When the rear door opened and the jury filed in, the courtroom was half-filled. All of the familiar faces were in their place. O'Brien was on the bench; his clerk sat directly below him. Between them and the jury was the court reporter, poised before her strange keyboard, like a church organist awaiting her cue. Against the far wall opposite the jury box, the judge's law clerks and externs watched wide-eyed. Against the wall behind them leaned a chart from the police shooting case marking a street corner and bullet trajectories.

Jeffries sat casually between Driesen and two associates, a gold pen twirling between his fingers. Two deputy marshals stood behind him, rocking back on their heels. Leslie Montaigne sat in the first row of the spectators' benches along with a line of reporters. Walter spotted Rachel Martin toward the back of the courtroom. Two other district judges at the back. Walter had never seen that before.

Walter had been told that if the jury was going to acquit they would look at the defendant but that jurors returning a conviction would avoid his eyes. Walter had never found the method very accurate but he always watched. Several jurors looked in Jeffries's direction but others avoided him.

O'Brien waited until all the jurors were seated and the courtroom was absolutely still to speak. "I have a note indicating the jury has reached a verdict in this case," O'Brien said.

Mrs. Thompson stood up from her seat in the front row of the jury box. "Yes we have, your honor." She held a slip of paper in her hand.

"The clerk will please receive the verdict," O'Brien instructed.

The clerk took the verdict form from Mrs. Thompson and handed it up to O'Brien. The judge spread it before him, looked it over, and then handed it back to the clerk. His face remained impassive.

"Mr. Jeffries, please rise," O'Brien said.

Ted Jeffries and Driesen stood to face the judge. The silence in the courtroom seemed to grow deeper and heavier. It was as if they were all paralyzed.

"The clerk will now read the jury's verdict," O'Brien instructed.

The clerk stood and held the verdict form in front of him. "We, the jury in the case of *United States of America* versus *Theodore Henry Jeffries*, do find as follows.

"Count one, conspiracy to distribute controlled substances. We, the jury in the above-titled matter, find the defendant—not guilty."

Someone in the back of the courtroom screamed.

"Count two, distribution of a controlled substance. Not guilty."

Walter just listened for the words at the end of the clerk's cadence. Each time but one they were the same: "not guilty."

"Count five, child exploitation. Not guilty.

"Count six, possession of cocaine. Guilty."

Judge O'Brien confirmed the verdict with the foreperson and asked the attorneys if they wished to poll the jurors individually. First Driesen, then Walter, refused. The case was over.

"Your honor, in light of the verdict in this case, I would move that my client be released on his own recognizance pending sentencing," Driesen said.

"Your honor—" Walter began.

"Your motion to detain was with regard to protecting witnesses *for trial*, counselor," O'Brien said to Walter. "The defendant is to be released forthwith. You will have to go downstairs once more, Mr. Jeffries. The marshals have paperwork that needs to be completed."

The background noise in the courtroom rose sharply as O'Brien left the bench. Leslie Montaigne rushed into the well of the courtroom past the startled marshals to embrace Jeffries. She was sobbing as she held him tight. Driesen stood behind the two of them, smiling awkwardly, waiting for a chance to congratulate his client. Reporters clustered around and shouted questions.

"Well, we tried," Matti said to Walter.

Walter felt the cold spread from his middle. It was the feeling of nothing, a vacuum. He could not manage a reply.

"God damn O'Brien. We could have done it with the second video," Curtes said. "Or a couple of little breaks. He knew what was going on, he was playing games. One of these days the people in this country are going to wake up and see what's really happening. I can't believe it, Walter. That asshole's gonna walk!"

A reporter stood close behind Walter and was tentatively, but persistently, asking questions. "Any reaction on the verdict, Mr. Buris? Did this come as a surprise? What will be your position at sentencing? I'd like to get some comments if I could."

Walter stood. "We of course respect the verdict of the jury after a lengthy trial. I remain convinced of the defendant's guilt and believe we proved it, beyond a reasonable doubt, on all charges."

Walter went up to his office and shut the door. He thought about crying but the emptiness inside swallowed everything. He wondered what he would do the next day. He would have time to go to the dry cleaner's for the first time in weeks. He could fix the TV antenna that had blown down in the Santa Ana winds a few days before. He wanted to forget, but the picture of Jeffries as he left the courtroom kept coming back to him. Jeffries had strolled down the marbled hallway surrounded by reporters and fans. Leslie Montaigne, her face streaked with tears, clung fast to one arm. He laughed and spoke as he went, answering questions and tossing off jokes like a politician who had just won an election.

"I'm not bitter. Life's too short for that," he said to one reporter.

"What did I learn? Well, that the food in jail needs improvement." Great laughter followed.

"My plans? To go home, take a long hot shower, and drink a cold beer. Maybe two. But nothing stronger."

A loud knock sounded at his door and Paul Curtes stuck his head in.

"Walter? Everyone wants to see you."

Walter waved them in.

Matti offered his condolences and then sat on a chair in the corner, his eyes on the floor. Curtes pulled hard at a can of Pepsi. Rachel Martin could not stop talking.

"You know I've been around. I've seen shit happen." She gestured wildly with her cigarette. "And you know I didn't agree about everything that happened on this case. But you guys—you guys nailed that son of a bitch. I mean who the hell did they think made that video? He had one in his car. We kill ourselves to bring him in. We find the house. We get one of the kids to testify. And he walks. I can't believe it. I just can't believe it."

"Shut up," Matti said quietly.

"We got him for possession," Curtes offered.

"And what will he get for that?" Rachel asked.

"Time served and a hundred hours community service, max," Walter said. "O'Brien will treat it like a shit case."

"So let's search the house," Rachel said. "Maybe we'll find something that'll get even O'Brien pissed off."

Matti shook his head, disgusted.

Walter closed his eyes. He just wanted to be done with it all. "Okay. Set it up for tomorrow," he told Matti. "Right now I need to be alone."

At home Walter unplugged the phone and turned down the sound on the answering machine. He already had five messages. As he sat in the living room drinking a beer he could hear the machine click on and off as it played and then recorded messages. Earlier he had left a message for Laura, but he did not want to talk to her yet. She might be sympathetic but underneath she would only pity his pigheadedness.

He turned on the television to watch the local news. The verdict was the lead story on all the broadcasts. All led with the same interview of Mrs. Thompson, the jury foreperson.

"It was a very difficult case, because the charges were so serious," she said. "And we recognized that Mr. Jeffries might have done some of the things they said. But the government did not prove it beyond a reasonable doubt. There were so many other people who could have been responsible. And none of the young people really—they didn't accuse him themselves, so it was totally circumstantial. We just had to acquit."

Walter pointed the remote at the TV and turned it off. He took a hot bath and went to bed. Although he was very tired, sleep came hard, and he listened to the broad whir of the attic fan until he lost himself in its sound.

NINETEEN

Matti picked Walter up at seven-thirty in his dark green Chrysler. He wore new blue jeans, dark sunglasses, and a dark blue windbreaker with FBI on the back in big yellow letters.

"I cannot fucking believe this," Matti began, mashing the accelerator as they headed down the hill. "Twenty-two years with the Bureau and after losing a case we do a search because of some lame-brained probation officer and when I ask for a little backup you know what my supervisor says? Sorry, everybody's on vacation. Even my own partner tells me he can't make it—he's got a doctor's appointment. I mean can you fucking believe it?" Matti glanced over at Walter, but Walter kept his eyes on the road. "You should have seen Martin's face when I had to rewrite the affidavit—you would have thought I was putting a mustache on the *Mona Lisa.*"

"She's worked hard," Walter said.

The day was sunny but it was not hot and the smog was still thin. Walter felt strangely disconnected. The pain of the verdict had still not hit him. Meanwhile he felt like he was playing hooky from school.

Rachel Martin sat in her VW bug down the street from the house, drinking coffee from a large Styrofoam cup. She joined them in Matti's car as they waited for Paul Curtes.

"I think we should just walk around inside a little before we do anything," she said. "Just kind of feel the place out."

"Oh damn," Matti said. "I forgot my crystals. You know—to get a feel of the place. You can't do a search without crystals. Did you guys bring any crystals?"

"Dan—" Walter said gently.

"But I think I've got a Ouija board in the back. Maybe we can bring back the spirits of residents past and they can tell us where to look," he said, taunting Rachel.

"Spoken like a true bureaucrat," Rachel replied.

"Lady, don't you ever fucking call me a bureaucrat," Matti replied, a finger in her face. "I do what I want, when I want, and I make the system work for me. And don't get any ideas just because you found this damn house. We could have found it anytime we wanted. It just wasn't worth it."

They lapsed into silence until Curtes pulled up in his new Toyota Supra a few minutes later.

"Wait here," Matti instructed.

Matti strode up the front steps, rang the bell, and then disappeared around the back.

"What's he doing?" Rachel asked.

"He's an expert lock picker," Paul said. "They teach it in Quantico. Actually, he teaches it in Quantico."

A few minutes later Matti appeared in the front doorway and waved them in. He looked pale and distracted.

"What is it? You find anything?" Walter asked.

Matti just shook his head.

Walter stopped in the tiled front entrance to get a picture of the layout. A large rectangular living room sunk two steps below the rest of the house lay to his left; on the right was a small dining room. Beyond the dining room lay the kitchen and laundry room. At the rear of the house were three bedrooms, a small den, an outdoor deck, and the pool. The house was clearly lived in—yesterday's mail sat on a front table (a phone bill, a Von's mailer, *Newsweek*, and two letters addressed to Mr. H. Sadet), dishes from breakfast (fried eggs, cereal) lay in the sink. In the master bedroom the bed was slightly rumpled. The place was otherwise immaculate; in the children's rooms the walls were clean, toys stowed in closets and boxes, beds made.

The house was furnished and decorated in basic modern American. Thick wall-to-wall carpet covered the floors except in the kitchen. The ceilings were sprayed stucco with glints of sparkle. Pictures of coastal scenes decorated most of the walls except in the kitchen, where studio photographs of the family hung.

Walter was not sure they had the right house until he saw the pool. He stood where Tommy and Eleana had embraced and found where the camera had been. "Get a picture of this," Walter asked Curtes. Curtes had brought a 35mm camera along, and the blue-white light of his flash marked his progress through the house.

After walking through the house a second time Walter sat down in the living room and watched the activity around him. Curtes photographed each of the rooms from four angles. Matti inspected closets, bureaus, file cabinets, prodded upholstery, and banged on walls. He paced off the dimensions of each room with his feet to determine if there were any hidden interior spaces. Rachel Martin wandered through the house as if in a trance, trailing her fingers over walls and furniture as she went. No one said very much.

Walter was out back, feeling the sun on his face, when he heard footsteps behind him. Walter pressed himself back against the wall and watched Matti step onto the rear deck. Matti looked around but did not see Walter, then took the path by the pool and disappeared through a gate on the other side. He walked with a brisk step, as if he knew where he was going. Walter followed and found the FBI agent at the bottom of a range of steps, admiring a small cactus garden. Matti looked up at him, startled.

"It's a nice collection," Matti said. "I've got some at home. Probably been here quite a while."

"Yeah," Walter said. He reached his hand over and gently touched a rounded globe of spikes. They were sharp and yet looked soft in the golden light.

"I guess I'll go back up and help," Matti said. He turned abruptly and brushed past Walter, taking the steps two at a time.

A few minutes later Walter heard loud voices coming from the house.

"I'm telling you, Rachel, that's beyond the scope of the warrant. And we don't have probable cause," Curtes said.

"And I'm in charge and I don't want you messing with anything. I told you before, look but don't touch," Matti yelled.

"Don't patronize me," Rachel said quietly.

Walter found the three standing over a phone answering machine in the front hallway. "What's the problem?" he asked.

"I just want to listen to the messages," Rachel said.

"It's not within the scope of the warrant," Curtes argued. "It's not a document and it's not an instrumentality. And don't tell me it's in plain view, because the message on the tape is not immediately apparent to the senses."

"You know, I've always thought the Fourth Amendment was overrated," Walter said. He hit the play tab.

The machine emitted static, and a series of clicks, before the tape engaged. "Hello, Mr. Sadet? This is Hillaway Cleaner. It is Tuesday. You have two suit that is ready. Please come get." A beep sounded and the next message began. "Hari, this is your mother. Call me." Another beep. The next message was short, the female voice muffled. "Harry, this is the company. Please call." There was a long period of static and then another beep. The same voice came on, this time much clearer. "Harry, I think you can expect visitors soon. Please clean up. And call me." The phone machine emitted three beeps in succession, signaling the end of the messages.

"Leslie Montaigne," Rachel said. "That's her voice. I've heard interviews with her. I'd recognize it anywhere."

"Leslie saying—expect visitors?" Curtes asked. "You're not starting that shit again, are you?"

"Okay, look. I've got a couple things I want to do," Walter said. "Then we'll sit down and talk." He waited until the others left, then returned to the kitchen. The day before she disappeared Eleana had talked to him about the house. At the time he thought she was just playing games because she would not tell him the address. She said that the studio was in the basement and the entrance was through a door hidden by the refrigerator in the kitchen. That struck Walter as too Hollywood, even for Jeffries. Nevertheless he gave the heavy appliance a series of yanks and shoves.

"What are you doing?" Matti asked, coming up behind him.

"If you were going to hide a door with this, how would you do it?" Walter asked.

Matti laughed. "Jesus, you're worse than that—"

"How would you do it?" Walter repeated.

"It would have to swing left," Matti said. "Which means the latch would be over here." He reached around the right side of the machine and produced a clicking sound. "Son of a bitch," he muttered.

He spun the refrigerator around easily to reveal a door.

"How did you know that?" Matti asked.

Walter shrugged. "Beginner's luck."

"Yo! Buried treasure!" Matti yelled to the others.

The door opened onto a steep stairwell. Walter followed Matti down, watching the spreading cone of light from his flashlight burrow into the ground. The air was still and cool and held the dusty tang of concrete and something else he could not place. Through a hallway at the bottom of the stairs a heavy door opened onto an enormous empty room, its high ceiling studded with small glittering objects. The room burst into brightness a few seconds later when Matti found the master switch.

"The studio," Walter said.

It was a broad open expanse of industrial gray carpeting with a high ceiling studded with studio lights.

"Unbelievable," said Curtes, coming into the room.

"Money, money, money," said Rachel behind him. "Hey, look at this." Rachel threw open an anteroom whose walls were mounted with divided shelves designed for videotapes. Against one wall stood a large modern refrigerator, empty except for a set of metal racks.

"To keep the film fresh," Curtes explained.

"They knew we were coming," Rachel said.

"Yeah, about six months ago," Matti replied.

Rachel ran her finger along the top of the refrigerator. "Then why isn't there any dust on anything? And watch this." She removed a vial of fingerprint dust and a brush from her purse and dusted the handle to the refrigerator. No patterns appeared.

"So they cleaned up when Eleana testified. Probably figured she'd told us about the house," Matti said.

"What about Leslie's message on the phone machine from yesterday?" Rachel asked.

"We don't know that that was her, or that it was yesterday," Curtes said. "We don't know anything."

"You can't be that dumb," Rachel said.

"And what is that supposed to mean?"

"Somebody around here's working for the other side," she declared.

"And you think it's me?" Curtes asked, his voice cracking.

"It's a possibility."

"No, lady, it's not. You think my wife won't talk to me anymore and sleeps with a fucking shotgun under the bed even though she hates guns because I sold out to Jeffries? You think I'd sell out high school, college, law school, and six years of practice for some sleazo producer?" He turned to Matti and Walter. "I told you she's crazy."

"You're running scared."

"I'm not!" Curtes screamed. "Now get the fuck out before I kill you!" The tendons in his neck stuck out like long wires.

"Rachel—why don't you wait outside. Please," urged Walter.

After Rachel's heavy footsteps on the stairs faded, Walter spoke. "You guys are probably right, there's probably nothing to it, but I need some time to think about it. Dan—if you could come in early tomorrow—"

"Jesus, Walter, I haven't had a day—"

"There's a grand jury coming in, I want you to give them a progress report."

"Have you scheduled time, is this one of the regular grand juries— I don't get it," Curtes said.

"I'll explain later. Now let's just finish up here. Okay?"

Driving back to the office, Walter tried to slow down his mind. It was hard because he had immediate decisions to make and too many possibilities to consider. It was like a chess game, where he had to think five or ten moves ahead, and he was terrible at chess. He was not patient enough.

Since Roscoe's death he had suspected and since the deposit box search he had known that there was something very wrong with the

[183]

case. While trial was under way there was nothing he could do; he could not even think about it and he barred the thoughts from his mind. When the case went to the jury, though, his doubts returned, now much stronger. Two days before the verdict he called an agent he trusted, Hank Lyle. He wanted to ask Lyle's advice but realized he could not. Instead he asked for help.

Lyle was in his late forties and still wore his hair combed back in a pompadour. His suits were made of synthetic blends and made him look even smaller than he was. Despite appearances he was the smartest agent Walter had worked with, and the least ambitious. He had seen duty in Vietnam and valued a quiet life. He was a veteran postal inspector, content to investigate postal carriers who pilfered mail and counter clerks who embezzled postal funds and save his greatest energies for his family and his record collection of fifties rock and roll.

Walter told Lyle he needed a favor. "I've got these grand jury subpoenas I need served on the telephone company for toll records. We need them right away," Walter said.

"For what kind of a case?" Lyle asked.

"Use of the mails to send obscene materials. Or anything else you want to call it. The point is I trust you and I can't trust anyone else. You may recognize some of the names on the subpoenas."

Lyle looked over the paper. "Rachel Martin, Daniel Matti, Paul Curtes?" He looked at Walter questioningly.

"Hank. I need these records and I can't answer any questions," Walter said. "I know it's a big favor and I hate to get you in this, but I need it. And don't say anything to anybody. No matter what."

Lyle just nodded.

TWENTY

Walter woke early the next day. Although it was still dark he could feel the day lightening around the edges; a bird chirped loudly in the tree that shaded his bedroom. As he thought about the day ahead of him he heard the newspaper arrive with a heavy slap on the driveway and he threw himself out of bed to pick it up. There were more allegations about secret arms deals in the Middle East, but it was hard to tell who to believe. Probably no one, Walter thought. The Dodgers had lost in eleven innings. He took a long shower, hoping the water and steam would strip away his fatigue. Today he had to be strong and sharp.

He spent his first hour in the office reorganizing his notes for the grand jury session. The grand jury was a body of twenty-one ordinary citizens who, under the direction of a prosecutor, decided whether to indict persons on felony charges. Convening the grand jury that had indicted Jeffries had not been easy. The grand jury had been informally discharged a month early in an economy move, and Walter had to call them in on his own, making all the calls and promising to pay the parking and per diem. Carlos, the grand jury clerk, was suspicious but said it was on Walter's head.

When he called they all wanted to know why they had to come in again, and what had happened with the trial. Walter asked them to come as a personal favor, assuring them it was important.

"You mind telling me what's going on?" Curtes asked, leaning against the door jamb. "That's not *any* grand jury you've got today. That's the Jeffries grand jury."

"That's right," Walter said.

"You're not just doing this for the House. We only did that yesterday. You set this up last week. I want to know what's going on."

"Fair enough. Take a look at these telephone tolls." Walter handed him the records that Lyle had obtained. "You'll note three calls between Jeffries's house and Dan's home during the course of the trial," Walter said.

"Jesus. What does Dan say?" Curtes asked.

"That's what I'm going to ask him this morning," Walter said.

"In front of the grand jury?"

Walter nodded.

"Oh no, Walter. Come on. He's one of the Bureau's best agents. I mean the best. He's risked his life, put it on the line, something neither of us have done. You need a hell of a lot more than this to put him in front of a grand jury."

Walter remained silent.

"Once you put this on the record, he's finished," Curtes said. "You know the way the FBI works. And he's not making it up about being in trouble with his superiors. Look, Walter, this has got to be explained. But let's just ask Dan and then if it doesn't add up we can take it from there."

"No," said Walter.

"What do you mean, no. You can't just ruin somebody's career like that, not somebody like Dan Matti. I won't let you do it."

Walter said nothing.

"This won't get you back in the office, Walter. In fact, you might lose everything, get disbarred."

"I know," said Walter.

"What about me? You think I'm in on this? Am I next?"

Walter said nothing.

"I'm going to Bridewell," Curtes said.

Walter shrugged. He would have to work even faster.

Walter went downstairs to greet the jurors as they came into the grand jury room. It was a simply appointed rectangular space with wooden courthouse chairs arranged in rows facing a raised platform at one end. The platform was shaped in a U, with the foreperson and secretary sitting at its middle, the prosecuting attorney at one end facing the witness who sat in a box at the opposite end. The court reporter sat in the well beside the witness to record the testimony.

"I didn't have a chance to bake anything nice, I've been so busy with family visiting that I just brought some leftovers," Mrs. Sudder, the grand jury secretary, said to Walter. She insisted, as she always did, that he take a cookie and then left them out for the other grand jurors. Henry Alter, the retired factory worker with an obsession for guns, came in with a copy of the new *Guns & Ammo* magazine. Alter played the role of grand jury character, always complaining that Walter and the other prosecutors were railroading the jury, although his only real complaint was that they did not handle enough cases involving firearms.

The foreperson of the grand jury was an insurance saleswoman, Annette Johnson, a solid woman in her forties who always wore business suits and white blouses tied with large bows. She took her work seriously and listened closely to what Walter said. She looked at him suspiciously when he told her he could not explain everything. He knew that she would give him a chance, but no more.

By nine-thirty they had a quorum, and Walter asked Mrs. Johnson to convene the grand jury.

"Ladies and gentlemen, I know you didn't expect to see me again," Walter began. "You've all heard about the trial and I'd be happy to talk to you about that after we're finished. Today we have some loose ends to tie up. There are some matters that need further investigation and you people, with your background in the case, are the right ones to hear about them. Our first witness today will be Postal Inspector Henry Lyle."

Lyle appeared to return the telephone tolls subpoenas to the grand jury. The process was a time-consuming formality made necessary by the legal fiction that the subpoenas were issued by the grand jury and not by Walter. Several grand jurors wanted to know what the subpoenas were about, but Walter said he would explain with his next witness.

Walter went out to the waiting room and found Matti there on one of the plastic chairs, dressed in a dark blue suit, his hair neatly combed. Sitting with his glasses off, Matti looked older. New lines appeared around his eyes and the shape of his face seemed subtly different. He had noticed the same thing in women in the months after giving birth.

"Come on in, Dan."

"What are we going to do?" he asked.

"Just lay down the foundation for future investigation. Either we'll extend this grand jury or we can use the transcripts to educate another grand jury."

"Whatever you say."

Inside, the grand jury secretary administered the oath to Matti.

"Would you state your name, your agency, and how long you have been with that agency?" Walter asked.

"My name is Daniel C. Matti and I'm a special agent with the Federal Bureau of Investigation, United States Department of Justice. I have been a federal agent for twenty-two years and seven months."

"What has been your recent assignment, Agent Matti?" Walter inquired.

"I am presently tasked to the child pornography unit in connection with the case against Theodore Jeffries."

"And in that capacity you have testified previously in front of this grand jury."

"Yes, I have. I recognize the cookies," Matti said, nodding toward the tin below him.

Everyone laughed.

"Agent Matti, our purpose here today is somewhat different than in the past. Pursuant to Justice Department policy I have to inform you that you may be the subject of this investigation. Your testimony here may tend to incriminate you criminally and therefore may implicate your constitutional right to remain silent. You have the right to remain silent here and you have the right to suspend an answer temporarily to consult with an attorney outside the grand jury chambers, is that clear?"

Walter looked up from his prepared sheet at Matti, who sat white-faced.

"Is this some kind of a joke?" one of the grand jurors called out. "Because if it is it's not very funny."

"It's not a joke," Walter said. "Agent Matti, do you understand what I just said?"

"Yes, I do."

"I am now placing before you grand jury exhibits 202 through 205 and would ask that you look through those." Walter put the telephone tolls in front of Matti and returned to his seat.

"Those tolls indicate three telephone calls between your residence and that of Theodore Jeffries during the months of July and August of this year, don't they?" Walter asked.

A long silence followed. Walter felt the sweat soaking through his undershirt and shirt into the armpits of his jacket. Matti kept his head down, studying the tolls.

"They appear to," Matti said finally in a thick voice.

"You never told me or anyone else involved in this case about those calls, did you?"

"No, I did not. But I have not done anything wrong and I have not broken any laws," Matti said. He coughed softly into his fist.

"In fact, you had a relationship with Mr. Jeffries prior to this case that you did not communicate to anyone else involved with the case, isn't that true?"

"I don't know what you mean."

"You recall that yesterday we participated in a search of a single-family residence located on South Hillaway Drive in the Hollywood hills?"

"Yes."

"Before yesterday, had you ever been in that house?"

"I don't know what you're trying to suggest," Matti replied.

"If I told you that Eleana Torelli, one of the residents of the House, recognized you from a meeting you had with Jeffries a year and a half ago, a year before the investigation began, what would your response be?"

"I would say that's unlikely."

"But not impossible?"

"Mr. Buris, you put me in a very difficult position here. I have good answers for all of your questions but they raise highly confidential matters that I am not at liberty to reveal."

"I see. But you are not exercising your Fifth Amendment rights."

"No. I have nothing to hide. I'd just like to speak to you privately."

"I understand that, Agent Matti, but as you know we are in a grand jury proceeding where all persons are sworn to secrecy. Any confidential matter you reveal will be kept confidential."

"I would greatly prefer to speak to you in private," Matti said.

"I'm afraid that's not possible," Walter said.

"Why not?" interrupted Mrs. Johnson, the foreperson. "We can vote to adjourn at this point. Maybe we don't need to hear his explanation."

"You of course have the option of doing that," Walter said, addressing the grand jury. "As your adviser I would ask that you do not because I need to have Agent Matti's responses on the record. The record must be explained in this case. But if you would like to withdraw so you can discuss the issue, we will."

"I'd like that," said Mrs. Johnson. A number of the other grand jurors nodded in agreement.

"Very well, we will be outside," Walter said.

Walter followed Matti out into the waiting area, a small square room whose bare walls were lined with plastic chairs. Matti suddenly turned and put his face inches from Walter's.

"He was my snitch," Matti said.

"I know," Walter said.

"How the hell did you know? Nobody knew that."

"Some things Eleana said, some things you did. The way you acted at the house yesterday, like you'd been there before. And I looked at your record. You broke an awful lot of cases involving people that Jeffries probably knew."

"So now what?" Matti asked. "You're going to crucify me because I had an informant go bad?"

"I want to ask you some questions about it, on the record," Walter said.

"Why? Just to bring me down too? Make sure everybody suffers? Whatever happened to going after the bad guys?"

"First you have to figure out who they are," Walter said.

"You know I always figured you were a lightweight but at least you knew your own limitations," Matti said. "Now I see you're the worst kind of lightweight because you don't know it. You don't have a fucking clue."

"Dan, I've already shown I know a lot more than you think. Enough to ruin your career. From here on it's a question of how you handle it. If we go back inside and you come clean, we can handle it internally. If you refuse, I'll go public. See, I don't have anything to lose."

"You're fucking worse than Jeffries."

"I'm working on it," Walter said. "It's a simple choice, Dan. Him or me."

"Jesus, tell me this isn't a nightmare," Matti cried, slamming a hand against the wall. "My whole fucking career down the tubes because of some dipshit pot-smoking prosecutor who lost a case."

"Him or me."

"I swear I haven't done anything wrong," Matti said.

"Then let's go," Walter said, gesturing toward the grand jury room. Matti nodded slightly.

As they approached the door they could hear angry voices from the other side. Walter knocked and they were admitted.

Walter faced the grand jurors. "I have spoken with Agent Matti and he has agreed to speak on the record. Agent Matti, please take your seat. You are still under oath."

The room was very quiet as they took their seats.

"Please tell the grand jury the nature of your relationship with Theodore Jeffries and when it began," Walter asked.

"For nearly fifteen years, off and on, Theodore Jeffries has worked for me as a confidential informant," Matti said. For the first time he was using his testifying voice. "Mr. Jeffries provided important information on a variety of cases ranging from narcotics to child pornography to international arms smuggling. Like many informants he was himself involved in criminal activity. Until this investigation began I had no idea how serious it was. For a variety of reasons I decided not to reveal the past relationship, but it in no way interfered with my handling of the case. We did have conversations during the course of the trial, but they in no way affected the case. I never gave him any confidential information."

"You say that Mr. Jeffries provided important information to you on a number of occasions. Did he do that out of the goodness of his heart?" Walter asked.

"No. At first I couldn't figure it out. He contacted me as part of a record industry payola investigation I was doing in the early seventies. He said he wanted to meet because he had some information. At that time he seemed like a legitimate businessman who was concerned about organized crime. I took him at his word. After he gave me more information on other matters he said that he enjoyed playing cop, and that seemed to be true. Lots of people do. But eventually I figured he did it because it gave him power."

"Did it give him power over you?"

"No. It gave him power over other people so he could manipulate certain situations."

"Did you ever do favors for him?"

"On occasion, yes."

"What kinds of favors?"

"Once or twice I talked to local cops about some trouble his kids had gotten into."

"Serious trouble?"

"Once it was pretty serious. A sexual assault."

"Did you do anything for him personally?"

"No. I guess that's what put me off my guard. See, most informants can't stay clean very long. So they do some work for you and then pretty soon they get busted. If it's not too bad and they're doing good work, you can put in a word. But most of the time you say tough luck—you did a crime, do the time. Jeffries wasn't like that. He always kept his nose clean. So I figured he was for real. At least I did for a long time."

"Did he ever do anything for you?" Walter asked.

"Not personally, no."

"For anyone you cared about?"

Matti hesitated and studied the pad of notes he had brought with him. "Once. About five years ago my brother was pretty sick and was in a little hospital out in the desert. He's had kind of a tough life and had a problem with alcohol. After his last business failed he went on a binge and his guts were rotting out. They did an operation but he kept getting infections. I went to see him, and they were doing what they could, but it was a little place and he was a charity patient. He didn't have any insurance. He was down to about a hundred pounds and he was dying and he didn't have to be and I couldn't do anything about it. There just wasn't anything I could do.

"I don't know how Jeffries found out but he did—I didn't tell him, I never would have told him—but anyway he came to me and said he could do something. I was desperate. He was my big brother and we couldn't afford anything and I couldn't let him die. So I said okay. Jeffries had him flown to Cedar Sinai and got him into intensive care, the best doctors. In three months he walked out of there like a new man."

"So you were grateful to Jeffries for that."

"Yes."

"Did he ask anything from you as a result?"

"All right. I'm going to tell you everything, things you would never find out. After he did that for my brother he asked me one thing. He said, 'Dan, just do me one favor.' He said, 'Dan, if you ever come after me, make sure it's for something big.' And I said sure. I mean that's the way it works anyway. You always give an informant a break, you just can't give away the store."

"I see," Walter said. "Before Roscoe Brown came forward with his allegations, did you have any idea what went on at the Hollywood House?"

"What do you mean?" Matti asked.

"Did you know, for example, that residents at the House were appearing in sexually graphic movies?"

"I knew Ted was making some kind of movies on the side. I heard things, he said some things. I never knew that he was using kids from the House."

"The possibility must have crossed your mind," Walter suggested.

"I don't recall that it did."

"What would you have done if you had thought about it?"

"Assuming I didn't have anything solid to go on, I probably wouldn't do anything except ask him about it. Nothing more I could have done."

"Did you know anything about drug use at the House?"

"No. I would have done something about that for sure. That surprised me. He really cared about those kids."

"Agent Matti, had you ever met Roscoe Brown before his involvement in this case?"

"No. Although I may have seen him at the Hollywood House once."

"You went to the House yourself?"

"Yes, once."

"So Mr. Brown may have known of your connection with Jeffries?"

"It's possible. I doubt it, but it's possible."

"Mr. Brown therefore could have had something on you."

"No, no way."

"At the time that the case against Jeffries became widely known wouldn't you say it was a fairly sensational case?"

"Yes."

"And you knew that it wouldn't look too good if it turned out that you had been doing business with Jeffries all these years, didn't you."

"Yes."

"And that's why you didn't reveal your relationship with him."

"Partly. I also didn't see the need."

"Agent Matti, did you tell Ted Jeffries where Roscoe Brown was living while he was under federal protection?"

"I did not."

"You recall that there was a beeper device found on his car when he was killed, do you not?"

"Yes."

"And you told me no law enforcement agency used a beeper like that, right?"

"I may have said that, I don't clearly recall."

"In fact, that beeper was one you had installed."

"I'm not sure. I often put a beeper on the vehicles of informants to keep track of their locations, however."

"Had you ever done that on a case where Ted Jeffries was your informant?"

"Yes."

"So he knew about your practice and could have used his knowledge to track Mr. Brown."

"I guess that's possible."

"You denied knowing about the beeper to avoid responsibility for Mr. Brown's death," Walter said.

"That's not true."

"Regardless of the beeper, you did not provide a high level of security for Mr. Brown, isn't that true?" Walter asked.

"We took a number of serious and expensive security precautions, but there were some we did not take."

"Why not?"

"There were several reasons. First, it was my judgment, based on my past association with Mr. Jeffries, and his association with Mr. Brown, that he was not likely to resort to violence. Second, it is my philosophy that efforts on behalf of an informant should be equal to the value and effort of the informant. It was my opinion, and still is, that Roscoe Brown was holding out on us. I thought he had more on Jeffries than he was saying and I wasn't going to go out on a limb for him until he came clean. Later developments in the case have confirmed my suspicions."

"So in fact you never took the safety of your informant very seriously."

"I didn't say that."

"When Mr. Brown was killed, though, you must have felt yourself in a very difficult situation."

"I felt bad about it. Personally and professionally."

"And that's when Ted Jeffries called you."

"Yes."

"What transpired during those conversations?"

"He threatened me."

"He threatened you?"

"Yes. He threatened me and my family. He wanted information but I wouldn't give him any."

"Didn't you call him once?"

"Yes. I called him after Eleana testified. I told him that if anything happened to her I would personally eliminate him from the face of the earth."

"And what was his response?" Walter asked.

"I can't remember exactly, but he got the message. He knew I was serious."

"Agent Matti, do you know where the films or videotapes that Jeffries made with his Hollywood House residents are?"

"No, I don't."

"Is there anything else that you think the grand jury should know about your relationship with Theodore Jeffries and your work on this case?"

"No. Although there are a lot of things that don't look so good now, I didn't do anything wrong."

"Thank you for your testimony, Agent Matti. Do any members of the grand jury have any questions?" Walter paused a moment. "Seeing none, we will conclude this grand jury session. I thank you for your cooperation."

Matti caught up to him on the stairs, yanking him back by the collar. "Hold it, asshole."

"You want something?" Walter removed Matti's hand.

"I want to know what your grand fucking plan is. I want to know how this little stunt is going to make it all better. I want to know how it's going to land Jeffries in jail or bring back your friend Roscoe. But maybe that wasn't the point. Maybe you're one of these types that has to have somebody to blame. You just want to be able to lay off Roscoe and losing the case on me. Well, it won't work. You're in it too deep for that."

"I don't have any grand plan," Walter said. "I just wanted to find out a few things. Which I did."

"You don't know shit."

Walter laughed. "You see that's where you're wrong, Dan. You don't have any secrets anymore. This is the way I figure it—tell me if I'm off base. A long time ago when you were really hungry you hooked up with Ted Jeffries and you made an amazing team. With his contacts and your ability, you got in places nobody else could and you did some righteous work. And best of all, you never really had to do much for him. A couple little things, but nothing major. You never had to stick your neck out. Then Roscoe started singing and that's when the trouble started. As far as you were concerned it was no big deal—some street kids doing drugs and making dirty movies. Nobody got hurt.

"But it got too big for you, too sensational. You had to ride it out. You got involved to do damage control. You weren't going to throw the case—you'd never do that—but you weren't going to help much either. You'd just let me and Roscoe screw ourselves.

"It probably would have worked out fine except Jeffries wouldn't play along. He whacked Roscoe and threatened everybody else. That made everyone else play hardball. That's when you started leaking information."

"Roscoe bought it because he was a cheat," Matti said.

"Oh right. Just another sleazoid dope dealer. And a colored one at that. You always underestimated him. He saw through you just like he saw through Jeffries. He told me once that Jeffries is the kind of guy that either you kill him or he kills you."

"What crap," Matti said.

"I saw your face when you took Tommy's stuff out of the safe-deposit box," Walter said. "You know what happened to him. You're just like Eleana and the rest of them. You don't want to admit it."

At that Matti turned and pounded down the stairs.

That afternoon Bridewell's secretary called and said he wanted to see Walter right away. Walter delayed until she called again, about an hour later.

Bridewell asked him to close the door and sat beside him in one of the upholstered chairs facing his desk. "I understand you've been tracking down some leads in the Jeffries case," Bridewell began.

"That's right. Turns out Jeffries and Dan Matti—"

"Yes, Dan told me about it earlier," Bridewell said. "It's terrible. There's something about undercover work that corrupts. It's ruined more good cops than anything else. But that's the FBI's problem. I'm more concerned about you. You look tired."

"I'm going to be taking some time off in a couple weeks," Walter said.

"Washington's taking a hard line on your situation. They want you to resign. Now."

"Do I have any choice?" Walter asked.

"Well, you can fight it, but you'll probably lose and ruin your career in the process. Walter, you've had a good five, nearly six years here. You're one of our very best trial lawyers. You've given more to this office than almost anyone. I'm really sorry that it has to end like this, but that's the way it is."

Walter noticed his hands were shaking. "If I could just have a couple more days—"

"No. This Jeffries thing has gotten to you. This is our standard letter. I'd like you to sign it," Bridewell said, handing it to Walter.

Walter looked it over briefly.

"I'll make sure that we follow up on everything," Bridewell said. "You did a fine job on the case, you really did."

Walter took the pen that Bridewell offered. "Say good-bye to everybody for me," he said as he signed his name. Walter rose and walked out of the office without ever turning around. He did not want Bridewell to see the tears in his eyes.

TWENTY-ONE

For nearly three weeks after he was fired, Walter stayed home. He did not answer the phone or the door. He changed the message on his answering machine to say he had gone out of town. Every day he read the newspaper carefully, took long baths and longer naps; he drank. At night he prowled the city on his motorcycle, sometimes slipping in to a movie that had already started and watching until it started again.

The full hurt of the case came down on him. It hurt so badly that at times he could not move; he had to sit and wait for it to pass. But he exposed it to thought, hoping that like a wound exposed to air it would scab over and heal. He tried to stay alert. Somehow he knew it was not over.

He was sitting in his kitchen late on a Friday night drinking beer when the doorbell rang. It was a loud flat buzzer, like the sound of a fly caught in a window screen, and it made him jump. He thought about who would want him dead. There were more people than he had realized.

He reached over to flip off the overhead light and crept quietly to the kitchen counter. By lifting himself onto the tile surface and craning his head around he saw through the edge of the kitchen window the backs of two dark figures standing at the door, one large and one small. The smaller one put a cigarette to its mouth, and in its glow Walter recognized them.

"Well whattya know," he said, flinging open the door.

"Hi," said Eleana.

"We were in the neighborhood and thought we'd drop by," added Dan Matti.

Eleana smiled, but she looked thin and tired. She let her cigarette fall and ground it into the concrete step.

"Come on in—I've been worried about you," he told her. "And you too," he said to Matti.

"Right," Matti replied. "Look, uh, I'm just delivering, okay? But if you've got a second."

"Ellie, why don't you go inside. I'll be right there," Walter said.

"I'll make myself at home," she said, smiling.

"She okay?" Walter asked, stepping out onto the front porch.

"Yeah. LAPD picked her up at the bus station on that material witness warrant you put out. It's probably no good now but I didn't see any point in telling her that. You know what she has in her pocket? An invitation to Jeffries's big birthday bash tomorrow night. I think that's why she's back."

"Shit."

"Yeah, you're right about them," Matti said. "They never learn."

"So what happened with you?" Walter asked.

"Lubbock, Texas. Special agent in charge."

"Could be worse."

"Yeah. You know I've been thinking a lot about what happened."

"Yeah?"

"I still think you're full of it. But I guess I see where you're coming from. I mean somebody's gotta believe that shit, right?"

"You're always inspirational, Dan. But I appreciate it."

"Yeah. And you look out for that girl," Matti said. "Remember Tommy."

Walter found Eleana at the kitchen table, finishing his beer.

"You look like shit," she said.

"I guess I should shave," Walter said, rubbing the stubble on his face. "I'm doing what we used to call getting my head together."

Eleana took a tour of the house just as she had on her first visit. Walter waited for her in the living room.

"You got fired," she said, looking around at the mess. "Or you quit."

"Right the first time," he said.

"Because you lost the case?" she asked.

"Not exactly. It's a long story. What about you? Where have you been?" he asked.

She sat on the floor, back to the couch, and he sat next to her.

"I went to the bus station, took a bus that was going somewhere. Got off in some dipshit town where it was totally flat and a hundred degrees all the time and they grew asparagus or something. I like small towns because somebody'll always take care of you. I got a job as a waitress," she added proudly. "It was great. Except the guys think they can feel you up if they give you a big tip."

"Yeah."

"Then I got bored. I mean on Friday night the kids go out to the airport to watch the planes land."

"Doesn't sound so bad to me," Walter said.

"Yeah, well the cops started hassling me. I needed some money and I gave some of the guys twenty-dollar handshakes. You know." Eleana gestured with her hand in front of her crotch.

"You look older," Walter said. "In a good way I mean."

"Look," she said proudly, showing off her fingernails. They were short but smooth and painted red.

"That's great," he said.

"Then I get off the bus and these motherfuckers goddamn arrest me when I haven't done a fucking thing. When I saw that turkey FBI guy I said I wanted to see you. They acted real funny about that, but, here I am."

"You came back for the party tomorrow."

"How did you know? Oh yeah, they searched me. Is that legal— can they just search you whenever they feel like it?"

"Are you going?"

"None of your goddamned business."

"Did Ted know where you were all this time?"

"Nope. But one of his guys tracked me down. I guess I called somebody or something and they traced it. He can find anybody."

"Eleana, you can't go, not after testifying."

"I want to find out what happened to Tommy," she said.

"Tommy's dead."

She shook her head, hard. "Everybody liked Tommy," she said. She dug through her bag and showed him a small photo album full of snapshots. The photographs lay in individual plastic wrappers in long rows on each side of the book. As she flipped them up he saw bits of life at the House: teenagers clowning for the camera, out-of-focus shots of a picnic at the beach, a picture of the residents and staff in a crumbling human pyramid in front of the House, and several of Tommy. One showed him standing beneath a tree with an arm wrapped around Leslie. She smiled shyly at the camera, looking nearly twenty years younger. There were two pictures where Tommy stood between Jeffries and Eleana, all of them beaming for the camera.

"He wrote me a letter," she said, producing a well-worn envelope.

"Hold on. I've got something to show you." Walter left for his bedroom and returned with the evidence envelopes from the bank. They were supposed to be in FBI custody, but Matti was sloppy about such things and had left them in Walter's office at the end of trial.

"Recognize this?" Walter showed her Tommy's driver's license in a clear plastic bag.

"Where'd you get this?" she asked.

"Ted had it. In a safe-deposit box. Along with this." He showed her the ring. "Is that Leslie?" he asked, pointing out the inscription.

"Yeah," she said, staring at the ring. "She liked him because he made her laugh." Her voice was faraway. A tear started down one cheek. "This doesn't prove anything. Maybe he forgot it or sent it back to Ted or something. He's alive, I know it."

"Ted killed Roscoe too."

"No! No! No!" she screamed, stamping the floor.

"What are you going to do?" he asked when she calmed down.

"I'm going to the party."

"Then I'm going too," Walter said.

Jeffries lounged in the giant spa that dominated his master bathroom and listened to the gentle sounds of the party below him. It was somehow the ultimate luxury to lie naked in the swirling water, knowing that so many awaited him. He smiled, imagining the problem his party had presented the city's Westside elite. The invitations had arrived when he was still in jail; most were declined or ignored. Now that he had been exonerated—that's what the headline in the *Times* read—the party figured to be one of the biggest celebrations of the year. Leslie said she was getting twenty calls a day from secretaries and assistants who claimed that there had been problems with the mail or that the invitation had been mislaid; several claimed they had burned in house fires. Leslie had never lost faith. She had kept the business running and never stopped work on the party. And everything had worked out, just as they had promised each other.

When he was finally dressed, Jeffries called for her. She appeared at the door almost immediately, her hands flittering over her jewelry, her hair, and her outfit. She was always nervous when they gave a party and believed she personally had to greet the guests, even when they numbered in the hundreds.

"Hey kiddo," he said as he turned in front of a full-length mirror. "I've got something for you. Two things actually." He took a package wrapped in tissue paper from the bed and handed it to her. "Be careful opening it."

Leslie gently tugged the wrapping from an old copy of *Ulysses* by James Joyce. "Oh my God. Is this the first edition?" she asked.

"The first Paris edition," Jeffries said. "I thought it was appropriate. You know, the guy who goes off, has all these adventures but finally makes it home."

Leslie laughed and nodded happily. "Ted, you shouldn't have." She kissed him warmly on the cheek.

"Maybe you don't want the other," Jeffries said, teasing.

"Give it to me," she said, laughing.

"You have to promise to be good," he said seriously.

"I promise."

From the pocket of his jacket Jeffries removed a small bottle of pills. "You have to make them last," he said. "It's the highest quality Dilaudid they make."

"Oh, Ted," she said, carefully examining the label. "I don't—"

"I know that methadone gets pretty dull. You have to promise me to go easy on it though."

"It's just I've been so good—"

"So you deserve a treat. Go ahead, it's a party," Jeffries urged.

"Well, maybe just one," she said. "I don't know . . ."

"You decide, Leslie. I just wanted you to have something special because of all the hard times. You know I—uh—I appreciate everything. I couldn't have done it without you."

"Oh, Ted, you know I'd do anything for you. Just promise me— promise me it's over. I just want a nice quiet life making lots of money."

"That sounds wonderful. Don't worry, all the excitement's over. It's going to be dull, dull, dull. Word of honor." He offered her his arms and when she stepped closer, wrapped her in a tight embrace.

Jeffries made a grand entrance coming down the front staircase, appearing to shouts and boisterous applause. Entertainment people always loved drama and the idea of historic moments. He noticed that Leslie was missing, which meant she was considering his gift. Jeffries knew what she would decide. Soon they would be back to their old ways.

Mark ran up to him as he moved out to the back of the house.

"Ted—"

"You're looking sharp, kid."

"She's here," he said breathlessly. "Eleana. She just walked in. And—"

"Hey, slow down. People will think you've got something to be excited about."

"Sorry." Mark caught his breath.

"That's better. You're still doing the acting workshop?"

"Oh yeah. Everyone says I've got presence. And you can't teach that."

"Damn right. I saw that about you right away. And as soon as things calm down, we'll get you working in front of a camera. First some supporting roles to build your chops and credibility. Then we'll find the right vehicle and make you big."

"Oh, man, that sounds great. I just want to make it, you know."

"You were going to tell me something," Jeffries suggested.

"Ellie—you'll never guess who she came with. That asshole law-yer, the guy who was trying to put you away."

"Walter Buris? The prosecutor?"

"Yeah, that's him. So what do we do?" the boy asked.

"Interesting. Very interesting," Jeffries said.

"We gotta call it off," Mark said.

"No. You take care of Ellie, just like we discussed. Say you want to talk to her about Tommy. Go out to the Cherry Orchard—discreetly. Take the back way. The security people will make sure nobody fol-lows."

"What about—"

"I'll take care of Mr. Buris," Ted said.

"You sure? I mean—"

"Mark, it's just right. When you get more experience in the business you'll learn to appreciate times like this. It's not planned, but you're open to the moment, you see that it's just right. So you go with it."

Something struck the car roof hard, and Rachel started, her hands flying to her ears to snatch off the headphones. She jammed them beneath her and then glanced up at the silver-haired, mustachioed man who peered at her from the passenger side, his broad mouth playing with a smile. At first she did not recognize him.

"Looks like old home week," he said.

Her heart jumped a second time when she recognized him. Dan Matti wore an expensive blue blazer, with open-necked tailored shirt and ascot. He had done something to his teeth so that it looked like he had a slight gap between his incisors.

"What are you doing?" he asked.

"Oh—nothing." It was a ridiculous statement, but she was a terrible liar in any case. She had told Walter it was crazy, him playing investigator, going in wired, and her listening to the transmissions, but he was absolutely determined and would have done it anyway. She had not considered the possibility that her presence could endanger him. Matti could only be working security for Jeffries. He would know what to look for. "Please go away," she said as firmly as she could manage.

Instead he grabbed the headphones and put one phone to his ear. "Who's in there?" he demanded. "Who've you got wired? It's not Ellie, is it?"

"Go away." She tried to roll up the window but Matti forced her hand away from the crank.

"Now let's be reasonable, Rachel. You're sitting in a parked car at

[202]

ten o'clock on a Saturday night, miles from your home, but only a block away from Ted Jeffries's birthday party, listening to the party on headphones. Something is going on. Either you tell me what kind of amateur cops-and-robber show you've got going or I blow you and your little scheme out of the water with a phone call."

"What are you doing here?" she asked.

"I'm going to the party. I was circling a couple times, just to get the lay of the land when I spotted you. You don't exactly blend in here."

"I don't believe you."

Matti laughed. "You always were a suspicious bitch. Little like me that way. Maybe you even had your reasons. But I'm on my own now. I just gotta tie up some loose ends. Come on—what's up?"

Rachel shook her head.

Matti put on the phones and listened. "It's fucking Walter! I'd recognize that voice anywhere. Move over," he ordered, removing the phones. "We have to get in there."

"No!" she yelled.

Matti slapped her hard, once, across the face, leaving white streaks in her reddish complexion. "Now move over. I don't have time to argue."

Walter tried to look unimpressed, but he had never seen anything like it. An enormous mesh canopy two stories high and the size of a small house had been thrown up over the patio of Jeffries's house and filled with the flora and fauna of a tropical rain forest. Monkeys of at least three varieties clambered up and across the trees, vines, and lattices that ranged throughout the upper reaches. Brilliantly colored parrots chattered and swooped; strange frogs, lizards, and snakes gave movement to the lower realms. The air was hot and moist, but fresh. It smelled of rain and rotting vegetation. From somewhere came the sounds of South American music, a quick, light drum and several wooden flutes. Many of the guests were dressed in costume, with slashes of fluorescent body paint across their faces and torsos, costumes that looked more like plumage than clothes. Waiters fanned throughout the space, bearing trays of champagne and food from around the world.

Walter walked on, avoiding the table of volunteers taking donations to save the rain forest, and skipping out of the way when a family of tapirs appeared before him.

The rear yard was left open. Long banners of brilliant red, green, and orange stretched high along one edge of the property, catching the sun and throwing richly colored light onto the gathering. Standing in a pool of reddish light was Jeffries, soon joined by Leslie Montaigne. He wore a white silk jacket over a tropical print shirt and dark pants. He glided between groups of new arrivals, greeting guests, exchanging bits of conversation, hugs and kisses. It looked like a group dance, a graceful whirl of engagement and disengagement.

Walter took a glass of champagne, sipped a little, and spilled the rest on his jacket. He circulated slowly through the rain forest, keeping an eye on Jeffries and Leslie from afar. The other guests looked him over as he passed by, curious if he was anybody. When they saw he was not they quickly turned back again.

He kept an eye out for Eleana. He thought he had seen her going somewhere with Mark, but in the commotion he could not be sure. In the car he had tried to tell her his plan, but she had been too nervous, smoking one cigarette after another and constantly changing stations on the radio. As soon as they were in the door she disappeared, saying she wanted to find out "who's around." He decided not to worry. Even Jeffries wouldn't try anything at a big party.

It was about ten o'clock when Walter noticed Leslie heading inside. He followed at a distance and watched her meet with two chefs in the kitchen. With their toques and coats they were striking white figures beside the diminutive woman in a dark pants outfit. Walter installed himself in an overstuffed chair in the corridor beyond the kitchen.

As Leslie passed him he spoke. "No hard feelings, I hope," he said, a little louder than necessary.

She stopped and her expression darkened, but something about her eyes made him wonder if she recognized him. "You weren't invited," she said finally.

"Eleana brought me. Did you know she and Ted were in touch?" Walter asked.

"I have nothing to say to you."

"You know Eleana thinks Tommy's still alive," he said.

"He is," Leslie said.

"Right. And I bet you've had a letter from him," Walter answered. "A typewritten letter that's fairly short and sounds like him but just gives a PO box in Boston."

Leslie looked at him coldly.

"I understand after you gave this to him Tommy never took it off." Walter showed her the ring. "We got it from Ted's safe-deposit box out in Malibu. The one he didn't tell you about."

Leslie looked it over carefully. She seemed calm, but Walter noticed a hard twitch at the corner of her mouth.

Walter took back the ring. "I'm afraid we have to keep this. Evidence, you know. You might want to ask Ted about it though."

"Ask me what?" came a strong voice behind them. It was Ted Jeffries.

"He's got Tommy's ring," Leslie said.

Jeffries shook his head. "Never trust a cop."

"I recognized it," Leslie said.

"Well, maybe Mr. Buris and I should have a little heart-to-heart," Jeffries said.

"He's dangerous," she warned, glancing at Walter.

"I'll be careful," Jeffries replied, a hand on her shoulder. "You go on back to the party." Jeffries waited until she was gone to speak again. "That was nasty," he said. "But you're learning. Attack the enemy at his weakest point. Come on upstairs, I have something to show you." He led Walter to his second-floor study, a large wood-paneled room done in the English country style. The glassed-in bookcases were lined with leather books. Jeffries poured out two glasses of whiskey from a bottle on the bar.

Walter downed his drink in two swallows and Jeffries refilled it.

"Probably oughta slow down," Walter said. "But what the hell."

"You know I meant what I said the first time I talked to you—remember that, in the men's room?" Jeffries asked. "I like to catch guys when they're fiddling with their dicks—kind of a moment of truth. But I meant what I said—I like your style. If you weren't such a goddamned fanatic you'd be really dangerous. That's why you got canned."

"I resigned," Walter said.

Jeffries laughed. "Yeah. Anyway, just to show what kind of guy I am, how about if I get it back for you? No deal or anything, I can just leak something about the drug test being a setup, something we did to help the case. Then if you say you're sorry and you test clean, nobody's gonna have any problem about it. You're back putting the bad guys away. What do you say?"

"Fuck you," Walter replied.

Jeffries shrugged. "No skin off my back."

"I can make a lot of noise about you killing Tommy," Walter said.

Jeffries laughed. "Let me show you something." He reached beneath his desk and pulled out a videotape, then swung open a bookcase to reveal a large-screen television and VCR. He dropped in the tape and returned to his seat, remote control in his hand. "Gary Driesen explained to me about not being tried twice. Double jeopardy, sounds like a game show, but it means you can't do anything about this. I gained a real appreciation for our legal system out of my trial." He grinned broadly and pointed the remote at the television. It came to life with a ping and a rustle of static. "This thing's my insurance policy. It means you guys'll never touch me."

A deep professional voice narrated the tape. "Some time ago in Hollywood, a select group of people from the entertainment industry gathered at a secret location in Southern California for a night of intimate fun." The screen showed a group of tuxedo- and evening gown-clad guests sipping cocktails at a makeshift bar in what looked like the studio of the house in the Hollywood Hills. Unlike the other videos the sound and light quality was poor. Walter guessed that the tape had been made secretly with a hidden camera and microphones.

"The cocktail hour lightened the mood and allowed all to become acquainted," the narrator said.

The camera closed in on two couples huddled around a small mirror, snorting cocaine.

"The fat one there's Marty Bransen," Jeffries said. "He's the head of Universal. And that's Patty Simmons, from the TV show. And to the left you might recognize several of our more prominent elected representatives."

The party was full of Hollywood, Sacramento, and Washington figures, with brief appearances by Mark, Eleana, Tommy, and others Walter did not recognize. The tape showed partygoers engaged in heavy petting and occasionally more. Tommy and Eleana were in great demand, hands groping for them when they went by. They always put themselves at their guests' disposal.

"Turn it off," Walter said.

"This is the good part," Jeffries replied, watching intently. "Where Eleana really gets into it."

The screen showed three overweight men greedily undressing Eleana.

"It's kind of like a ten-year-old's fantasy," Walter remarked. "Dirty pictures of your friends. Don't you think it's just a little—pathetic?"

Walter caught Jeffries's eyes and saw that his remarks had found their mark.

Suddenly the door behind them flung open and Jeffries jumped for the remote, switching off the set.

"What are you doing?" demanded Leslie.

"Just having a little chat," Jeffries said.

"You were showing him something," she insisted.

"I'll explain later." He made a move with his hand under the desk.

"Why did you invite Ellie?" Leslie asked, her voice cracking.

"She's a friend," Jeffries responded. "Now Leslie—"

"And why did you give Mark that gun?" she demanded. "I saw him with it earlier. You said it was over!" she screamed.

"It is, dear," Jeffries reassured.

Two dour-faced men appeared at the door, and with a move of his chin Jeffries indicated Leslie. "She needs her medicine," he said. "And see that we aren't disturbed."

Leslie allowed herself to be led out of the room.

"She's been under a lot of stress lately," Jeffries said.

"Who hasn't," Walter replied. "Well, it's been nice talking, but I really have to go," he said, standing up.

"But we haven't finished," Jeffries objected.

Walter thought he heard the click of a lock from the other side of the study door.

"It's a funny thing—when you were a fed you were untouchable," Jeffries said. "But a burned-out hack who drinks too much, smokes dope, and has no judgment—that's different."

"You're so full of shit," Walter said.

"You know it takes a lot of education to be as stupid as you are. You wouldn't last two days on the street. Sit down. I'm going to show you something like you've never seen before. Something you'll never forget." He reached into the desk and produced another videotape. "I never should have kept this. But I have this part of me that likes to keep things for posterity. I don't care what they say about me when I'm gone, I just want them to remember." He put the tape into the machine.

"It was a kind of screen test for a serious drama we were going to do. Or at least that's what we told Tommy." Jeffries turned on the machine.

The screen came to life, showing Tommy and Mark in folding chairs in the studio, facing the camera.

"Is something going to happen?" Tommy asked, looking around.

"You're supposed to look at me, dummy," Mark said. "And look at this." Mark produced a large gun, which he pointed at Tommy's head.

Tommy leaned forward. "I'm sorry, Ted. I won't take any more drugs, I promise. I won't hustle anymore. I won't see Ellie. We're finished anyway. Whatever you want. I owe you everything, I know that."

Mark giggled. "That was pathetic."

"Hey, it's real," Tommy protested. "I'm not acting. I'm scared."

"What do you think, I'm going to blow you away or something?" Mark laughed sharply, a kind of barking sound.

"Please," Tommy said, his eyes pleading, but not with Mark. They were focused directly out toward the screen.

[207]

There was a flash and a bang and Tommy's head fell back in a strangely slow motion.

Mark turned toward the camera, his expression earnest.

"Did I do okay?"

Then he turned back. "Okay, Tommy. You can get up now." But Tommy did not move.

Jeffries switched off the tape and Walter sat rigid, more scared than he had ever been. Jeffries would never have shown him the tape unless he were going to kill him.

Jeffries gave him a shy smile and twirled a pen between the fingers of his left hand. Walter could see that he was doing something with his right, maybe getting something out of the desk. He tried to think of something to do, but his mind was a blank. He wished he had had more time with Sara. He wondered how she would turn out.

Then came a thumping sound beyond the door, and a rough cry, a half-shout, half-scream. Walter turned around in desperate hope, but found himself in a black space of pain starting from the back of his head. Jeffries must have hit him, and hit him in the best spot, where the cerebral cortex lies closest to the surface of the skull. But his brain was like a motor after the ignition was shut off, continuing for several revolutions. There was more sound at the door, louder, and then a voice, incongruously bright and familiar.

Walter sensed nothing after that, a nothingness like the static of a television tuned to a blank channel, a nothing that faded to an even deeper nothing.

Mark and Eleana sat beneath the oaks on a high knoll that backed up against the scrub brush of the canyon. The sunset made the hills strange purple shapes against the sky. The sound of the party drifted up to them, fading in and out like a distant radio station.

"I used to come here with Tommy," Eleana said.

"What a creep," Mark said.

"You said you knew where he was," Eleana said.

"You're sitting on him." He laughed at her reaction. " 'Course it was dark, almost like it is now, so I can't tell exactly where we stuck him, but it's around here. The guy was about to go to the cops, run us all in." Mark fell silent. He drew an automatic pistol from beneath his shirt and pointed it in Eleana's direction.

"I was supposed to scare him," he said, as if to himself. "Ted said the gun was loaded with blanks, but it wasn't. He wanted to make it easy for me—that's what he said after. You do it once and then it doesn't bother you. Taking care of Roscoe was a piece of cake. I was in and out of there in five minutes. You should have seen it. It looked like

[208]

one of those modern art paintings, the way he was spattered all over the wall."

"You're sick," she said. She wondered how dark it was and whether he could see her hand reaching down.

"I figure it's good experience, you know, for when I'm in the movies. I mean even most of the big stars, you can tell they don't know what they're doing when it comes to real action. But when the camera comes in on me for the close-up in the big scene at the end, where the good guy has to take out the bad guy, everybody's going to see it in my eyes. Experience comes through the eyes, you know. I'll be the only leading man who actually knows what it's like to blow someone away." He giggled.

Her fingers settled around the familiar plastic handle. With a practiced motion she drew the knife, flicked out its blade, and pressed it against Mark's face, its tip at his eye.

"You can kill me, but I'll scar you for life. I'll make it big and nasty so no doctor can fix it," she said. "No one'll even put you in a commercial."

He held still.

"Drop the gun," she said, pressing harder.

His breathing became labored. Out of the corner of her eye she could see the gun rise and then drop from his hand. She kicked it beneath her.

And then she slashed him, an ugly cut from cheekbone to mouth. A little something for Tommy.

TWENTY-TWO

"I hope I'm not interrupting anything."

The words came back to Walter as they pried at him, disturbing his rest. Where had he heard that voice and what did it mean? He remembered the sounds at the door and then that voice.

"I hope I'm not interrupting anything."

Walter felt himself in a strange, ugly place where there was nothing, but it was all right there and he wished they would leave him alone. They wanted him to come out where it hurt.

"Walter, can you hear me?"

"Walter, it's okay."

He opened his eyes and the room appeared blurry, as if underwater.

"Walter, are you okay?" It was a woman's rough voice, vaguely familiar.

"Huh?"

"It's Rachel."

"What are you doing here?" Walter mumbled.

"I was supposed to listen, remember? To your wire. They must have hit you pretty hard."

"Mmm. The tape—" he said, pointing toward the shattered television.

"We've got it," Rachel said. "Along with all the others. That double jeopardy stuff Jeffries said, he's not right about that, is he?"

Walter managed to sit up. The pain was becoming intense. "No. See, it all depends on whether it's the same offense," he explained. "The test is whether each offense has an element that the other does not. It's the Block—, Blockburger. But the issue here—"

"Walter, enough," Rachel said. "Do you know what day it is?"

"Sure—it's today. Right?"

"I'm going to get you a doctor," Rachel said. "Don't move."

"Eleana—" he called out, but Rachel was already gone.

Walter heard voices again and saw a tall man with an entirely bald head and rounded black glasses peering over him. "I'm Dr. Reaper," he announced. He crouched down and examined Walter's face and skull. "Look at me now, eyes wide. Oh yes. I think maybe just a little trim on that nose, maybe a little tuck down around the chin. I'm one of the best plastic surgeons in town, you know."

"Doctor, he's hurt," Rachel protested.

"Oh, yes, a minor concussion," the doctor replied. "Nothing serious. Drink plenty of fluids, lots of rest, and no German philosophy for at least a week." He laughed heartily.

When Rachel helped him downstairs, the party was louder than he remembered, despite the clumps of uniformed police that moved through the front of the house. Walter caught a glimpse of Jeffries and Mark sitting silently in the small dining room, facing each other at one end of the granite slab table. From the way they sat, with their heads slightly bowed, they could have been saying grace, except for the awkward position of their arms, bent behind their backs, joined at the wrists in metal handcuffs. Half of Mark's face was covered in a bulge of gauze and tape. The man who had blocked the door in Jeffries's study was also at the table, handcuffed.

Eleana and Leslie sat silently in the front hall.

"You okay?" Walter asked Eleana.

"Sure," she said brightly. "I can take care of myself. But they took my knife. Can you get it back?"

Walter tried to smile. "I'll see what I can do," he said. "Nice to see you again, Leslie."

Leslie made no sign that she heard him.

"Yo, Walter! You goddamned cocksucking amateur fuck-up! Don't you ever learn?" It was Matti, but he looked different somehow. "If I hadn't spotted your trusty companion out there, listening to music in her car, there'd be a couple corpses here tonight."

"Hi, Dan," Walter said.

"I gotta tell you, Walter, that was the stupidest goddamn piece of cowboy law enforcement I've ever seen," Matti said. "But damn it, it worked. We've got this sucker cold."

"What happened?"

"What happened is that they were about to blow your fucking head off when your local representative of the Federal Bureau of Investigation, United States Department of Justice, ordered them to cease and desist. I'd like to take credit for Ellie, but she took care of things herself."

"I guess I owe you," Walter said.

Matti shook his head. "We're even."

A short time later Matti took Jeffries outside and Walter followed, steadied by Rachel.

Jeffries stood motionless beside Matti at the front of the house, staring at the ground. A steady stream of expensive cars came and went through the long circular drive. A mariachi band, seven musicians in black and silver-studded outfits with broad black sombreros, strolled among those waiting for their cars and alternated love songs with vigorous upbeat numbers. Jeffries eyed them with evil intent as they neared, but they ignored him, launching full-bore into a raucous corrida.

"Shut the fuck up!" Jeffries shouted at the band, and the two trumpeters, who had set off on a wild high run, sending shining notes into the night sky, suddenly broke off, leaving a jagged edge of sound behind. The mariachis moved away.

Leslie came out of the shadows and Jeffries immediately yelled at her. "Call Driesen, tell him what's happened."

She did not react.

"It's all bullshit. I'll be back before the party's over," he said.

Leslie still said nothing.

"They'll be coming for you too, you know," he said.

"You promised," she said quietly.

Walter felt the night's cool breeze wash over them.

A large American sedan stopped in front of the steps and the valet looked expectantly for a tip, which Rachel finally supplied. Matti put Jeffries in back between two Beverly Hills patrolmen and drove off. Walter watched the winking red light of a plane move slowly across the sky. Although he felt as if someone was pounding nails in his head, he did not mind. It seemed like a very peaceful night.

On a Sunday in January, nearly six months later, Walter went out to Topanga with Laura and Sara. They had not been for a long time, and with the recent rains he thought the hills would be green again. The day was overcast, the light made soft and milky by the ocean's mist.

"I don't see why they don't give you your job back," Laura said as Sara scampered ahead on the fire trail. "After what you did . . ."

"Well—I actually talked to Curtes about it—he has Jackson's old job now. Apparently Washington thinks it would set a bad precedent now that the war on drugs is at a critical stage."

"A critical stage?" Laura asked.

"It's an election year."

"Nothing ever happened to that FBI agent, even though he lied to everybody about Jeffries," she said.

"Yeah, but he saved my life."

"Except, Walter, it's because of him you were in that situation. He's out there peddling his life story to the networks. One of the big agents at ICM is representing him. Everybody's talking miniseries," Laura said.

Walter shrugged. "It's a good story."

"Oh come on, Walter. You got screwed—you're still getting screwed. Don't you care?"

Walter smiled. "You sound like Rachel. She's always calling me up and telling me to sue somebody or something."

"So why don't you?"

"I got what I wanted—most of it anyway. Jeffries'll spend the next ten years in prison at least. He's facing the death penalty if they ever put the case together on Tommy. Mark is doing time. Even Leslie's facing five years." He paused. "You think I'm ridiculous."

"No. Just old-fashioned. That's what I liked about you."

"Thanks. I think."

"What are you going to do now?" she asked.

"I've been taking some appointed cases. Criminal defense."

"You said you'd never do that," Laura said.

"I guess I'm not feeling as self-righteous as I used to."

"Daddy, Daddy—you can't catch me," Sara called out.

Walter set off after her, his arms windmilling. He nearly caught up with her at the crest of the next rise.

"I beat you," she crowed.

He had to rest for a moment against a tree. He had been thinking more and more about Roscoe. He had stopped blaming himself for what happened, but that only dulled the pain. Walter still missed him. If he had lived he would have been the first to take on Hollywood. Walter could imagine him pitching a roomful of movie executives, thrilling them with his adventures. He might even have played himself, he had that kind of appeal. Laura was right, it wasn't fair.

The sun was starting to break through the haze and Walter felt its warmth on his face. He decided he was not going to be depressed, not today. He was alive, the land was green and bright, and his daughter wanted him to chase her.

"Watch out, here I come," he yelled, and Sara squealed with delight.